THE WAY
OF THE
GREYHOUND

THE WAY
OF THE
GREYHOUND

A MAGICKAL JOURNEY
OF SELF-DISCOVERY

GINAMARIE TALFORD

ONCE IN A BLUE MOON | Massachusetts, USA

Once in a Blue Moon
Massachusetts, USA

Hardcover ISBN: 979-8-9856085-8-8
Paperback ISBN: 979-8-9856085-4-0
Audible ISBN: 979-8-9856085-0-2
Ebook ISBN: 979-8-9856085-3-3

Cover design by Christina Thiele of kn literary arts,
Ginamarie Talford and Lynn (Talford) MacGill
Interior design by Christina Thiele of kn literary arts and Ginamarie Talford
Once in a Blue Moon Publishing logo by Ginamarie Talford
Illustrated chapter sketches by Ginamarie Talford
Editorial production by kn literary arts
Author Photo by Colman O'Connor

Printed in the United States of America
First Edition
Book One

DEAREST READER,

Are you a believer in *Serendipity*? I certainly am, and the fact that this book is in your hands is serendipitous indeed! *The Way of the Greyhound* is the story of a lost Greyhound's Magickal Journey of Self-Discovery and her search for a new home while suffering the effects of deep loss and of being bullied. The Greyhound teaches us how to quiet our mind, listen to our intuition, find our authentic voice, and begin to heal the scars we carry. As she deepens her connection with Nature (*the Tao*), *the Way* leads her to awakenings of self-acceptance, self-worth, and opens her heart to love.

For clarification, my spelling and capitalization of the word *Magickal* and other words is intentional. I have morphed the meaning of the word *Magickal* so as to relate to the *Tao*, or *the Way*. Aleister Crowley brilliantly defines Magick in his text *Magick in Theory and Practice*:

"Magick is the Science of understanding oneself and one's conditions. It is the Art of applying that understanding in action. . . . One must find out for oneself, and make sure beyond doubt, *who* one is, *what* one is, *why* one is. . . . Magick will show him the beauty and majesty of the self which he has tried to suppress and disguise."

This is the Greyhound's journey. This is our common journey.

In the midst of the bustle of our daily lives, we forget to *breathe* deliberately and deeply. I must gently remind myself to take a deep *breath* often. When I finally do, I feel much more mindful of *the Way*—I am calmer and better able to return to the present moment. As the Greyhound journeys through challenges, she is taught how to *breathe* by the Moon. Imbedded throughout the story are times when she is reminded to take a deep *breath*. I humbly suggest that as you read, when you come across the italicized words *breath* and *breathe*, you allow yourself to take a deep, cleansing *breath* along with the Greyhound. My hope is that you feel a sense of calm wash over you as you experience quiet internal peace.

Peace,

Ginamarie

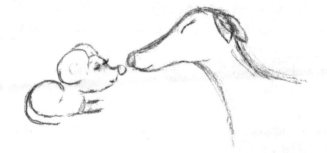

TO MY DAD

The Way of the Greyhound is dedicated to my dad, Eugene (Gene) D. Talford, who passed away on the snowy Thursday morning of February 6, 2020. I began writing this story in the first few months following my dad's departure. Time spent literally putting pencil to paper served as moments of respite from the heaviness of the grief and loss, not only of my dad but also of a decade long relationship that ended in a heartbreaking good-bye.

My dad's passing was extraordinarily difficult for me. He was a kindhearted, quiet, and honest Spirit. "Teach Peace" was his mantra, and he personified it. His zeal for life was extraordinary! He took nothing for granted, especially the people in his life and life itself.

He loved my first Greyhound, BrindleMars (the protagonist of this story), and my current Greyhound, SweetP (who, serendipitously, is BrindleMars' niece!). I never knew how he loved Greyhounds and secretly always wanted one, until he met BrindleMars. Dad always had a special connection with dogs. As a child, I thought he was Doctor Dolittle. It wasn't until much later in life that my sister and I discovered he carried dog treats in his pockets, which naturally drew dogs to him. Without anyone noticing, he would sneak dogs a treat and they loved him for it and we him. That was his Magick!

I miss you every day, Dad. Say hello to the Moon for me. I love you, and I'll see you on the other side.

ACKNOWLEDGMENTS

—

Dr. McGonagle, thank you for never giving up on me these last eleven years. Doc, you gave me hope and helped me find *the Way* out of the darkest times in my life. Without your support, gentle nature, and wisdom, I would not have had the courage to continue on or heal those parts of me that were deeply wounded and scarred. You taught me how to be more mindful and kinder to my Self, and helped me find my voice again. The affirmations you've offered me throughout the years have become an integral part of my daily healing practice and this story. I am grateful you came into my life at precisely the right moment. You are an Earth Angel who saved me.

Mum, thank you for being the first person to lay eyes on my story, for editing my first draft, for loving it and me. You taught me how to bend—not break—and how the world is not so black and white. I love you!

Mr. Compagnone, thank you for editing the second draft of my story and always believing in me. When I was a senior in your honors English and creative writing classes, you inspired me to follow in your footsteps and become a high school English teacher—a career that gave me purpose and joy for decades. You have been my surrogate father through thick and thin. You are my confidant, my Moon, and I love you.

To my sister, Lynn Rose MacGill, you are my North Star. You are a sweet, special soul that sees the good in everyone. Thank you for all the times you calmed me during a panic attack. You have always believed in me and in my healing Journey. Thanks for helping me with my cover design. You are impressive in every way, Sis! I love you to the Moon and back.

To my tribe of Warrior Women: Lynn Rose MacGill, Kristen (Lehman) Schwabe, Collette Sengupta, Taylor Skye (Schwabe) Feathers, Maria Rumasuglia, Melanie Sandford, Karen Kenney, Celeste Steffenson, Nancy Quevillon, Joanna Hunt, and Whitney Stewart, you all inspire me with your courage, fierceness of heart, and love. Thank you for accepting me as I am and for being my Soul Sisters. I love you all truly and deeply.

Guy Moore, thank you, thank you, for reading my novel, and for all your help with editing and tweaking syntax. The last thirty-three years with you in my life have taught me so much about true friendship, self-reliance, and the importance of laughter. You are a steadfast friend and one of my Earth Angels. Love you—always.

Dr. Pirrotta, you taught me how to *cry gently* and that I am worthy and deserving of great love and happiness. Thank you for your practical guidance and healing words of wisdom. I am forever grateful to you.

Phil Messina and John D'Agata, thank you from the bottom of my heart for taking a true leap of faith, believing in me as a writer, and helping introduce the Greyhound to the world. I am in awe of the artistry you both possess.

To Kelly Notaras and the talented editors, designers, and staff at kn literary arts, thank you: Jason Buchholz, my developmental and managing editor, your thoughtful comments and expertise in writing and storytelling strengthened the Greyhound's journey and gave me the courage to publish it. You are a kindred Spirit I hope to meet someday. Kelly Bergh, you are a brilliant line editor. You made me a better novel writer during the most challenging phase of my writing journey. Jennifer Sanders, my concierge, thank you for walking me through this complicated process. You are a delightful spirit and I am grateful to have been on this self-publishing journey with you by my side! Elisabeth Rinaldi, my copy editor, thank you for catching errors I missed. You are a grammar-smith! Your comments at the end of this writing journey helped me tremendously. Erin Seaward-Hiatt, thanks for the initial contributions you made to the cover. Christina Thiele, my book designer, thank you for bringing my design vision to life. You are incredibly brilliant at what you do. Helen Burroughs, my proofreader, what can I say, but thank you! You see what no one else sees.

Thank you, Reid Tracy, president of Hay House, and Kelly Notaras, owner of kn literary arts, for inspiring me to put pencil to paper during the most challenging year of my life and tell my story. You both know your craft well and continue to inspire writers to write.

CHAPTERS

—

ONE	THE CAGE	12
TWO	THE HOME	40
THREE	THE HILL	54
FOUR	THE ESCAPE	68
FIVE	THE ESCAPADE	80
SIX	THE CHALLENGE	96
SEVEN	THE CHOICE	110
EIGHT	THE STARS	118
NINE	THE MOON	122
TEN	THE ACTION	132
ELEVEN	THE ANGELS	140
TWELVE	THE SCARS	152
THIRTEEN	THE KISMET	162
FOURTEEN	THE KISS	194

ONE

—

THE CAGE

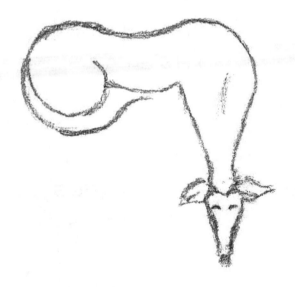

YOU ARE NOT ALONE

And so it was . . . An obedient, gentle Greyhound found herself in a strange, cold, corner Cage. She had never been so cold. Her bones absorbed it and ached because of it. Fresh cuts and deep lacerations covered her battered body, appearing as though she had been afflicted by some ancient plague. She had so many wounds and Scars, and not all were the visible kind. Her ears twitched. Why was she here? Where was here? Where was the Track? Where were all her racing mates? Her Owner? Her Trainer? Where were her celestial friends—the Sun, the Stars, her Moon? When she raced, she used to see the Sun, and she'd see a portion of the Moon through the small window near her Cage, but now they were hidden from her. The absence of windows and the dingy, concrete walls amplified her gloom. She felt uneasy—alone, abandoned, and hurt.

And what about all the strange creatures in the adjoining Cages? They were so different from her own kind—each unique in composition, varying in body structure, color, and texture of fur. Their whimpering and barking burdened her heart, and because of it, thoughts of the dark ride that had brought her to this place bombarded her brain, as did the Bee that buzzed about her head and unquieted her mind. The sharp unfamiliarity of the place made her head throb, which the incessant buzzing of the Bee bumbling about her Cage did nothing to alleviate. Trying to comfort herself, she turned her attention to her wounds and licked them, soliciting some relief from the pain.

Exacerbated by the Bee's presence, the Journey had been a long and exhausting one. She didn't want to think of that terrible truck ride now, but despite her wishes, flashes of the images inside the truck were too vivid to ignore. She remembered being carried in her Cage one night, and upon approach, the dark truck seemed to disappear and blend into the night, undetected, except for the loud rumbling of its engine and the stench of its exhaust fumes. This had had an unsettling effect on the Greyhound. She shivered at the thought. Instead, she focused on figuring out where she was and how to get back to the Track so she could run again.

Here she was so alone. The mini but mighty Mouse that had slipped into her Cage at the Track before all the Cages had been loaded into the truck was nowhere in sight. The Greyhound figured the Mouse had stayed silently unseen during the lengthy ride here—wherever here was—so the driver and the Bee would not discover it. Many times the Bee had threatened to sting her and the Mouse if she didn't listen to it, and it told her its sting was deadly. She was truly fearful of it. The Bee bumbled about her, flitting in and out between the bars of the corner Cage.

"You could have been the best!" the Bee buzzed. "They never should have sent you away because you faltered a few times. Usually, your execution was flawless."

For a moment, the Greyhound, exhausted and in pain, felt a puff of pride, but soon she succumbed to the doubts the Bee's droning conjured. The Bee's half compliment compounded her feelings of inadequacy, adding to the pounding in her head and the new ache in her belly.

I clearly did not do enough to continue racing or to succeed, and now the life I led yesterday is gone—cruelly and unwillingly taken from me, she thought.

Racing had facilitated the necessity to endure the head pain, which had come on ferociously and without warning some time ago when the bullying began, but the fresh cut on her belly and the strange stitching that held her skin together hurt more than she could bear. It felt as though someone had torn her insides out and made her unwell. Something was wrong—terribly wrong. Mental and emotional conspiracies commingled with her physical anguish. She had never experienced such an unquiet mind. Was her body failing her? Was her mind? The sharp pangs pummeling her Spirit and proclaiming she would never be whole again seemed to indicate as much.

What did I do wrong? she thought.

She remembered winning the last race and faltering at one point on the turn, and there had been reason enough for that, but the sequence of events was too foggy to focus on now on top of the belly pain that was worsening. The Greyhound didn't share her missteps and maladies with anyone other than the Moon, though the Bee was somehow privy not only to her strengths but also to her weaknesses. The Greyhound remained humble and silent, preferring introspection over the obsessive sharing others deemed compulsory when in company. Observing life suited her more than talking or gossiping about topics that lacked substance. It was customary for racers to spend most of their time in a Muzzle, which prohibited them from speaking; that's why long ago she had learned to listen, observe, and reflect more intently on her experiences and focus on how to improve her performance.

After analyzing the previous day's race, questions remained.

Is that why I was sent so far away from the only place I've ever known? she thought. *How could my Owner send me away? She told me I was one of the best racers she had ever known—a master racer.*

"So she said," interjected the Bee, crashing into the Greyhound's thought process. "You did everything your Owner and your Trainer asked of you. They had no right to treat you with such malice and cruelty."

Could the Bee be right? the Greyhound thought.

She had done absolutely everything asked of her. Everything—even when it hurt her to do so. The Bee continued stroking the only semblance of pride the Greyhound ever held dear—her eighty-one career races. Running was her life; it was in her blood; it coursed through her veins. She had run for more years, and in more races than most other Greyhounds, with a record of thirteen wins! Placing in the top three forty times stood as an outstanding accomplishment for any racer. Pride overshadowed humility for a moment.

"It was a good feeling to place so often, wasn't it?" The Bee goaded her.

"Yes, those were good days," the Greyhound answered, mustering a momentary half smile as she remembered the exhilaration of crossing the finish line and the thrill of winning.

Accomplishing something worthwhile outweighed the difficulty of the preparation she had endured. She had done her job—a job she loved. When she placed first, her Owner and her Trainer gave her quick pats on the back in front of all the other racers and praised her profusely. They paraded her around the Track as the crowd cheered loudly, "Mars! Mars! Mars!" Why they yelled "Mars" had always remained a mystery, nevertheless, her tail helicoptered wholeheartedly as circles of dust ascended in the air behind her. She had never been given a proper name and believed everyone deserved one, as did she for her unwavering obedience. In her world, certain words commanded action. That's all she knew. Obeying those commands was part of her job. It was her duty to do as she was told and not to questioned why.

The Greyhound had no idea there was only one reason she was useful until, late in her career, she overheard the Trainers say they were glad they had bet on her to win.

The Bee had added its own explanation at the time. "Your Owner was only happy because she had made all those people, including herself, a great deal of money and notoriety every time you placed. They used to bet on you. That's why the Owner lived in a mansion on the other side of the property. I hope you don't really believe they cared about you. Do you?"

That aspect of the Greyhound's world was foreign to her. After listening to the Bee's explanation, it was clearer why she had been teased by the other racers who always made fun of her gullibility and the fact that she was nice, even to those who hurt her. They were relentless, telling her she was too humble—too trusting—to recognize when she was being taken advantage of for her talents and nothing beyond that. Before hearing the new information the Bee had spouted, the Greyhound had viewed life and the Track—the only world she had ever known—with rainbow vision. She beat herself up for her naïveté, and as the bullying intensified, color faded from her world.

The Bee's voice continued reverberating against the cold steel of the Cage as confusion crushed the light countenance the Greyhound had briefly worn. She questioned her own worth and the reason her Owner and Trainer had disowned her, but she could not concede to any reason they had put her on that awful truck following the last race.

How could they cast me aside like that—like garbage? How could they discard all of us in that way without a second thought? Why was I abandoned without warning, without a word, or without a good-bye?

JUST ONE LOOK

And so it was . . . Waiting for the Handler to lead her outside made the morning hours burdensome. She did not like this place. The Greyhound's belly bellowed for some semblance of relief. Her priority was to quell the pulling and stabbing sensations she felt inside and out. She tried not to lick the huge wound or the many cuts and scrapes that had accumulated during her last few races. The tendency to ignore discomfort and carry on without complaint was her way. Long ago she learned how to stuff the pain deep down and remain stoic so nothing interfered with the protocols of daily life. Silent and increasingly despondent is how she remained as the early morning hours wore on.

Finally, one of the Handlers cautiously approached her Cage with the Greyhound's leash and racing Muzzle clenched in hand. Confounded by his fearful energy, she looked up at him, doe-eyed. His energy shifted. He entered her Cage and closed the door behind him so she couldn't escape.

Quietly he said, "Hey, Girl. It's time to go outside."

He crouched down on one knee and secured the muddied black Muzzle to her snout. She was used to the black Cage on her face, and its familiar scent of the Track, and offered her snout freely.

Click. The sound of the leash clicking in place on her collar was a signal all Greyhounds knew well—the signal to fall in line beside the one who held the power—the power that kept the racers in their proper place.

"Take it slow. That belly of yours will hurt for a while. You were severely injured when you arrived. Just take one step at a time."

He's kind enough, she thought.

And he was right. Getting up was extremely difficult and extraordinarily wrought with shards of pain, as if a sheet of glass had shattered into a million pieces, imbedding themselves all over her body. She wanted to wince but did not allow herself such a blatant display of weakness.

The Handler led her to a set of heavy, black doors that opened to a small courtyard. A tall, chain-link Fence enclosed the empty courtyard on three sides, while the tired, old building served as the anchor wall. The Fence resembled the one that outlined the boundaries of the property beyond the Track. Both towered above her. She wished for a way out— for a break in the fencing at some indiscriminately weak point in its construction; but wishing was futile.

The chirping of a tiny Bluebird, who had landed in the branches of the lone Pine Tree that graced the aging courtyard, caught the Greyhound's attention enough for her to lift her head. The Sun had risen that morning, though it refused to shine through the thick canvas of clouds that cloaked the rays that could have provided some warmth for the cold Greyhound.

Maybe the Sun wishes to be shielded from all my pain, pondered the Greyhound as she looked at that place in the sky where the Sun might be hiding. *Why do I always feel so blue under a cloud-covered sky?* she wondered.

The Bluebird's song comforted the Greyhound somewhat as she stood there, finally able to catch her *breath*—a welcomed respite from the musty, dank air in the building and the even staler air that lurked in the corner of her Cage. Inhaling again, she picked up on the Bluebird's sweeter scent, which combined with those of other animals, some of which resided inside the building and some of which she could tell had long ago left this purgatory. While the Greyhound wished she were somewhere else, a second Handler approached, reminding them their time was almost up. She hung her head again, wondering why there were no other animals in the courtyard with her. Perhaps it was due to the abdominal wound that had appeared when she awoke that morning in the corner Cage, or perhaps she was being punished.

"Maybe they are afraid of you," offered the Bee. "You do have that eyesore on your stomach now."

I know I have so many Scars, and this new wound is hideous. I don't blame them for not wanting to be near me, but why would my Owner abandon me and allow strangers to slice me open?

The Bee whispered in her ear, "You were expendable. You served your purpose well and once you became badly injured, they couldn't invest in the time and resources needed for your rehabilitation. They won't ever allow you to race again. You are a liability. Don't you see? But, I can help you, if you listen to me."

The Greyhound shook her head. The Bee backed off. Its explanation stung more sharply than her physical pain. The Greyhound tried to piece together the events of the previous day.

I remember winning the race, then I passed out from the pain. When I came to, I was being loaded onto the black truck. When I arrived here, I was carried into a brightly lit room and lifted onto a cold, steel table. Someone replaced my mask with a different kind and placed it over my mouth. I woke up this morning with a fresh wound on my lower abdomen. What do you mean I will never race again? How can you say that to me? You know how much racing means to me.

"Okay. Do your business," the Handler said.

The Handler's command crashed through the confusion in her brain. Nature called. She *breathed* in the cool, damp air one more time and held her *breath*, savoring it. As she followed the Handler into the building, she looked back and nodded at the Bluebird, who had helped her forget the pain for a moment. The Bluebird nodded back and took flight, disappearing behind a cotton field of clouds. An undeniable pang hit the Greyhound's heart as she watched the Bluebird go.

Back in her corner Cage, the Handler gave her some medicine to help ease the pain.

"I'm so glad you found your way to our Rescue Shelter," the Handler said. "You can recuperate from all your injuries while you are here. You have been bruised quite badly, and you will need your rest. Go to sleep now. I'll take you out again tonight, after dinner."

The Greyhound cocked her head to one side, then the other. *Rescue? Am I in need of rescue? Rescue from what? From whom? I was fine the way I was. Now I'm not. Will I ever be okay again?*

She was too fatigued to fight off the medicine's effects. Through the heavy fog of sleep, she heard a familiar voice say, "You are not alone. I am with you always, DearOne."

She could not muster a response as she drifted to the netherworld of Night Terrors. Unwillingly, she slept most of the day.

PATIENCE, DEARONE

And so it was . . . The next two nights elapsed ever so slowly, and the Greyhound's mood darkened in the Moon's absence. The Greyhound was kept sedated most of the time in order to speed up the healing process, which progressed at a snail's pace. She didn't like the groggy feeling she was forced to feel.

On the third day of her stay, an elderly Couple visited the Shelter. They entered through the large, glass double doors that the Greyhound could see from her Cage.

"Welcome to the Northern Massachusetts Rescue Shelter." The Handler smiled as he led the frail Couple through the double doors and down the long hallway of Cages. "We hope you find the dog that fits your family best."

From the Greyhound's vantage point, she could see the three walking around the horseshoe-shaped room. Their conversation echoed off the bare walls.

"It's so loud in here," said the woman. "Are the dogs always this riled?"

"Only when visitors come," the Handler answered.

I guess he isn't around at night when they whimper and moan, thought the Greyhound.

"Well, our dog will not be allowed to bark without a proper reason," the woman remarked. "We are looking for a rather large dog to take with us. This German Shepherd here is quite stately in appearance."

"Yes, she certainly is," commented her husband. "But Shepherds usually develop hip dysplasia, and we won't be able to take care of a dog with any outstanding ailments."

The Greyhound could not see the German Shepherd's face, but she empathized with the creature. She knew the Couple's comment must have stung.

If these people are unwilling to accept the Shepherd, who has no visible flaws, how will they ever want me? I have Scars I cannot hide.

As the Couple made their way to the Greyhound's Cage, the Greyhound heard the woman, who was pointing a finger at her, ask, "How about that one in the corner there? What's its story?"

The Couple stopped in front of the Greyhound. "What kind of odd creature is this?" asked the woman.

The Greyhound had curled herself up tightly, positioning herself intentionally to hide all the Scars on her underbelly and legs.

"That's a Greyhound—quite an elegant species," replied the Handler. "This particular Grey is a racer from the Southern Greyhound Racing Track."

"Hmmm, a racer you say? She looks like a tiger with those black stripes," the man commented. "We'd like to see her up close."

The Handler unlocked the Cage and entered, unafraid this time. He secured the Muzzle and leashed her. *Click.*

"Why the Muzzle?" asked the woman. "Does it bite?"

"It's her original racing Muzzle. We were told by the Track's Owner to always secure it," the Handler explained. He led them to an observation room that was much larger than the corner Cage, but its walls were made of concrete nonetheless. Once inside, the heavy, steel door closed behind her with a thud. Even though the Handler had unleashed her, the Greyhound simply stood still with no idea what to do or why they were looking at her.

"Mars, Mars! Come over here. Now!" the Couple shouted.

Were they from the Track? She wondered why they were shouting the same word the spectators at the Track had yelled when she was paraded around as the victor. Glued to the corner of the room, silent and stoic, her fear mounted. *I can't let them see my Scars.*

With arms folded, the Couple paced back and forth, inspecting her. She did not care for the Couple's energy. Something about it felt off. Judgment oozed from their eyes and pursed lips. Sleep seemed to be the only remedy for the situation. Her belly ached, and her head pounded. She was desperate to yawn, but the dirty, bloodstained Muzzle prevented her from such an instinctual action. She had grown accustomed to the cumbersome contraption that had been an appendage for as long as she could remember, but it kept her from being able to drink freely. It kept her from expressing herself. It kept her silenced.

"She's too lanky and much too delicate. There's nothing but skin and bones about her. You can see all her ribs protruding from her sides. Quite unattractive, to say the least. Is she lame? Deaf? Can she see us? Why won't she come when called?" asked the woman.

Before the Handler could respond, the Couple noticed the round Scar on the Greyhound's back right hip. "Look at that burn mark! She must have been abused. Damaged goods by the looks of her. We can't take a chance with her. Sorry. Good-bye!"

The Couple huffed off. The Greyhound was glad.

"Poor thing," remarked the Handler as he led the Greyhound out of the observation room. "You do have so many wounds and Scars, and it's too bad you will never have pups now that you've been spayed. Don't fret. You are gorgeous and graceful, GentleGiant."

The dejected Greyhound felt profoundly sad as the door to the Cage closed behind her. *Click.* Not even bothering to get up on the raised bed, she lay on the cold concrete, lowered her head, and quietly licked her wounds. Out of the corner of her eye, under the bed, she could see a tiny tail moving back and forth. The creature attached to it looked at the Greyhound empathetically.

At least you *haven't left me yet,* she said. *I can't fathom why you would want to stay with me,* the Greyhound communicated to the Mouse.

The words the Handler and the Couple had uttered resounded in her mind. She ignored the tugging from the stitches on her stomach. All she could do was tend to the gouges in her legs.

I didn't ask for any of this to happen to me. This is worse than one of my Night Terrors. I want to leave this place and never come back.

Just as the Mouse opened its mouth to speak, the ever-present Bee began to taunt the Greyhound. The Mouse, unseen by the Bee, scooted back against the wall, under the raised bed, to its safe spot, nestled in the darkness.

"I guess they did not want you, eh?" buzzed the Bee. "It must be all those Scars, and now this news that you can't ever have a litter of pups. It all must have frightened them. You really should get away from these humans. They don't have your best interest at heart. They never have. If you come with me, you can run wherever and whenever you wish. You could be Cage-free!"

Though she did not like the Bee when it was so brutal, the latter ideas intrigued her. Maybe she would be better off alone. At least she'd be able to run again. She was consumed by what the Handler had revealed—the news she would never have puppies devastated her, dashing her dreams of having a family of her own. Now she had to let go of the stories she had overheard her Trainers tell—tales of ex-racers who had been adopted by families and had found loving, forever homes.

The Greyhound could only muster a three-word response, "Leave me be."

The Bee buzzed off as the grave misfortune that had just befallen the Greyhound ushered in a deep melancholy.

They all are right, she thought. *I am damaged. I can't race. I can't even have pups. What good am I anymore? I have lost everything. I have nothing left to give. I am broken.*

The Greyhound fell into a deep depression. Neither food nor water appealed to her, and sleep refused her plea. So she cried softly, dampening her whimpers into the scratchy underbelly of the bed so they could not be heard. There had always been consequences for crying, but she didn't care. Her Spirit was broken.

She missed her Moon. He used to keep her company most nights and listened to her whenever she felt like sharing. The Moon had always been her confidant—her protector. She thought him to be Magickal as he was able to adjust his shape and the intensity of his light seemingly at will, and she loved how it appeared as though he was able to dodge in and out of the clouds at whim. He was her everything! He did not judge her, instead, he seemed to understand her the way no one else could. He accepted her the way she was with all her Scars and imperfections. He was her constant companion—her saving grace.

Overwhelmed by the cold, the Greyhound moved on top of the faded, red bed—the only speck of color in the nondescript place. Its short legs stood only a few inches from the floor, barely making a difference in the temperature. At the Track, the racers' Cages were stacked. Hers was on top. It had always been too warm up there, but she minded the warmth less than the constant chill of the current climate.

She wondered what the remaining racers back at the Track were doing. Several of them had not been selected for the extraction—her sister being one of them. She wondered where the other racers who had accompanied her on the terrible truck ride were now. Thoughts of Track life melded with the melancholy of the moment. She remembered how the racers used to communicate with one another by whispering. The racers couldn't speak too loudly, especially at night, or it would ignite the wrath of the Owner, so they learned to whisper to one another. It was similar to the sound of a purring cat. She knew what cats were. Several felines were allowed to roam the Track grounds freely, unlike the Greyhounds, who remained in their Cages, barring a training session or race, the only time they were allowed to run. When they were let out of the building twice a day to attend to business, the cats would strut by and hiss at the racers. She often wondered what it would be like to be a cat—to roam wherever she pleased.

Greyhounds! That's what the Trainers and Owners called the racers. They all carried the title without question. It was the title with which they were born. It had nothing to do with their fur color because not all Greyhounds were grey. Some of her fellow racers had fur that looked greyish-blue, but that was just a coincidence. Her fur wasn't grey at all. It was a lovely brindled color—a wonderful combination of various shades of brown and black. Even the elderly Couple had noticed how the unusual black stripes that flanked her body resembled those of a tiger. It was one of the kind Trainers who had first made mention of them when she was a pup. A bright white patch of fur in the shape of a heart adorned her chest, and the tips of her long tail and all four paws looked as though they had been kissed by the same white Stardust.

Thoughts of fellow racers made her nostalgic. Once upon a time, the Greyhound had become very fond of one of her former bottom Cage Companions. She still missed their late-night discussions about life and their shared passion for running and the giggles they shared. The Companion was caramel-colored, like the Fawn they both had witnessed hop one of the Track's Fences after it had become disoriented. This had not concerned her Companion, but the creature's mishap had concerned her. She remembered how they were impressed by the agility and grace of the fine creature and amazed how easily it could dodge between the Trainers who failed to catch it. They giggled at the absurdity of the Trainers' attempts to trap the wild animal.

Nature's wild creatures cannot be tamed, she had thought at the time.

"They must be crazy if they think they can corral and catch him," her Companion had said.

She smiled at the thought of the Fawn jumping over a bent portion of the Fence and how happy they had been to see him escape. That was a special day they had shared. Their romance had been short-lived, but she didn't want to think about those trying times right now. Sometimes, she still dreamt of scaling that Fence when the pain penetrated the silence of the night.

Why does everyone abandoned me? she thought. *Are you there, Mouse?*

"Patience, DearOne," whispered the Mouse, remaining hidden under the raised platform.

I AM OKAY
HOWEVER I AM RIGHT NOW

And so it was . . . As the Greyhound lay on the hard bed, she stared at the steel bars that kept her from running free. She had lived her entire life behind bars, muzzled and tethered to a lead. Freedom had come only on training or racing days when she could run. She loved and lived to run. It was thrilling! Fulfilling! When she ran headlong into the wind, she felt as though she were a bird, flying high above the ground—above the fray of her life. The fresh air invigorated her, and the feeling of the firm, warm sand beneath her paws put her at ease. She never grew tired of the hot Sun that warmed her back as she ran. She loved the Sun, even craved it. On that Track she was at peace—until she wasn't.

Much love, or what she had mistaken for love, had only been shown to the Greyhound by her Trainer when she placed in a race. Simply being noticed was worth the sharp pains she felt in her eyes, lungs, and aching muscles that followed each race; the attention was worth the cuts to her paws, face, and underbelly from the debris that assaulted her when she fell behind the other racers or when one tragically faced its demise in front of her as she leapt over its mangled body. It burdened her heart to witness such a sight without being able to stop and help her distressed comrade, but she had to win or suffer a similar fate, so she did everything she could to make sure she was the best there was, no matter how she suffered. But now, her battered body, overwhelmed by the devastating effects of years of racing, was no longer serving her. She tried not to lick her leg wounds, though she needed to find some relief, somehow.

"Maybe that's why no one wants you," said the Bee, returning to pester her.

She looked up at the Bee with sad eyes. Listening to its buzz drained her emotionally. She felt useless, worthless, and unlovable. At the Track, she would overhear her Owner and Trainer say that she was their finest specimen and that they were so impressed by the spectacular job she was doing. Now what was she doing? Nothing.

I don't know what to do now. It's clear that I am not wanted at the Track anymore, but if I don't go back, where will I go? I don't even know where I am. How will I ever race again? Oh, she sighed, *I need to race again. I don't know how to do anything else. I don't even know what anything else looks like. I just want to run without restrictions or the backlash of pain. I just know I am cold and I am lost—so lost.*

This was the time when the Shadows usually appeared. She didn't know their names or much of what they looked like, except that they were the color of night, difficult to discern in a Moonless sky. She had learned to predict their arrival by the heaviness in her heart and the onset of her head pain, and she knew their proximity when she felt dizzy or nauseous or lost her *breath*. In the past, she had avoided being consumed by them. Dribbles of joy throughout her life had kept the Shadows mostly at bay, but there were times when she couldn't muster the strength or will to confront and escape them. They fed off her fears—her insecurities—her Scars. They were able to take her *breath* away so that her *breathing* became labored and distressed. Now she feared she had been scarred too many times, in too many places, both inside and out, to hide from the Shadows any longer.

I just want some peace, she thought as she forced her eyes closed. *I just want to be okay the way I am.*

As she fell asleep, she heard a calming voice in her head repeat: *Say to yourself, I am okay however I am right now.*

MOST CURIOUS

And so it was . . . By the appearance and disappearance of the dismal light that snuck through the small, rectangular window at the end of the long hallway of Cages, the Greyhound knew another day had ended. It had not ushered a single visitor from the Track, like she hoped it would.

Day by day, the pain in her abdomen had begun subsiding, allowing her to focus her attention on the other strange, caged creatures. The one advantage of being stuck in the corner was the sight line it provided to several of the pens down the hallways to the right and left of her. The Greyhound was curious by nature and a keen observer of her surroundings and had heard some of the Handlers call the other captive creatures dogs.

Odd, she thought, looking up to her right. Her ears twitched, then her right ear stood straight while the other flopped over at the midpoint and partially covered her left eye—a reflexive posture she held when pondering a puzzling problem. *Dogs? But I'm a dog. How could all these creatures be dogs too?* She was baffled.

In this new place, the Greyhound learned there were many kinds of dogs, each so different from her. The dog down the dingy hallway to her right was referred to by the Handler as the Yorkshire Terrier. He was a tiny, light-brown-furred dog afraid of anyone who walked by, and it scrunched itself into a ball, burrowed his itty-bitty body in his blanket and disappeared into the confines of his Cage.

The Greyhound felt a familiar pang in her heart. Not knowing why this happened, she just accepted that it did whenever she observed any creature in pain. She wished she could break the bars, protect, and comfort the timid, frightened dog. Even though Greyhounds were bred to chase small creatures around the Track, she had no such desire to hurt them. Most of her fellow Greyhounds surely would have eaten the Yorkie for the win, but she couldn't conceive of such an act of brutality. To harm another living thing wasn't in her true Nature. She could just about make eye contact with the little one and tried to reassure him that he was safe, but the poor, fearful fella just recoiled deeper into the Shadows.

Located two stalls down the left hallway, the great German Shepherd was talking to the Bulldog in the adjacent Cage, who stared up at the Shepherd with wide eyes and a furrowed brow as drool dripped down its chin. It was a one-sided conversation at best. The Shepherd was a strong, proud princess who stood up straight with her nose in the air and her chest puffed up whenever anyone passed by her. The Shepherd spoke with an accent quite familiar to the Greyhound. Some of the Greyhound racers from the Track were from across the Pond and sounded just like her.

"I worked in the Search and Rescue Unit," the German Shepherd touted. "I had a very important job, working for Scotland Yard—a position my father held before me. I was the finest K9 the country ever had! The Met Police never could have done its job without my expertise."

The Shepherd took a deep *breath* and lifted her chest even higher, then continued all in one *breath*. "I found any missing person or criminal they instructed me to find. I just needed an object the suspect had touched, and poof—I could follow that scent for miles! I would successfully lead the Met Police to the suspect's hiding place, or I'd locate a key piece of evidence that would solve the case! Everyone wanted my help. I was in great demand, you know."

The Bulldog barked incoherently in response, "Ar-rooff!"

"I'm pretty sure he's trying to say something." The Greyhound's eyes widened, surprised she had said this out loud. What the Bulldog meant, the Greyhound couldn't say for sure, but she tried to translate for him.

"Pardon me," the Greyhound continued. "Excuse me, Miss K9?"

Ignoring the Greyhound's presence, the Shepherd continued, "I received the queen's medal for valor and extended service, but my strong hips gave out on me, and now I am unable to run, but I am extraordinarily proud of my accomplishments. They remain unmatched."

"Huh?" the Greyhound gasped, though no one noticed. *Not run? How awful. I can't imagine not being able to run again.* Her heart ached for the Shepherd, even though the dog had ignored her.

The Bee reappeared just then.

"You won't ever be able to run again if you are confined to a Cage," it bumbled. "I can show you a place where you won't have a care in the world."

"Shhh," whispered the Greyhound, who was genuinely interested in learning about the other dogs and how they had found themselves in this place.

The Shepherd, with conviction, continued, "Regardless, I still hold the title for solving more crimes than any other Search and Rescue K9! Enough now." The old Shepherd, winded, added, "It's time to rest these hips of mine. The pain is much too much to stand any longer." She limped to the back of her Cage and delicately lay on her bed.

The Greyhound empathized with the Shepherd's pain, but was relieved the chatter had ceased. She diverted her attention to the left of the medal recipient, where an elegant creature stood, watching the activity. Its fur was pure white, like the clouds that hovered near the Sun on a pleasant morning. The people who took care of cleaning the Cages called the dog a West Highland White Terrier. The Greyhound vaguely remembered seeing the dog on her hazy first day in the Shelter. She had been baffled about why the word *white* had been a part of the dog's name, because at the time its fur was clearly a dirty grayish color. But now, after having been bathed, the Westie was a wonderful specimen. Her ears were perky and her eyes were kind, but her tail was stumpy, as if someone had prematurely cut it off when she was a puppy.

Why would someone do that? the Greyhound thought. *Why is there such needless cruelty in the world?*

The Greyhound tried to speak with the Westie, but the dog stayed silent. The Greyhound could relate to the demure creature. She herself rarely spoke anymore. Those around her did all the talking. First, it was nearly impossible when muzzled, and second, no one listened to her anyway when she tried. Long ago, she had learned that it was much too dangerous to speak her mind. There had always been repercussions whenever she had done so, and being made fun of by those around her shackled her speech. Or maybe being muzzled her entire life was the reason she didn't know what to say when given the chance. Hypotheses mounted in the Greyhound's mind.

Perhaps the Westie was afraid to speak up for fear of retribution from others as well. Their Cages were within each other's sight line, and there was an unspoken understanding between the two—each knew the other had endured painful experiences. Sometimes, no words are needed to understand another's heart, the Mouse had told her.

THE UNDERDOG

And so it was . . . Noontime had arrived, and all the animals were released briefly into the courtyard. This time, the Greyhound was allowed to join them. None wore Muzzles. Her belly was healing slowly, and the pain was subsiding, though she knew the Scar was permanent. Keeping to herself, the Greyhound stood with her side against the building, admiring a tiny, white flower growing out of a small crack in the concrete. The juxtaposition of the delicate flower surrounded by the harshness of the concrete touched the Greyhound in a way she had not expected. Moved by its beauty, she took a reactive, deep *breath.*

It's quite amazing how something so small has the incredible strength to grow in such a hostile environment and still be so delicate and beautiful, the Greyhound thought.

Scanning the courtyard to see if she could spy any other miracles of Nature, the Greyhound noticed the Westie sitting quietly by the lone Pine Tree. The Greyhound was just about to walk over to her to see if she would be amenable to sharing space in the Sun's light, when she overheard the Yorkie being bullied by what the Handlers called the Rhodesian Ridgeback whose Cage sat to the left of the Yorkie's. The Greyhound and the Shelter dogs had learned the hard way that the Ridgeback loved to bother dogs smaller than she. They said she felt superior to the others because of her heritage, boasting how her ancestors used to chase lions. The Ridgeback was a proud one, but her type of pride had horrible consequences for those around her.

"Why are you so small? You are so insignificant," the Ridgeback barked provokingly as she gnashed her powerful teeth at the tiny dog.

"Why don't you stand up for yourself? Why won't you fight back?"

The Ridgeback moved closer and closer to the Yorkie, until the tiny dog, shaking like a brittle leaf, was backed into the corner of the courtyard against the chain-link Fence.

"You're so small. I could devour you completely! I think I will!" the Ridgeback said viciously.

At that moment, the Greyhound felt something nudge her. Without hesitation, in one powerful leap, she sailed over the Husky and the Shepherd, and found herself between the terrified, tiny thing and the raging Ridgeback. She surprised herself by how high and how far she had leapt.

"Grrrrrr!" She growled so forcefully that her own voice was unrecognizable.

The Greyhound had no idea from whence the sound had come. She had never growled at anything in her life, but she had to save the Yorkie. The growl had affected her posture. She stood at attention with her chest lifted high like a soldier ready for battle. All four of her legs were balanced and locked in place, ready to shift her stance if the situation escalated or necessitated a different posture. The execution of a leap in any direction from this position was possible. One of her ears faced forward while the other turned to the side so she could hear each noise made and every word uttered by those around her. Her eyes were laser focused on the Ridgeback's, but her extraordinary peripheral vision allowed her to see what was happening all around her, except for one blind spot directly behind her.

Perhaps it was the Greyhound's guttural growl that day that stymied the bully's intention to cause harm, or maybe it was how the Greyhound towered thrice over the Ridgeback. Or had it been the intimidating Scars on the Greyhound's face, legs, and underbelly that had frightened the Ridgeback? Whatever the cause, she was thankful it worked—the Ridgeback retreated. The Greyhound would make sure the Yorkie was never bothered again.

SLEEP OR LACK THEREOF

And so it was . . . Later that afternoon, back in their respective Cages, the Greyhound glanced over at the young Yorkie. Their eyes locked in mutual respect. The Yorkie finally stopped shaking, and the corner of his mouth lifted into a half smile. It was as much of a smile as the lad could muster. The little one eventually fell asleep, but there had not been much sleep for the Greyhound since she was no longer being given medication for the pain.

Time wasted away while she observed the other dogs. Down the hallway to the right and next to the Ridgeback was where the Husky resided. He was snoring unabashedly. She admired the dog's gorgeous, thick, black-, brown-, and cream-colored coat, which covered its entire body and kept him warm.

I wish my own fur protected me from the cold that has invaded this place, thought the Greyhound.

"You envy the Husky, don't you?" buzzed the Bee.

Unlike all the other dogs in the Shelter, the Greyhound had no fur on her belly or thighs due to living a life in a Cage and on concrete floors. She had been losing more fur as time passed, but it only happened when she thought of the Bee, who remained a consistent bother. Her sparse fur was one more defect that set her apart from the others and reconfirmed the feeling that she did not belong.

"You don't belong here," the Bee chimed in, reading her thoughts of inadequacy.

"Please, please, leave me alone," she pleaded.

The Bee's presence made it nearly impossible for her to fall or remain asleep. It complied with her request this time, for it needed its own rest. It flew off somewhere, but not before uttering its nasty promise, "Soon enough, I'll be back—soon."

The Greyhound was a restless Spirit, and sleep had always been a taxing necessity. Back at the Track, the other racers slept most of the day, every day, but she felt like she would miss out on something or that she should instead prepare mentally for the next race. If she slept too deeply, the Night Terrors and the Shadows surfaced. Those kind of dreams felt so real. If she let herself drift into the netherworld, she would have dreams of never returning to this one. Sometimes, she did not wish to return and feared she'd be okay with that outcome.

Will there ever be a time when I will be able to sleep deeply—peacefully? she thought, looking down at the Mouse tucked under the raised bed. It poked its head out, but said nothing.

THE SWEETNESS OF SILENCE

And so it was . . . The bluster of the dogs wore away the Greyhound's tolerance all afternoon, and she could tell even the setting Sun was happy she didn't have to listen anymore. The Greyhound's mind drifted back to the Track, to the times when she had needed a reprieve from all the barking in the kennels too. The barking had been incessant but not as bothersome as the buzzing of the Bee, which reached the deep recesses of her weary mind. Both sounds nagged at her, hurt her head, and pounded on her eardrums. Craving the sweetness of silence, she would often stay up later than her racing mates, just so she could listen to the stillness of the night. It was one of the only times the pesky Bee wasn't bothering her with its relentless prattle or hampering her thought process. Her hypothesis of whether the Mouse kept the Bee at bay, or if it was the other way around, needed proper attention at another time.

Oh, that Bee! She shuttered at the thought of it. A few fur hairs floated to the filthy floor. *I hope it has flown away forever. That would be a welcome boon.*

The silence afforded her peace. With it she could *breathe* deeply as the world around her slept and dreamt. The darkening of the light reminded her of the times, not long ago, when she could see a sliver of the Moon from her Track Cage. She felt less alone when she saw any portion of him or his light. She was deeply grateful for his company and unconditional love. They often communicated—she and the Moon. He knew her *by Heart*—every facet of her personality, every weakness and strength, all her secret desires, all her darkness and all her light. He knew it all, and still he did not judge any of it.

The Greyhound had only ever told one other soul about this secret relationship. After being bullied by the other Greyhounds and her Trainer for so long, the oppressiveness of their treatment of her became too burdensome to bear alone. On a night following a day of racing that had ended with yelling and sharp criticism regarding her performance, she was gazing at the Moon. It comforted her somewhat, but during that time she craved the comfort of another more. She told her newest Companion, the handsome one who she had loved deeply, how she felt about the day's disturbing events and how they had adversely affected her. At first, he seemed outraged enough at their mistreatment of her, but his demeanor changed abruptly as he ranted and blamed her for allowing the bullies to get to her, as if she had done something wrong to instigate their anger; as if she had done something to instigate his. He said it was her own fault that head pain plagued her.

The Greyhound took his criticism to heart, upset not only because of his cruel accusations, but also because he was frustrated by her chronic pain. She did not want to make him unhappy. She loved him. She did everything she could to please him. Wanting to focus on his sympathetic side and calm him, she decided to share something positive and dear to her. It was then that she took the risk of opening her heart even more, desperate to believe he cared about her as much as he cared about himself. Maybe that's why she overlooked his unpredictable mood swings. Maybe that's why she believed his promises of a life together and his charming protestations of true love. He was a charmer for sure. All this, combined with her desire to be loved completely, outweighed the risk of being hurt, over and over—the madness of love.

She hesitated in that moment, then opened up about her fantastical connection with the celestial orb. As the words slipped out of her mouth, she knew instantly she had made the mistake of being vulnerable and honest. The shift in his demeanor and the energy surrounding him darkened as his condescension and dismissive air rose against her. What followed had become predictable over time, though she wished it weren't so. As her partner battled against the simplicity of her honest nature, she locked eyes with the Moon's, praying for the waking nightmare to stop. Soon after that night, it did. He left her for another, swiftly erasing her from his life as if she had never existed—as if they had never loved one another for all those years—as if they had not survived going through Hell and back together—as if all his words of loving her had never been uttered. Why had he given all of his attention to another Greyhound, in an instant, instead of to her? He gave it all away, to someone else. It was the attention *their* love had needed; the attention she begged him for to make their life together better, so they could stay together. He shattered her heart into a trillion little pieces with his broken promises.

Their love had begun as a Magickal knowing, the kind in fairy tales. But the odds that the complicated circumstances and the malevolent influences would cease suffocating their love were sadly insurmountable. These outside forces, always lurking close by in the Shadows, relentlessly fought to tear them apart. Stopping them was beyond the Greyhound's control. The two Star-crossed lovers had done the best they could at the time. She decided to keep the loving, caring parts of him and the memories of the good times they once shared in her HeartBox for safekeeping, never to be opened again.

The Bee, too, had made fun of her that particular evening when it caught her still gazing at the Moon after her Companion's tirade had ended and everyone had fallen asleep. The Bee told her she was crazy if she believed the Moon actually cared about her enough to converse with her or considered her anything more than an insignificant speck on Earth's surface. It made sure she knew that she would never be loved by her bottom Cage Companion or anyone else the way she hoped. Love like that just doesn't exist, the Bee had said. After that night, she never shared her relationship with the Moon with anyone for fear she wouldn't be believed and that she'd be laughed at for having a connection with a celestial being.

Now, in this dank building, the dogs slept, snored, and whimpered. The Cage bars reverberated in response. The Moon's waxing crescent light had barely been discernible through the cloud-covered sky when the Handler had let the dogs out earlier for their evening stretch, adding to the Greyhound's despondency. She pined for her Moon.

Why wouldn't I have a connection with the Moon? She tried to convince herself. *I was born on a Moonlit night. It feels quite natural to have a close connection. He is a part of me.*

"He certainly is," peeped the Mouse, popping its head out from under the coarse blanket. "The Moon has always been with you ever since you were born under his full light. He has been rock steady in his love for you and a true guide."

The Greyhound thought about how the Moon comforted her during difficult nights when she couldn't tolerate the head pain caused by the Trainers' bullying and reprimanding during the day or her handsome

34

Companion's shouting that came late at night. She shared her misfortunes with the Moon. He listened with love. No other being had ever loved her the way she felt loved by the Moon. She clung to that feeling as it carried her into a semi-slumber.

BELIEVE IN YOUR OWN MAGICK

And so it was . . . The next day came and went, despite the Greyhound's desire for it not to come at all. It was a busy day in the Shelter. One by one, each dog was rescued. The German Shepherd princess, the reticent Westie, the meek Yorkie, and even the rowdy Ridgeback had all found their forever homes. Only the bewildered Bulldog and the humble Husky remained, but the location of their Cages was not conducive to conversation.

The blanket scraped against the Greyhound's underside as she lay there. At least the stitching had been removed from her belly and no longer painfully pulled at her insides as it had when it entangled with the fibers of the blanket. She questioned the reasons she had been overlooked by all the families that had come to adopt the others. It was becoming clearer to her that she was so damaged even her Owner didn't want her back. The Greyhound wallowed in a whirlpool of worrisome thoughts. Each dropped into the next, encircling her mind. *Why hasn't anyone come for me? Do my Scars make me as unattractive as the Bee claims? The Bee must be right. I know I'm not perfect. That's what got me here in the first place. I don't belong here. I don't know where I should be anymore. I don't really want to be anymore. Something's gotta give. Maybe if I try harder to get adopted, someone will want me despite these ugly wounds. There must be someone out there who is gentle and kind—someone who doesn't mind the presence of Scars. Maybe there's someone who is just as lonely and alone as I am. Maybe that someone needs my companionship. Can I take that chance again—of being with someone new? I need help. Mouse? Moon?*

"Just believe it to be so," the Mouse answered. "Connect with your imagination via your heart. Think it. Feel it. Believe what you feel in your heart to be true and *breathe* it in. Believe the impossible is possible, DearHeart. Possibilities are like Stars—infinite and available to anyone who believes in the manifestation of their Magick. Believe in your own Magick."

The Greyhound didn't quite know what Magick was but wanted to believe anything was possible. *I want to believe. Truly I do, but I am afraid of being hurt again, and so soon. Am I ready? I've already lost so much—everything. Do you think I am strong enough?*

"Only you can answer that, DearHeart. You must come to know this of yourself, in your own time, at your own pace. You know well that every race is run alone. No one can run in your place. You must take each step, whether *the Way* is fraught with challenges you must face or easily trodden, no matter how sure or unsure you are. You know this truth truer than most."

Teach me how to believe in myself again. The Greyhound gently nosed the Mouse's side. They lay quietly together. The Greyhound mused the future's possibilities.

BRAVE ENERGY

And so it was . . . Cluck, click. Cluck, click. A Girl with long, curly, dark-brown hair and hazel eyes approached the corner Cage, making a clicking sound between her gapped front teeth. The Girl reached her hand beyond the bars as if she were trying to touch the Greyhound, unfazed by the Greyhound's wounds. The Greyhound was afraid if the Girl saw all the Scars on her worn body, she would be frightened by them and leave. The Mouse touched the Greyhound's back leg, then snuck beneath the bed. The Greyhound decided to show her true Nature to the calm Girl by walking back and forth, rubbing against the cold, steel bars, and touching the Girl's hand with each pass. The Girl remained close and did not recoil. Incrementally, the Greyhound's brave energy surfaced and reached her vocal chords.

The Greyhound grunted, "Hello, you seem very nice. I am a Greyhound." The only audible sound was *purrr, purrr, purrr.*

The Girl called for the Handler who habitually jingled the Cage keys, which he kept on the large ring around his wrist. The rattling of the keys meant the Greyhound was being taken to the large room again. Could this be her chance to be freed from this Cage? Any place was better than here. The current conditions were unsustainable. She had to be on her best behavior.

Will she accept me with all my imperfections? she thought as the uncertainty surged.

"I wouldn't get your hopes up!" the Bee replied as it flew into the darker recesses of the Cage. "You just need to follow me out of here. I'll show you a place where the pain inflicted upon you by humans can't touch you. There's a better place I can offer you than any human ever could. How can you trust this one? You haven't been able to trust any human being. You can trust me! I promise."

"Come on, SweetOne," said the Girl to the Greyhound. "Come on, it's okay."

There is something special about this Girl's energy, thought the Greyhound. *She seems like a sweet Spirit.*

The Girl's demeanor was gentle. Even the heavier energy of the Cage had become less oppressive in her presence. The Greyhound's body relaxed to a degree.

"Don't trust her," the Bee said in a hushed tone.

Shush. The Greyhound motioned with the swipe of her tail.

She obediently followed the Girl into the room where she had met the elderly Couple. Sunshine streamed into the space. Her Muzzle was removed at the Girl's behest. The Greyhound was surprised by the Girl's insistence. As soon as the Greyhound felt the tension of the leash release, she scampered over to the two large windows at the far end of the room, overlooking the parking lot. Some smelly old toys and a frayed gnawing rope lay in a bin below them. With her head uplifted and her eyes closed, the Greyhound leaned her body forward as a flower does as it reaches for the Sun. She absorbed as much of the warmth that radiated through the windows as she could. The Sun's salutation revivified her, and the cleansing *breath* she took was audible.

The tall Girl joined the Greyhound and immediately bent down on one knee and said, "I love the Sunshine, too, SweetOne, especially on a chilly October day like today."

They both looked out the window. The moment was quiet and still. Their energy commingled as though parts of their Spirits had been reunited after a lifetime apart.

"Look, you can see my little black Jeep from here," the Girl said. "It's the one right in front of us under the Oak Tree."

"Purr," the Greyhound replied. She was very familiar with Jeeps.

Many of the Trainers and workers at the Track owned them.

Maybe she's from the Track, and she's come to take me back, thought the Greyhound.

Her hardened heart clung to one strand of hope as she stood eye-level with the Girl. The Greyhound's jaw trembled once or twice, but she did not dare wag her tail for fear of being seen as too rambunctious or needy. Plus, she did not trust the outcome of the situation quite yet. The Greyhound looked into the Girl's kind eyes and was comforted by them. Their hazel color reminded her of the green needles of the Pine Tree in the courtyard.

She purred again, "Purrr, purrr."

The Girl pet the Greyhound's neck gingerly and stood up. After noticing the Scar on the Greyhound's hip and learning from the Handler that the Greyhound most likely had been burned by a cigar, the sympathetic Girl tried stroking the hip where the burn mark was etched into the Greyhound's furless skin. Cowering, the Greyhound retreated a few steps with her head down but her eyes cast upward. She felt the Girl would surely reject her if she allowed her to touch the Scar.

"It's okay. You are safe. I'm not going to hurt you. I'll never hurt you, SweetOne," the Girl whispered reassuringly as her outstretched hand reached to touch the Greyhound's head.

The Greyhound, pacified by the honest tone of the whisper, offered her head for a few more significant strokes. She was not used to the delicate attention. It felt good. The Girl's touch was soothing, but the Greyhound backed away each time the Girl tried to touch any of the Scars scattered about her body.

Suddenly, the Handler reattached the leash and positioned the Muzzle in its proper place. With a *Click*, the Magick spell was broken. She was being led somewhere else. Where now? She could see the Girl leaving. Her heart pounded, and she began to panic. Was she being taken back to the corner Cage? She couldn't let that happen. She was tired of being alone.

"Don't go!" she barked. The first bark was muffled by the Muzzle, which prevented a true outcry, so the Greyhound cried out again as loudly as her vocal strength allowed. "Please don't leave me!"

The Girl looked back. "Don't worry, SweetOne. I'll be right back. I'm not leaving you here. I promise."

The Greyhound took a deep *breath*, which calmed her nerves slightly.

I want to believe you, she thought. *I really do, but promises made to me are always broken.*

Hope abated as the Greyhound waited for the Girl. The Greyhound felt suspended in time as it pass over her in waves, while the bustle of activity in the Shelter continued nonetheless. With official papers and the Greyhound's leash in hand, the Girl finally returned. The Greyhound couldn't believe her eyes. Though her stomach was too tender for her to truly jump for joy, she poked the Girl's hip and leaned into it with all her weight. Her jaw trembled a little more—in the Greyhound's world, *nitting* was a true sign of affection.

The Girl reached down and patted her back. "Okay, okay," said the Girl. "We're going home!"

TWO

—

THE HOME

OPPOSING BUT BALANCED FORCES

And so it was . . . Puzzled by the term the Girl had used, the Greyhound questioned the possibilities. *Home? What home? Is she talking about my forever home? Was she sent by my Owner to take me back to the Track? Will I soon run again? I desperately need to run.* She wanted to feel hopeful but didn't trust the emotion.

Together they walked out of the cement building to the Jeep parked under the Oak Tree. The first thing the Greyhound noticed was the colorful flower on the tire cover. The symbol was pleasing to look at, and the swirls of circles that sprang from each of the petals in the design distracted her from all the questions rambling through her mind.

"I saw you looking at the flower," the Girl said, "Do you like it? I painted it. I have the same one on my classroom door. The yin-yang symbol is in the center there. It represents two opposing but balanced forces," the Girl offered. "Yin represents stillness in energy, like the Moon, and Yang symbolizes movement in energy, like the Sun!"

The Greyhound tilted her head, absorbing what the Girl said. She thought of the Sun and her Moon and how each was represented in the symbol. She thought of how the Bee challenged her own balance. *I wonder if that's* the Way *everything in the universe works,* thought the Greyhound.

The Girl opened the hatch at the rear of the Jeep and up went the wide window. The Greyhound looked towards the Girl for help. Any other time she would have hopped into the Jeep with ease. After all, she was used to jumping pretty high to reach her top Cage, and this wasn't nearly as high, but her belly still ached, especially after the leap she took last week over the dogs in the courtyard. She'd need another day or two before she could execute such a feat on her own.

"I've gotcha," said the Girl. "I'll be careful not to touch the Scars on your belly and hip."

The Girl gingerly lifted the Greyhound and placed her in the Jeep.

Before the Girl closed the hatch, she removed the Greyhound's Muzzle.

"How's that? Is that better?" the Girl asked. "That's gotta feel better."

The Greyhound did all she could not to focus on the Girl's comment about her Scars. Her heart hurt a bit, and her insecurity regarding her Scars magnified. She didn't even realize the Muzzle was missing. Its heaviness remained upon her.

It's obvious the Girl is repulsed by my Scars. I knew she'd have a problem with them. The Bee said as much, the Greyhound thought. *Sadly, she's just like everyone else.*

Her thoughts of dejection didn't linger as her attention diverted to the Jeep's soft floor beneath her feet. Several layers of blankets covered the back portion of the Jeep. She couldn't believe the Girl had done this for her. The Greyhound made a few circular passes, almost touching the roof with her head, then settled comfortably.

On the ride home, she was astounded by all the sights she spied through the large windows. It was a new, exciting world she never imagined existed. In one of the vehicles that passed them, a young child smiled and waved. In another, she saw a dog resembling the Westie from the Shelter, but the vehicle sped by too quickly to be certain. The Greyhound saw people doing this or that. One woman, looking in a small mirror, fixed her hair. The passenger in a bright yellow car chatted with his driver, and an occupant in another vehicle was talking on his phone. Yet others, those who gazed beyond the roadway, the Greyhound imagined were lost in contemplation of the gravity of their own lives. The Greyhound wondered what their lives were like, if the gravity of her own life was equal to, any better, or just worse than theirs.

A plethora of Trees in the distance caught her eye. She was astonished by the sight. The Greyhound had only ever seen one or two Palm Trees near the Track.

There are so many Trees. Too many different kinds to count, she thought. *I love Trees! They are so tall and can see everything. I wonder what they see. I wish I could see as they do.*

It amazed her how colorful their leaves were. Hues of Sunshine yellow, burnt rust, and crimson dazzled the Greyhound. She wondered what the Sun thought of the yellow leaves, but she still preferred the green Pine Trees above the rest. She felt a little guilty preferring one Tree over an another.

The Girl rolled down the windows. "Go ahead, Girl, stick your head out the window. It's okay."

How did the Girl know I wanted to smell the air? she thought.

The Greyhound stuck her long snout out beyond the window well and smelled all the inviting and not-so-enjoyable scents carried by the breeze. Though unsure of what all of them were, she inhaled each deeply anyway and took in every facet of the moment fully. The Greyhound experienced sensory overload as they continued driving. The Girl giggled at the Greyhound's wiggly nose.

"I never knew any of this existed. How could I have? I've been in a Cage my entire life!"

An unexpected little grunt slipped out. Not realizing she had said all that out loud, her throat tightened. It closed any time she became emotional or wished to voice her opinion but dared not. It was the significance of the word *Cage* that had begun to morph into a new meaning for the Greyhound, who realized there was an entire world that had been kept from her intentionally. Another uneasy feeling seeped into her heart. Maybe she didn't want the Girl to take her back to the Track. Now that she was free, she had a strong feeling she did not wish to return to the place where people had limited her life experience. She had no desire to go back into a Cage any time soon either. It felt too good to be free, to move about unimpeded by a Cage or a Fence. Could it be that her entire life had not been her own?

"What do you smell?" asked the Girl.

"Well," purred the Greyhound, "I smell something quite noxious. I think it's emanating from the black roadway. It's not pleasant at all. Wait, I can smell apples too! Yes, apples!"

Apples were her favorite! They were given to the racers when they won a race, but only if they had proven themselves worthy. As the Jeep rounded a bend in the road, an expansive orchard came into view. Dozens of perfectly aligned rows of Apple Trees dotted the field.

Apples grow on Trees? the Greyhound questioned. *How odd. I know coconuts do, but apples too? What else does? What else don't I know?*

"I smell a wonderful scent coming from the front of the Jeep," the Greyhound cooed. She sniffed at the Girl's shoulder, "Oh, that's you. You smell so nice."

The Girl responded to the Greyhound's cooing, "What? You like how

I smell? It's vanilla bean and bergamot. If you love these scents, you'll love all the scents at home too. The cinnamon spice I boil on the stove makes the house smell so delicious," the Girl said, *breathing* in deeply, as if she could smell it.

The Greyhound sniffed audibly too. The Girl giggled.

"It's Autumn, ya know. My favorite time of year! Most of the leaves on the Trees are changing color now, and some of the Trees are just beginning to drop their leaves. Oh, and the air is so crisp this time of year! There are even some flowers still in bloom," said the Girl with a sweet enthusiasm.

The Greyhound thought the Girl's voice sounded as lovely as the Bluebird's song. The Greyhound decided to maintain her position between the two front seats. The view was better and she could be close to the Girl. As the Greyhound steadied herself, the Girl offered her right palm to the Greyhound, who hesitated, thinking she was still muzzled. Realizing she was unencumbered, she placed her jaw in the palm of the Girl's hand, relaxed, and kept it there. Her heart swelled. Could it be she was beginning to feel safe?

She had never felt safe before—always worried about being the best and proving to everyone around her that she could do anything was her normal. Feeling safe was rare. She always felt the ground beneath her would give out for one reason or another, especially when the bullying began without warning, or if she unknowingly said something wrong to the Trainer, who didn't like her, or to her handsome Companion. Feeling safe enough to be who she really was had never been an option. She wished she had one of the loving, more caring Trainers that the other racers had.

In front of her on the floor, the Greyhound saw the Mouse pop its head out from one of the two front pockets of the Girl's Lucky denim bag it had slipped into back at the Shelter. The Mouse blinked and smiled. The Greyhound remained still in the Girl's hand. Savoring the moment, she blinked back.

The Girl's hand flinched suddenly, which startled the Greyhound and triggered a flashback. She was transported to a time when she had been wary of those who wanted to harm her and impede her success. Specific occurrences of malfeasance by fellow racers were wrought upon her all the time. Sometimes, the racers would bark all day and night so she would lose sleep and not have much energy the next day, or her Trainer and handsome

44

Companion would be in such bad moods that they'd yell at her without warning, for no reason at all, then blame her for their unprovoked outburst. It was quite unsettling and disturbed her Spirit every time it happened. The anxiety and the emotional exhaustion each left its own signature mark on her mind and body and affected her performance as well.

The Greyhound thought about how the Bee and her Companion had said it was her own fault that her Trainer's rage reared and roared, but she could never figure out what she had done to cause it. In her heart, she knew that no one should ever be yelled at in such a frightening manner, not ever. The Bee blamed her for most things that went awry in her life. Subsequently, she would blame herself for not trying hard enough to please those around her and feel even worse—less than enough. She was always so hard on herself. Thinking about those times exhausted her now and sapped the newfound joy she had been experiencing on the ride.

The Girl spoke again, breaking through the torture in the Greyhound's mind. "You need a name. Your racing name was Mars, but that's not your real name. It isn't personal enough. It's just the name on the roster the spectators yell so you're not distracted when racing. It doesn't quite suit you, though I do like anything celestial. That fur coat of yours is brindle in color. Hmm. I'll have to think about it . . . "

"Purrr," the Greyhound whispered. "Purrr."

She finally understood why the spectators and the Couple at the Shelter had yelled the word *Mars*, and she was quite pleased to hear that she would finally be getting a name. It felt good to have someone care about her enough to want to give her a name. At the Track, she was a number and it had always been, "Get over here!" or "Come!" or "Hey!" It had hardly been said in a kind tone. It was forceful and generic—not personal and loving. There, she was just a Grey with a job.

She looked up and blinked slowly at the Girl as the feeling of being wanted for who she was and not just for what she could do washed over her. Not trusting the emotion completely, the Greyhound didn't allow it to linger. She retreated to the back of the Jeep.

The Bee, which had been hiding in the back corner, buzzed softly in the Greyhound's ear so as not to be detected by the Girl. "She'll never accept you with all your Scars, you know! Remember, you are riddled with them. We both know only some are visible, and they hide much deeper wounds!"

The Bee was right. A sigh escaped from the Greyhound's throat. She was well aware of the wounds and Scars that dwelled on the inside, deep down in the recesses of her broken heart and battered body. The Greyhound questioned why the Mouse had not come to her defense, but, had stayed quiet and out of sight. Had the Bee purposely been keeping the Mouse at bay? How could that be?

NEW PLACES
OFFER NEW OPPORTUNITIES

And so it was . . . They arrived at their destination.

"We're here! We are home!" The Girl smiled.

As she opened the rear hatch, the Bee flew out, almost colliding with the Girl's forehead.

"Ugh," the Girl shouted. "I don't like Bees! I've never been stung by a Bee, and I hope I never will be." She giggled. "Ha ha, I just made a pun!"

The Greyhound didn't yet know what puns were, but she liked when the Girl laughed. She wasn't used to people laughing for good reasons. Usually they laughed at her expense.

Click! The Girl attached the black leash to the Greyhound's black collar and lifted her out of the Jeep. Immediately, she led the Greyhound to a small yard bound by a large stone garage on the left and a chain-link Fence on the other three sides. The Greyhound sighed as she studied the Fence. There was one Pine Tree and other unfamiliar entities the Girl called flowers in the yard. She thought of the white flower growing out of the concrete and sighed again. As the Girl led the Greyhound around the humble space, she identified each object so the Greyhound knew what she was seeing.

"That's a young Eastern White Pine Tree in the center," said the Girl. "I love Pine Trees! They smell so nice. Their pine cones and pine needles are beautiful and have healing properties too." Picking up a few of the Pine's needles off the ground, she smiled and said, "Oh look! Right there. It's a HeartStone. See it? It's imbedded in the ground at the base of the trunk. HeartStones are Magickal!" The Girl left the HeartStone undisturbed. She gently broke the pine needles in half and took a deep *breath.* "Ahhh." The Girl bent down and held the broken needles near the Greyhound's nose. "Smell that? Nice, huh?"

The Greyhound *breathed* in the aroma and purred. The Girl pointed to one of the giant Trees that partially cascaded over the enclosure on the other side of the Fence. "That huge Tree is a White Oak Tree, one of the strongest Trees in existence, and next to it, in the neighbor's yard, is a Lignum Vitae Tree. Bumble Bees love that Tree come Springtime."

The Greyhound shivered at the news. A few of her fur hairs fell to the ground.

The Girl continued, "Those are flowers along the Fence. These white ones are Montauk Daisies, one of my favorite kinds of flowers, and over here are Cosmos. They are quite colorful, and I love their name. That huge stone structure is the garage, which houses the Jeep and various yard tools. Beyond the Fence is the Ballfield, where the neighborhood kids play baseball. This small yard is the place where you can watch the kids, and you'll take care of your business over there," said the Girl, pointing to a particular spot in the corner. "Do your business, Girl. It has been a long ride. It's okay. You're safe."

The Greyhound did as she was told. She was an obedient one. She looked around. It was a lovely area, though not large enough to run and certainly not long enough to sprint or gallop.

Where am I supposed to run? she pondered. *Surely, I cannot run here. I could probably run in the Ballfield, but not if I'm tethered to this leash.*

As the Girl coaxed her around the enclosure, the Greyhound felt something soft and cushy underfoot. She lifted each foot awkwardly as though the ground would open up and consume her.

The Girl undoubtedly saw the Greyhound's uncertainty and smiled to reassure her. "That's grass; it won't hurt you; it's a part of the ground. I will never let anything hurt you."

The Greyhound was relieved. Nothing she had ever walked on had ever felt this soft, and she preferred the ground's green blanket more than the concrete that hurt her wounds and made her bones ache.

I could get used to this, she thought, but she couldn't help but wonder why she was here—with this Girl, and why a field, with no Track, was over there. She certainly didn't miss the excruciating daily workouts or the screaming that came at her from the woman in charge of her training. Not all the Greyhounds were yelled at—mostly it was directed at her. If she won, she was praised, and her fur was stroked for a few seconds; but if she didn't place, she could barely sleep on those nights as she relived the race step by step and identified each failure made. No one paid any attention to her on those days, unless it was to criticize her. She feared losing too often, because she didn't want to disappear like so many of her friends had after having lost consecutive races. Where had they gone?

Have I disappeared now too? She tried not to think about the past as she continued assessing the yard, but she was still attached to the leash in the Girl's hand. The Girl led her around until it was time to go inside.

THE NEWNESS OF THINGS

And so it was . . . The Greyhound followed the Girl out of the small enclosure and across the driveway, where an aromatic Cedar gate affixed to a post was attached to the garage on her right and to the house on her left. *Click!* The loud sound of the gate closing behind her echoed in her brain. It was the same one the kennel door had made in the evenings, when the Trainers left and locked the racers in their stacked Cages. The Greyhound could no longer see the Ballfield, now hidden behind the Cedar gate. That concerned her. She inspected the larger yard. Life at the Track had taught the Greyhound to be extraordinarily adept at judging distances.

I wonder if she'll let me loose, thought the Greyhound. *At least here, there is enough room to stretch my legs. I could probably eek out two strides or so. It certainly isn't expansive enough for me to run outright. Ugh, I don't want to be fenced in anymore. I want to run and roam free like those Squirrels in the Tree. Why are they free and I'm not? Why are Birds free to fly at will, but I am bound by a collar, a leash, and a Muzzle? Why am I always held captive behind Cages and Fences?*

"Look over there, Girl," said the Girl pointing to the left corner of the yard. "That's a Weeping Cherry Tree, and the flowers beneath it are Gerbera Daisies—my favorite. They are devoted to the Sun and have the power to help ease our sorrow. Unlike the Montauks, they have just about outlasted their bloom cycle."

Pointing to the right, the Girl continued, "That small opening leads behind the garage to the area we just came from, overlooking the Ballfield.

That's how you will get to your business spot."

The Greyhound sighed with relief. The Bee, buzzing about the Daisies, was watching her closely. The tall, Cedar Fence surrounding the backyard turned into a chain-link Fence as it met the entrance behind the garage. As she peered into the opening, she was transported back in time to the starting gate at the Track, which was only a tad wider than this space. Her muscles tightened as she remembered how exhilaration and fear filled the starting gate before each race, and how the sound of the crowd cheering and the muffled barking of the muzzled racers resounded in the metal Cage that surrounded her. Standing there, peering behind the garage, she envisioned the Track perfectly groomed, prepared for her to tear through with each stride. She reveled in the anticipation of that gate opening as the lure was released.

I miss racing. She let out a meager bark. "Ruff." She could have cried, but didn't.

The Bee buzzed closer now. "Go ahead, you can cry if you must, but it won't give you what you desire. I can make your desires happen for you, not at the Track, but somewhere even better without Fences!"

"It's okay, Girl. You'll fit through just fine. You can test it tomorrow," the Girl said as she stroked the Greyhound's back. Let's go inside. That Bee is bugging me."

The Girl opened the back door. The Greyhound noted how the door was made of heavy steel that had a reddish hue, was worn, and bent somewhat in the bottom corner. Beyond the door, it was warmer, but the Greyhound stood in shock, looking up at the insurmountable mountain that loomed before her. Her jaw dropped.

How am I supposed to get to the top of that? she thought.

"These are stairs. Come on, Girl! Follow me," said the Girl.

Stairs? the Greyhound questioned. She had never seen stairs before now. She imagined what the Bee would say right about now: *You'll never be able to climb those stairs! Not in your condition. You're not strong enough or brave enough.*

The Greyhound looked into the Girl's hazel eyes, then back at the stairs.

The Girl's voice broke through the Greyhound's mounting fear. "Don't worry, you can stay down here until you heal. I'll just set up the extra Cage. Here's some water and a biscuit."

The Greyhound refused both. She was not used to being given anything before her nighttime sleep, so she watched the Girl build the Cage, which took longer than expected.

"It's getting dark now. It's been a very long day, and you need your rest." The Girl set up the Greyhound's Cage by layering it first with thick foam then a white sheet. "You will be comfortable in here."

The Girl had such a tender tone, but the Greyhound's head ached as a new reality presented itself. She was being put into yet another Cage!

"Here, Girl. Go on in," the Girl said.

The Greyhound obeyed, as she had been taught to obey those who commanded her. Slowly, she walked into the black, steel Cage, turned around, and lay her tired body on the sheet. Her nose faced the Girl. The dejected Greyhound looked up with sad eyes, but she was too exhausted to confront the fierce feeling that she would never be free.

The Girl placed a soft, blue blanket on the Greyhound. "This will keep you warm tonight, SweetOne."

The Girl's voice began to fade as sleep shrouded the Greyhound. She faintly heard the Girl say, "I'll see you in the morning," but she could barely open one eye to see the Girl disappear up the long staircase. She fell hard and fast asleep that night and drifted into a dream state.

NIGHT TERRORS

And so it was . . . The night lingered as the Greyhound continued dreaming. She dreamt of a Moonless night where Shadows watched her through the darkness. Though they had no recognizable features, she knew them well for they visited often. The heaviness of their presence was undeniable. The frightening feeling of being captured was deeply imbedded in her bones. She found herself at the Track in the starting box again. It was sweltering, and the metal, scorched by the Sun's rays, was hot against her sides. Being inside the mechanical gate was a familiar place, but something was disturbingly different this time—she was trapped! The Shadows had trapped her! The Greyhound knew she had to break free and run to safety or the Shadows would destroy her. Strength was her strong suit, but the threat of getting burned intensified.

"You must save yourself. You can do it," a muted voice whispered from just outside the confines of the gate.

Strangely, the voice reassured her. She scrunched as far back in the chute as she could without touching its sides, then leapt forward with such force that the swinging doors burst open the moment her muscular body made contact. Freedom was hers. However, the Shadows followed and would be upon her imminently.

"You don't belong here!" They cackled. "You are of no use to us anymore! We are done with you! We never wanted you here. We only used you. You did everything we needed you to do, so now you are expendable, and we will dispose of you! Now, you will disappear forever—without a trace—as if you never existed!"

The more she listened to the Shadows, the more she felt her body freeze and her throat tighten. She tried to move but was paralyzed by the fear.

A familiar voice drowned out the others. It was a comforting voice that urged her, "Run, run, run! Keep running! Don't stop! Run! Get away from here—far, far away, and never look back. Don't worry, I am always with you."

How can I run in the pitch-black? she thought. *How will I know which way to run? How will I find* the Way *out of this darkness? How? It's impossible!*

"You will know *the Way*." The voice neared, as did the shouts of the Shadows. "You will know *the Way by Heart*, DearOne."

Looking down in the direction of the faint voice, the Greyhound felt something tug at her paw. Still unable to see in the lightless night, she lowered her snout and took a sniff. That scent! Yes, she recognized it. It was the Mouse from the Track.

"What are you doing here?" whispered the Greyhound, for fear of being heard by the Shadows that tormented her so.

"I'm here to help you, of course. Why else would I be here?" said the tiny creature. "There's no time. You have to go. Now. Run! Run as if your life depends on it. Save your Self. No one can save you but your Self."

"But I don't know *the Way*," said the Greyhound with an audible turbulence in her voice. "I can't move. I'm in so much pain. My eyes ache. My head is heavy and feels like it's going to explode! My legs are cut and bruised all over. I can't move. I can't see *the Way*."

"You know *the Way*," the Mouse went on, "You know this Track *by Heart*—*by Heart* you will know *the Way*."

It was true. The Greyhound did know the Track. She had run the Track thousands of times. She knew every inch of it—where every hole tended to form, how the dirt was softer in some places where the lure glided along the rail and harder closest to the apron where the spectators sat behind a Fence. She knew how many strides it took to complete the front stretch and exactly when to make the turn. She even remembered where she had seen the golden Fawn fly into the air and leap over the Fence to freedom. The spot was located directly after the tote board but before the escape turn where the lure disappeared at the conclusion of a race. The Mouse was right—she knew it *by Heart*.

"There's no more time to waste. You've been here long enough. You've done all that you were meant to do here. The time has come to go—to say good-bye to the life you once knew. It's okay. . . . It's okay to go," the Mouse encouraged.

The Shadows were upon her. Their darkness hovered above her—all around her. If she did not run, they would surely reach her, consume her, and she would not survive. The Greyhound knew what she had to do. All her weight shifted to her hind legs, which bent a bit, and with all her might, she hurled herself into the dark sky. By her third leap, the Greyhound was a quarter of the way down the front stretch. Six more strides and she'd be at the turn. Three last strides and she'd leap to the right at just the precise moment to clear the Fence. She ran along the rail. The Shadows fell behind. As she sailed over the Fence, she looked up and saw the Stars and the Moon shining brightly. The Shadows were disappearing, but how could she land firmly on the ground if she couldn't see it? Why wasn't the sky light enough for her to see the ground? She was falling now—falling, falling so fast! The Greyhound cried out in her sleep, *Help me. Please. Help me!*

"Wake up. Wake up, DearOne." A tiny voice broke softly through the Night Terror. "You're having a bad dream. You were running in your sleep again. You're okay now. I am with you."

The Greyhound awakened from the Night Terror quite relieved the Shadows hadn't really devoured her. It had felt so real. She spied movement out of the corner of her eye. It was a tiny tail. The sweet scent was unmistakable. It was the Mouse from her dream—the Mouse from the

Track that always seemed to be close by whenever she found the courage to ask for help. She was not alone.

THREE

—

THE HILL

IN THE STILLNESS IS KNOWING

And so it was . . . The Greyhound gently lifted the left corner of the blue blanket with her teeth to uncover the Mouse.

"It is you!" whispered the Greyhound.

"Of course it's me," muttered the Mouse. "Who else would be here with you?"

The Greyhound shrugged. "No one, I suppose. I'm just glad you made it inside the Girl's house." She paused. "I have a question."

"Anything," said the Mouse.

"Why did you sneak into my Cage at the Track that night? Why would you want to make that terrible Journey with me?"

"Why wouldn't I? I am always with you," peeped the tiny creature.

"Where were you hiding?" the Greyhound asked, confounded.

The Mouse explained how it had remained hidden under the tattered paper in the Cage the day the Greyhound was forcibly removed from the Track. The Greyhound remembered how uncomfortably tight the Cage had been, how dark it was in the truck, and how the stench was inescapable in the absence of fresh air. Racers wailed in pain and desperation. Some were injured like herself—some more so, some less, some clung to life, some didn't. She shivered as she recalled how several of them had succumbed to their fate over the course of many hours spent in agony. No sleep had been possible on that trip. The Greyhound might have rested if she had seen the Mouse.

"Why didn't you say anything?" the Greyhound groaned.

The Mouse mused, "It isn't up to me to reveal myself. It is up to you to become still enough to hear me—to become still, even amid the chaos that surrounds you. In the stillness is knowing. In the knowing is the peace you seek. Know I am always with you."

The Greyhound was too tired to figure out exactly what the Mouse meant, but its words consoled her.

"Be sure to stay hidden so no one sees you—especially the Bee, who may wish to hurt you," cautioned the Greyhound. With that, the unlikely companions curled up close as the Moonlight of the waxing crescent Moon shone through the small basement window, encasing the two in its healing light. The Greyhound fell asleep, comforted by the fact she was not alone.

TETHERED

And so it was . . . Early the next morning, the Girl fed the Greyhound a warm meal. Surprised by how delicious it tasted, the Greyhound's tail twitched. It had been such a long time since she felt delighted enough to wag her tail, but she caught herself and stopped the motion, unsure of how the Girl would react. Even though the Girl had been nice enough so far, trust was difficult to embrace after all the Greyhound had experienced. She was not ready to trust just yet. Luckily, the Girl did not notice the moment of vulnerability. The Greyhound was relieved.

Following the meal, the Girl leashed her, led her to the driveway, and helped her get up into the Jeep. Though the Greyhound was healing well, the Girl said she did not want to risk opening the wound on her lower abdomen. The Bee flew in unnoticed and landed on the side window just as the hatch closed.

Is she taking me back to the Shelter? Did I do something wrong? the terrified Greyhound panted as her fear presented worst-case scenarios.

"She probably saw all the Scars on your underside and knows you are damaged," the Bee proclaimed.

The Greyhound tried to remain calm, but the Bee aggravated her nerves.

"Don't worry, Girl, we are going someplace special. I want to show you one of my favorite places," the Girl said excitedly.

"Why would you want to stay with her anyway?" the Bee quietly questioned the Greyhound. "She has put you in a Cage on a concrete floor just like all the others. You are not free as you so desire. You are not even allowed to roam alone in the yard. The Girl has kept a watchful eye on you since your arrival yesterday. No good will come of your stay here. You should come with me! I will show you what true freedom is, and you will be able to run as you wish. I promise."

The Bee's buzzing dizzied the Greyhound as fear mounted and confidence faded. The Greyhound wished it were the other way around.

"We are here." The Girl's voice broke through the tumult that twisted in the Greyhound's tortured mind. She parked the vehicle under a beautiful Sugar Maple Tree that must have been at least a hundred years old. The hatch opened, and for a moment, the Greyhound wished the Girl would just let her jump out of the Jeep on her own accord, but to her dismay, just as the Bee had predicted, that sound, *Click*, made it clear she was not free.

"I told you so," the Bee taunted.

The Greyhound's ears flopped, and some fur fell to the ground as she shook her head. The Bee backed off. The Girl led the Greyhound down a narrow, paved walkway that eventually blended into the green grass, which was beginning to brown in patches, here and there. Looming ahead of them was a high Hill bedecked by gorgeous Zinnias, Sweet Alyssum, Cosmos, and Daisies—"The last of the Autumn flowers," the Girl said. The Girl named the various flowers and Trees as they walked partway up the Hill. It was an arresting sight! Struck by the brilliant beauty of Nature, the Greyhound's jaw remained open in awe of the Hill. Her past world had not been so beautiful, nor as colorful.

The Greyhound stopped. The Girl stopped too. The leash went slack as they stood there. Sniffing the clean morning air, she and the Girl each took a deep *breath*. In that moment of stillness, the Mouse appeared at the Greyhound's foot, hidden in the Cosmos. It remained unseen by the Girl. The Greyhound didn't even need to look down, because the feeling in her heart made the Mouse's presence apparent. She was becoming more aware of that gentle prodding.

I've never seen anything so beautiful, the Greyhound thought. *The Hill is so pretty!*

"It is beautiful," the Mouse agreed. "There's nothing more moving and inspiring than Nature and her wondrous beauty."

"Ahhh," the Greyhound inhaled deeply. She had never smelled anything like it. It was so grounding to feel the Earth beneath her instead of concrete and so energizing to *breathe* in clean air that had no trace of Track dust. She relaxed.

"Let's rest for a moment," the Girl said. "I don't want to push you too much."

I'm fine, the Greyhound thought. She was stronger than the Girl realized but acquiesced anyway. They sat and watched the Squirrels collect nuts on the ground that had fallen from the Oak and scurry up and down various Trees that traced the Hill's side. She had just begun enjoying the moment when the Squirrels started squeaking and mocking her. The Greyhound wished for a moment when she wasn't attached to the leash so she could chase away the Squirrels that gawked at her annoyingly. Knowing the Greyhound could reach them if she wanted to, the Squirrels taunted her from afar as the pesky Bee began to bounce about her head once again.

"Look at the poor Hound—tied up and can't run away," the Squirrels squawked. "Look at the pathetic pup—simply so sad today!"

The Bee joined in their derision. "You could be free all the time you know. I can help you escape. You wouldn't have to be bound by that leash. You'd be able to go anywhere you want. Unfortunately, you now belong to the Girl just as you belonged to the Track. You are being controlled now just as your Owner and Trainer controlled you."

"Be quiet!" begged the Greyhound. "The Girl cares about me! I think she might love me."

"Love?" questioned the Bee. "What do you know of love? Being bound is not love. Being free to do what you wish is love."

"I know about love. I've loved before and have been loved too," gruffed the Greyhound.

"By whom?" asked the Bee.

"My bottom Cage Companion loved me—and the Moon loves me too!"

"This foolish infatuation with the Moon must end! And you call what that racer offered you love? He would charm you then criticized you at every turn and he used you to satiate his own needs. And when he couldn't get what he wanted from you any more he—"

"Don't say it. Don't you say it," the Greyhound warned.

The Girl tugged at the Greyhound's leash, pulling her attention away from the Bee.

"Let's go, Girl."

They continued walking, but they weren't headed in the direction of the Jeep. The Greyhound and the Girl made their way along an old cobblestone path. The Girl stopped at the entrance of a large Circle of tall white bushes.

"They're called Hydrangeas," the Girl offered. "Aren't they beautiful?"

They are beautiful! There are so many of them. They look like puffy white clouds. This is a perfect place to stretch my legs and run! I could run about nine strides—the length of the Track, the Greyhound thought. She was ecstatic and ready to run. She felt strong.

"Please let me loose! Let me loose! This is the perfect place!" the Greyhound pleaded with the Girl. "Woof, woof."

She pulled lightly at the leash, forcing the Girl to take a few steps forward past the entrance of the Circle.

"No, Girl, I can't let you go in there. I can't take the chance that you might run away. The Handlers at the Shelter said I should never let you run free if there is no Fence. If you get loose, you will just keep running, and you'll get lost." The Girl gently tugged the leash, and the Greyhound, with her head hung low, followed at her side obediently.

But I want to run! I need to, she thought. She couldn't make another sound. Her throat tightened in disappointment.

"I was right," the Bee said condescendingly. "The only way you'll ever be free to run is if you follow me. Meet me tonight in the smaller yard when she lets you out for the last time. Trust me. It's for your own good."

Noticing the Bee, the Girl quickened their pace. It continued to follow them as they headed for the parking lot. The unrelenting Bee did not stop its brutal mental attack on the Greyhound. It planted seeds of doubt in her muddled mind. The discouraged Greyhound became more amenable to the musings of the Bee as they walked. Her Spirit sank. She indulged the Bee and listened intently to its machinations to escape. Freedom would be hers, like it was for the Birds and the Squirrels. The Bee tempted the Greyhound, and the madness of its plan somehow made sense. She was torn between the possibility of having the kind of love with the Girl that she had heard the dogs in the Shelter describe and the freedom the Bee was promising.

I wish the Bee would go away, thought the Greyhound.

They reached the Jeep. The Mouse appeared from behind the wheel well. "Don't fret, DearOne. The Girl truly cares about you. She's a sweet soul who understands those who have lost *the Way*. Deep down you know you would be happier with her. Trust that feeling. Know it *by Heart*."

"I'll try, but what if the Bee is right?" the Greyhound asked.

The Greyhound questioned everything. She even asked why it was so that the Bee disappeared when she listened to the Mouse speak. The Mouse wouldn't say. All it said was that she had to discover the reason on her own. The Greyhound was not glad about answers that remained in the stratosphere. The conversation would need to continue at a later time. She tried to ignore the perpetual pounding in her head. The ride home, with the windows rolled down, provided some relief.

DOUBT DOUBT

And so it was . . . As the Sun lay below the saffron-and-plum-colored clouds of the afternoon sky, the Girl cleaned the Jeep, and the Greyhound reposed on the green grass overlooking the Ballfield. The breeze was unusually warm for a late October day. A few leaves fell, here and there. One scarlet leaf landed on the Greyhound's nose. The Mouse giggled affectionately as the leaf teetered on the tip of her long snout. The Greyhound blew it off, but the leaf lingered in the air, levitating for a moment before gliding to the ground.

Looking up at the limb that had dropped the leaf, the Greyhound followed its course. It led to a larger branch that arced over the Fence. The branch was attached to the massive trunk of a White Oak Tree. The Greyhound was impressed by the grandeur of the Tree and asked the Tree politely, "Excuse me, but why are you losing your leaves? Does it hurt? Are you dying?"

"No, DearOne," the Oak replied in a raspy tone. "It does not hurt, and I am not dying. I am preparing for Winter. My leaves are completing one of their Autumn tasks. They not only provide me with food to sustain my existence, but they also release oxygen into the air for all living things to *breathe*. Once the cooler air arrives, my leaves change color into the extraordinary deep purple and reds you see, become undone, and float to the Earth where they can nourish it."

"That is gracious of you and them," the Greyhound humbly replied, though she had no idea what the word *Winter* meant. The synchronicities of Nature astounded the Greyhound with each new revelation. The thought that this particular place could become her favorite crossed her mind.

Neighborhood kids played ball as she watched. She loved how the children were free to run the bases once the bat met the ball and sent it sailing into the sky. The Greyhound was intrigued by how the ball was thrown from one child to the other with such accuracy more times than not. She smiled at the joy on the faces of the elated children, playing on the playground adjacent to the Ballfield. Particularly, the Greyhound liked watching the kids on the swings, and how they rose up to the sky like the Bluebird had, and how they swung back to the Earth without crashing to the ground. She imagined how incredible it would feel to see the sky, or her Moon, up close.

They are so free and happy, she thought. *I wish I were free and happy.*

Their giggles were infectious, the sound quite pleasing, and it made the Mouse, which was partially camouflaged by the colorful leaves, giggle too. The Greyhound could not wait for a child to notice her. She hoped one would come running up the slight incline leading to the yard and gently pet her through the Fence. She really wished there were no Fence at all.

I want to run, she thought.

"I know you do, DearOne," said the Mouse.

But when will I be able to? she asked.

"You must be patient, DearOne."

She enjoyed seeing the clusters of people gathering on blankets and lawn chairs. The Girl called them families.

The fresh scent of food wafted in the air, and her senses heightened. "Sniff, sniff."

"What do you smell?" asked the Girl from the driveway. "Oh, I know. You smell the hamburgers and hot dogs. I like the smell of popcorn popping best."

The bustle of activity was reminiscent of racing days at the Track. The bittersweet nostalgia hit the Greyhound's heart hard just as she was beginning to enjoy the moment. Unfortunately, the Bee was close enough for her to hear its buzzing. The Bee was steadily breaking down the Greyhound's defenses. The Bee had been with the Greyhound for a very long time—ever since she was a young pup. It was aware of the many hardships the Greyhound had endured but showed little empathy. It preyed upon her emotional exhaustion. That's when she became the victim of the Bee's pandered protestations of freedom.

The idea of escaping from the yard and truly being free settled in her mind. *What if the Bee is right? What if I could be happier beyond the boundary of this Fence? What if I were free to run wherever I wished and do whatever I desired and not be accountable to anyone? What if true freedom is out there somewhere, and I am missing out on what life has to offer? So many what-ifs!*

A deluge of doubt distracted her as she contemplated how much better her life would be if she were cut off from human interaction. After all, every human being she had encountered or trusted had let her down in some cruel, compelling way either by making fun of her, bullying her, or lying to her straight-faced. They had hurt her, both physically and emotionally. They had broken her heart, controlled her, or tricked her into trusting them only to brutally betray and abandon her once she had shown them her heart. Why had she believed them to be as sincere as she? Even the Girl, though kinder than the rest, kept her in a closed Cage, tied up, and fenced in as she was now.

Maybe I am better off without the Girl, or without anyone at all, she contemplated. *Humans always hurt me when I let them near. Why would I believe the kindness of the Girl isn't fleeting as well?*

The Greyhound's vulnerability always piqued the Bee's interest and drew it to her. Though she had not invited the Bee to be near her, it floated close to the prostrate Greyhound and landed on a Montauk Daisy that had snapped off its stem. The Bee buzzed in the Greyhound's ear.

"What are you doing here?" the Greyhound asked, annoyed. "I'm busy trying to enjoy myself."

"Ha!" the Bee began, despite the Greyhound's half attempt to shoo it away. "You don't seem to be enjoying yourself. You are tethered and imprisoned by this Fence. Wouldn't you prefer to be free from these constraints? If you follow my escape plan, you'd be free to run in the Circle you so adored today near the Hill. There you could see the Daisies dance at dawn, and I know *the Way*. I could show you *the Way*. Trust me."

The Greyhound sighed. There were those enticing words again, *trust me*.

"How would I get over this Fence? There is no way I could push through this monster, nor could I jump over it."

"It would be easy," the Bee gloated." The Fence doesn't impede your freedom. You do. You have sufficiently healed from the operation and your injuries. There are no excuses for inaction now."

The Sun sank into the horizon, and the plum-colored clouds morphed into a bright strawberry-orange as the Bee dribbled some doubt on the Greyhound's desire to be content with the Girl. It continued, "You are right! You have been immensely injured by human beings and your own kind your entire life. They only take, take, take! They let you down and pretend to be your friend and prey upon your kindhearted, generous nature. They've never appreciated your loyalty *or* your love. You don't need anyone anymore. You'd be better off on your own! Don't you agree?"

The Bee's torturous tirades tired the Greyhound, tempting her with its grandiose plan but leaving her too conflicted to fight off thoughts of a new life far away. She wondered where the Mouse had gone. She needed its help to unravel her twisted thoughts. Had it abandoned her too? Whenever she sensed the Mouse was close by, the Bee would warn her that she had better stop looking for the Mouse or it would get stung. The Greyhound wouldn't be able to cope with that tragedy, so she obeyed. More and more the Greyhound was becoming defenseless against the Bee's bidding.

"It's dinnertime, Girl," the Girl said as she untied the leash from the metal stake anchored in the ground and walked the Greyhound into the larger yard that hemmed the house.

The red-hued door opened, and the Bee flew undetected above the Girl's head into the basement. The Greyhound noticed that it landed on the shelving unit next to the Cage and hid in a rusty tin can. It was time to rest. She crawled into the Cage without having to be commanded.

The Girl fed the Greyhound before walking up the stairs, disappearing as she had done the night before.

The Greyhound wondered what lay at the top of the stairs behind the wooden door.

"You see?" said the Bee from inside the tin can. "She's left you locked in this Cage again! This is your new life. You may be in a new place, and the Cage may be a different size, but it's still a Cage."

The Greyhound's head pounded profusely, while the Bee's words echoed in the tin can.

There was no denying her situation. The Bee was right. This was not the life she had imagined. She was desperate to sprint. Her muscles ached from not being able to run for so long. Running away was the only solution. The Greyhound finally agreed to meet the Bee later that evening when the Girl let her out for the last time.

HUGS HEAL THE HEART

And so it was . . . A shaky anticipation marked the arrival of the Girl, who led the Greyhound out the heavy, steel door.

"Go do your business, Girl."

The Greyhound slowly made her way towards the path at the back right corner of the yard. She stopped short, where the Fence line disappeared behind the stone garage.

"What is it, Girl?" the Girl asked.

It was obvious to the Greyhound that the Girl was becoming increasingly concerned for her. She couldn't help it and looked back with an overwhelming sadness that lodged in her throat and stomach and shrouded her Spirit. She could feel, *by Heart* that the Girl was an empathic soul. She was compelled to turn and walk back to the Girl, who was waiting in the dimly lit doorway. The two met in the middle of the modest yard. The Girl knelt in the grass and outstretched her arms. The Greyhound accepted the invitation gladly as the Girl wrapped her arms around the Greyhound's long, elegant neck. The Girl gently hugged the Greyhound, and the Greyhound leaned in, allowing the burden of her weight and troubles to be supported by the Girl.

"I love your hugs," said the Girl loud enough for the Stars to hear her. "You give the best hugs!"

The hug lasted a long minute. The Greyhound did not want her to let go, and a part of her wished the Girl would just take her back into the house straightaway and thoughts of this zany plan would disintegrate into the Cosmos. She leaned more heavily against the Girl.

"What's the matter?" asked the Girl. "What's wrong? It's okay, Girl. There's nothing to fear. Don't worry. I'll wait for you. I love you!" the Girl whispered those last words in the Greyhound's ear.

And with those words, the Greyhound adjusted her weight, knowing it would cause the Girl to let go. She swallowed her tears and made her way towards the narrow opening. She looked back one last time at the Girl, who managed a half-smile, and nodded for her to go. The Greyhound knew it would be the last time she would see the kind Girl. This time, she felt as though *she* was the one letting someone down. Nausea negotiated its way into her throat. The Greyhound hung her head, defeated by the guilt and the dream she had deferred. Her nose grazed the grass. She hopped up the stone step the thoughtful Girl had made for her and vanished behind the Shadow of the garage, while the Girl waited in front of the open door. Once in the smaller enclosure, the Greyhound could see the yellowish light above the red-hued door, shining through the wooden planks of the Cedar Fence. The Bee's plan needed a quick execution or she would lose her nerve.

THE FENCE

And so it was . . . The Greyhound stood silently in the middle of the space and peered into the darkness. She looked up but didn't notice the waxing Moon, only the monstrosity of the Fence and how its top rail was illuminated by the Moon's half light. While the Girl waited for the Greyhound, the Bee acted swiftly and baited the Greyhound by petting her pride.

"You have effortlessly jumped that high in the past. You jumped over racers when they tumbled to their demise in front of you. You jumped even higher into your stacked Cage at the Track. Don't forget, you jumped over those dogs at the Shelter. Surely you can jump over that Fence! Do it."

The Greyhound was barely listening, withdrawn in thought regarding the Girl.

"There are so many interesting places in the world to explore, my friend," needled the Bee. "You can run whenever you want."

The valence of the moment burdened the Greyhound. Why was she leaving? Why was she running away? She thought of her warm food, her comfortable blue blanket, and that hug. She couldn't think straight, as the humming of the Bee grew louder and more prominent.

"Hurry! We must leave. Now! It's your only chance!" blasted the Bee.

Suddenly, she remembered the Fawn who flew over the Fence at the Track and how she herself had escaped the Shadows in her Night Terror. The Greyhound felt the Shadows hovering over her now. She couldn't help but hear the buzzing in her brain, impelling her to go.

"Jump! Jump! Now!" exclaimed the Bee.

Reflexively, she leaned back on her hind legs, gathered all her strength, and hurled herself into the night sky as if she were on that swing in the Ballfield. She was flying—flying over the Fence!

"Don't stop!" commanded the Bee, who could not contain its delirium. "Keep running! You'll find me. Don't worry."

The Greyhound did as she was told. She had always done as she was told. She knew no other way.

FOUR

—

THE ESCAPE

I AM FREE

And so it was . . . The Greyhound made her great escape. She ran down the slight incline on the other side of the Girl's yard, straight across the Ballfield, over the pitcher's mound, then over third base. She ran through the playground, jumped over the swing and across the parking lot to the familiar neighborhood streets where she and the Girl had gone on a walk. She did not stop running! The Greyhound ran away from the Girl, who called out to her with a faint crackle of consternation in her voice, which the Greyhound likened to the same grief she herself had expressed back at the Track when the one *she* loved had left her forever.

"Where are you, Girl? Where did you go?" the Girl called out in heart-wrenching desperation. "Come back! Come back home!"

It was just too much for the Greyhound to handle. It broke her heart to hear the sad tenor of the Girl's cries, but she couldn't understand why the Girl was crying.

She couldn't possibly be crying for me, the Greyhound thought. *I am too unlovable with all these Scars.*

She kept running as swiftly as she could, although she was not sure from what, from whom, or why. As she ran across town through more neighborhoods and various parks, she faintly heard another familiar voice whisper, "Listen, *by Heart.*"

The words echoed what the Mouse had told her in her Night Terror. But where was the Mouse? The Greyhound dug her claws into the ground and continued running into the cool, October night. The Girl's cries soon became inaudible, so the Greyhound concentrated on the grandiose tales the Bee had told her of a place far away from anyone who could hurt her, and wide, open spaces where she'd be free, not forced, to run as fast as she pleased, and roam as far as her heart desired.

I'm free! she thought. *I must keep going.* Her innate speed brought her quickly to the outskirts of town. The Greyhound's heart still ached, so she kept running. Two hearts broke that night.

THE DEAD OF NIGHT

And so it was . . . The Greyhound stopped running at full gait, slowing slightly, keeping clear of the peril of the main roadway. Echoes of the past and her caramel-colored Companion's death cries reminded her how dangerous vehicles of any kind could be. The incident happened one foggy night at the Track—her Companion had gotten loose while being brought in at night. He had taken the opportunity to escape. He often spoke of escaping but had promised he would take her with him. His offer had come at a time when the bullying had begun affecting all aspects of her life. Instead of being by his side, she and her fellow racers watched as he shot like an arrow out of the enclosure in the direction of the parking lot. The Trainer who had left the gate ajar was fired on the spot. She would never forget the sound of the supply truck's screeching tires and echoes of the piercing cries that emanated from her wounded Companion. She recalled the flurry of activity they all heard coming from the Trainers' cabin.

Someone yelled, "Get the buckshot!"

One of the Trainers grabbed the buckshot—the most feared object a Greyhound could encounter. There was chatter that the Trainers and Owner had found the downed racer still wildly wailing in pain. An unbearably loud bang rang through the air, rattling all the Cages and drowning out the Nightingale's song. A deafening silence ensued.

Her heart pounded fiercely and sank. Her first love was never seen again. She didn't know where they had taken him, but shovels were used in the process. Devastated by the loss and profoundly changed by his absence, she had not placed in the next day's race. His yelping and wincing were etched in her brain for months following the unfortunate twist of fate. She could no longer feel his presence as time passed, though she longed for some sign that he was okay in the afterworld.

So much had happened since that terrible night. The vacancy on the racing team prompted the search for a new racer and, after a good amount of time passed, one was placed in the Cage below her. He was quite charming and handsome. She and her new bottom Cage Companion took an immediate liking to one another. It was love at first sight. But, to this day, if memories of her caramel-colored Companion, her first love, invaded that remote part of her mind where she housed them, she could still hear her caramel-colored Companion howling in pain. Thoughts of his audible pain gave her the same sinking feeling she had felt when she heard the Girl crying out to her.

Will I miss this place? Will I miss the Girl? Did I make the right decision by listening to the Bee? Where is the Mouse? Why has it abandoned me? What have I done? she thought. Her sight was blinded by tears, but she swallowed them whole, knowing they would never stop if she let even one tear drop. She continued running into the dead of night.

HEED THE WARNINGS

And so it was . . . Once she felt far away enough to do so, the Greyhound's gallop turned into a trot, which waned into a walk. She was tired, thirsty, and noticeably alone. When she came upon the Hill where the Girl had taken her the day before, her heart fluttered. Why had she gone to that spot? Had she subconsciously or consciously chosen that familiar place where she, the Girl, and the Mouse had shared a happy time together? Did she secretly hope the Girl would look for her there and bring her back to the house? Was the Girl even looking for her? The Greyhound doubted it. Only the damn Bee's buzzing was reliable.

The Circle of Hydrangeas was partially illuminated by the half Moon, rising in front of her as she came down the Hill. She remembered them fondly, but it was too dark, and she was too tired to run right now. Their white bunches of flower heads also reflected the Moonlight and appeared Starlike, but the flower heads had begun to sag.

Are they dying? She wondered. *Why do things have to die?*

In unison, bass-toned voices answered her. "We are not dying, DearOne, in the manner of death as you understand it. We are preparing for Winter, whose mightiness slowly approaches."

"Oh," the Greyhound responded, astonished the Hydrangeas could actually communicate. She regulated her *breathing,* then continued speaking. "Winter? What is Winter?" she asked, remembering she had forgotten to ask the Oak Tree the same question.

"Winter is a wondrous force that turns Nature inward, except for the Evergreens, of course."

"Why are *they* special?" the Greyhound inquired.

The Circle continued in concert with the Crickets' chirping in the distance. "The Evergreens have been marked by Winter, for they are allowed to keep their green hue all year long. We eventually will lose our green leaves and our white blossoms will change."

I wish I were special, thought the Greyhound.

"Winter's chilling *breath* will harden the ground beneath you and blow the cool, Fall air far away for a time. He will cloak the Earth in snow so Nature can sleep deeply below Winter's white blanket. She requires respite from the toil of prior seasons," the Circle explained.

The Greyhound did not know what the Hydrangeas meant by *snow,* but she noticed it was much cooler here than at the Track. She had never been cold there. Realizing how chilly she had become and that her core temperature had fallen fast following her long run, desperation settled in as her exhausted body pleaded for rest and water. She knew she must keep moving and find shelter or perish.

"Winter will command attention, DearOne! If you do not heed his powerful presence, you may find yourself trapped in his cold clutches with nothing to do but sleep—a sleep unlike the Earth's, for it is one that offers no awakening. Seek shelter before mid-December, DearOne! Pay special attention to your surroundings on your Journey."

The Hydrangeas' foreboding warnings made the Greyhound shiver. She thanked them for the information regarding Winter but wondered what they meant by the latter advice.

Haven't I always been aware of my surroundings? she questioned.

"Farewell, DearOne. Until we meet again!"

As the Greyhound walked away, the last words uttered by the Circle faded into the silent night.

BE AWARE OF
YOUR SURROUNDINGS

And so it was . . . The exhausted Greyhound walked into the Forest to find a resting place while she waited for the Bee to arrive. Early on in her career, she realized rest was vital following a race or great expenditure of energy. A sprinter by nature, long-distance running was not her forte.

Her aerodynamic body was made to run in short bursts, and it could reach incredible speeds, but for Greyhounds, generally speaking, endurance was challenging. The Greyhound had heard the Track crew tell stories of the speed and agility of her kind and their masterful hunting ability, though she had never hunted herself.

To puff up her pride when she had wavered about its escape plan, the Bee had told her tales of other fast animals and explained that very few animals on the planet could run faster than she. It explained how a hare was quite fast and could reach high speeds in just a tail's length, and how a lion was as fast as she, but exhibited even less endurance. A Greyhound, the Bee boasted on her behalf, could beat a lion in a race but never a cheetah.

The Bee had promised to show her an open field where she would be able to run without the fear of a turn or the need to come to an abrupt stop. She imagined how that freedom would feel as she walked into the black Forest, which, in the absence of streetlights, grew ominously darker with every step. Rest was paramount! She knew her body was about to fail her. Her eyes ached, her head pounded with grief, and her legs had become weary. Extremely aware of most of her limitations, she did not allow herself to dwell on them or she'd be wrought with a fusillade of emotion. She had always pushed through challenges regardless of their physical or emotional effects. Now was no different from then.

I AM PROTECTED

And so it was . . . As the witching hour approached, the Greyhound became increasingly fearful of the choice she had made to leave the Girl. The Hydrangeas' warning to seek shelter soon played on a loop in her mind.

I'm so cold, she thought. *Why is it so cold out here? What happened to the hot days and the comfortable, warm nights? Why hasn't the Sun been working properly during the day? Why is it so dark now? I need light! Dearest Moon, where have you gone?*

As if by some Magickal force, the Trees shook and swayed, allowing the light of the Moon to shine on the Greyhound. She looked up. The Moon made himself known to her. A meager smile emerged despite the cold and her declining mood, both of which prevented her from smiling fully.

"You are here," the Greyhound whispered.

I am, glinted the Moon silently.

The two had always understood one another, even without words, ever since she was born. As a puppy, she was able to see most of the Moon's light out of the large window in the Breeder's barn. It shone on her most nights. They spoke to one another often. The other pups poked fun at her for doing such an outlandish thing. They didn't believe the Moon spoke to her. They simply thought she was crazy.

"I am lost," whimpered the Greyhound.

So you say, communicated the Moon.

"I don't know where I am or which direction is *the Way* I should go. I am afraid. It is so cold and dark here," the Greyhound confessed.

It is true. It is growing much colder than you are used to, but you will find the Way, DearHeart. And remember, should is an obligation; it is not the Way. This is your life—your HeartChoices—the Way you seek can only be known by Heart.

He had always called her DearHeart. The endearing term soothed her. There hadn't been many things that could comfort her throughout her life thus far, but the Moon could. The Moon had always been there for her. He was her light in the dark monotony of melancholy, her confidant when she could trust no other, her protector as she slept, and her dream companion—sometimes. He was the keeper of all her secrets and he knew all her pain.

Fear fell away as the Moon instructed her to follow him. The waxing light of his current phase was just powerful enough to flit through the dense Trees and illuminate the Forest floor in front of the fraught Greyhound. He led her through the Forest until she came upon an inviting grove of Pine Trees.

"You will be safe here tonight," said the Pines, swaying their branches and creating just enough space for the Moon's light to illuminate a safe spot beneath the largest among them. Its branches brushed the ground, creating a cave-like sanctuary for the poor creature. She bowed her head to the Tree, indicating her thanks, crawled under its soft canopy, and leaned her back against its trunk. Though she could see well enough behind her, the one blind spot she had was protected by the Tree's trunk. The Greyhound wasn't sure how she'd stay warm enough to survive the chilly night air.

Remember the White Arctic Fox from your dream, the Moon softly reminded her.

"That dream was so vivid!" she responded.

What did you learn from it? asked the Moon.

The Greyhound thought back . . .

FEAR NOT THE SHADOWS

And so it was . . . She had met the White Arctic Fox in a dream—not so much a dream as another Night Terror. A long time ago, when the Greyhound was at the height of her racing career, Night Terrors began plaguing her and continued for much of her racing years when the bullying had escalated. In this particular dream, foreboding Shadowy figures chased her so deep into the darkness and frightened her so much so that, according to her handsome Companion, she audibly yelped in her sleep.

In the Night Terror, the Track wasn't where she knew it should be. It had disappeared. Fear seeped in and consumed her. The Shadows made her quiver, and she knew instinctually that if she didn't run away they would surely destroy her. Dreading they would harm her irreparably, the frightened Greyhound ran as fast as she could, ending up in no man's land trapped between the Shadows and a White Capped Mountain.

The Shadows forced her to run towards the White Capped Mountain. The white stuff on the mountaintop piqued her curious nature, but there was no time to ponder her inexperience—the Shadows were much too close. Continuing in the darkness, she spotted a small, White Arctic Fox barely discernible, camouflaged against the whiteness of the frozen ground at the base of the mountain. It was no taller than the black cat that strutted around the Track. The White Arctic Fox stood at attention on its hind legs in front of a small arched opening in the Mountain's side as though it had been awaiting her arrival. A reassuring nudge inside her signaled she could trust the tiny creature, so she chose to follow it. She ran full gait through the entrance, which seemed to Magickally widen to accommodate her tall frame. Fear flared within her as she imagined the Shadows being able to fit into the Cave as well.

"They won't follow you in here," said the fluffy White Fox.

The years of bullying the Greyhound endured had stripped her of the ability to trust anyone or anything, except her Moon, so trusting the White Fox pushed the Greyhound beyond her comfort zone. The sureness in the Fox's voice quelled the Greyhound's fears enough for her to listen to the creature, drawn by its gentle energy. Perhaps it was the brilliance of its pure white fur that made it appear Angelic or maybe, since it had just saved the Greyhound's life, that random act of kindness was as good a reason as any for the desperate Greyhound to trust it. The choice was made.

The Greyhound followed the White Arctic Fox through a complex series of tunnels where quite an impressive manipulation of the ground had occurred long ago, most likely built by some ancient civilization or perhaps by the Arctic Fox itself. It led the still-quivering Greyhound into an interior Cave that had many egresses. The Cavern was astonishing! Gigantic Crystals hung from the ceiling and jutted every which way out of the igneous granite that covered most of the Cavern's floor, walls, and ceiling. Spellbound, the Greyhound forgot about the Shadows. The moment was too Magickal to think any dire thoughts, and she grew calmer with each *breath* as they walked deeper into the Crystal Cave.

"The Quartz Crystals will do that to you," said the White Arctic Fox, affirming the Greyhound's easing anxiety.

"They are magnificent!" said the Greyhound, still gazing at the extraordinary formations.

Nothing surpasses their beauty but that of the Stars and the Moon, she thought. There was no direct light source in the Cave, nevertheless, the Crystals glittered and glowed and generously enlightened the space and her Spirit.

"I have to go!" the Greyhound exclaimed. "The Shadows are still waiting for me at the entrance of the Mountain! How am I going to escape them? I'm trapped."

The White Arctic Fox calmly said, "Shadows are not allowed in here, DearOne. This space is sacred. They know better than to cross the threshold of my Cave, for they will be consumed by the light if they choose to do so."

The light? What light? the Greyhound wondered. "The light from the Crystals?"

"No, DearOne, the light within," explained the White Arctic Fox, who was keenly aware of the Greyhound's confusion by the look on her face and the tilt of her head.

"The light within what?" the Greyhound asked.

"You and me," the White Fox answered. "The light within has Magickal powers. It can dissolve Shadows so they can no longer hurt you."

"But how?" asked the bewildered Greyhound.

"The Shadows are nothing—only fears personified. Fears are nothing. They can't hurt you. How do you see it?" the Fox now questioned her.

"I guess you are right. Nothing can hurt me," acknowledged the Greyhound, not quite grasping the complete profundity of her own answer.

"Exactly," said the White Fox.

"What do you mean *exactly*? I understand *nothing* can hurt me, but Shadows are something," said the Greyhound, now even more perplexed.

"Shadows are cast from your fears. If you have no fear, they become nothing, and nothing can hurt you," the White Fox proclaimed with staggering certainty.

"I know about fears," said the Greyhound. "I have many more now than I've ever had."

"I know, DearOne," the Fox empathetically offered. "Your fears are chasing you. You will learn to confront your fears as *the Way* out of the darkness is revealed to you. Be not afraid. Now, you must rest."

The coldness of the Cave began to creep into the Greyhound's bones. She recalled how she overheard the Trainers exchange Greyhound facts they had researched. They discussed how Greyhounds burned calories even as they slept, and how Greyhounds had a very low percentage of body fat, and though this low percentage aided them in their capacity to race, it was not meant to keep them warm in colder climates. She needed warmth. The White Fox had an abundance of thick fur covering its body. Even its paw pads had fur on them, so it was always warm. The Fox graciously showed the Greyhound how to keep warm. The Cave also offered its gift of healing to her. While she slept, the clusters of Quartz Crystals cleansed her aura, soothing not only her physical body but also her Spirit. The Fox explained he would show her *the Way* out of the Cave the following day. She would be ready to face her fears in the morning's light.

GRATITUDE BEGETS GRACE

And so it was . . . Now, beneath the cascading Eastern White Pendula Pines, she remembered how, in her dream, the White Fox had shown her how to curl her body and angle her front paws beneath her with the right one upside down, cradling her head. This would keep her head from touching the cold ground as her long tail covered her nose. Her exhalations harbored additional warmth. Tonight, her bed was made of blue pine needles, which, despite their name, were surprisingly soft. Desperate to sleep, she would thank the Pines properly in the morning for their gifts. Once in position, and feeling safe enough to release into the moment, she drifted off, but not before managing an upward glance to see the Moon gazing lovingly at her. The Moon compassionately kept watch over the poor Greyhound throughout the night with the Mouse hidden beneath the Pine's needles.

The Moon waited patiently for the Sun to greet him and awaken the Greyhound. Then, he said his good-byes for the time being. The Sun and Moon had an understanding: She reigned over the day, he over the night. The Moon understood it was the Sun who graciously gifted him her light, and for that he was indebted to her to keep watch over the night. If the Greyhound looked closely in the distant sky at dawn, she could sometimes see the Moon, a guardian of the Earth, bathed in Earthshine.

As the Sun's rays warmed the Forest floor where the Greyhound lay, the Greyhound began to stir. She jerked upright, forgetting where she was for a moment until she found her bearings.

"You're okay, DearOne," consoled the Pines.

"Thank you kindly for allowing me to rest beneath your canopy and for your protection. You are quite generous," the Greyhound said with heartfelt thanks.

"You are more than welcome. It was my pleasure," exclaimed the tallest Pine, "but it was not I who guarded you. I only afforded you shelter. It was the Moon who kept faithful watch over you as you dreamed, DearOne. You seem to have won his favor."

"I have?" The Greyhound felt her heart grow with wonderment.

"You *have*," emphasized the Pine. "Not everyone is so special as to have the bond that you and the Moon share. It is rare. It is a Magickal gift!"

The Greyhound was astonished. She had always treasured the Moon's presence, but she never felt worthy enough to imagine he felt the same way about her. She was just a simple Greyhound who did her best to be kind, honest, and true. It was her way—the only way she knew how to be.

"Thank you for sharing your insights with me," the Greyhound said. "I appreciate it, truly. I will not take what you have told me lightly."

With this newfound information and warmth in her heart, she stretched her long, lean body forward and back, bowing in gratitude. She said good-bye to the Pines, and the search for the Bee continued.

FIVE

—

THE ESCAPADE

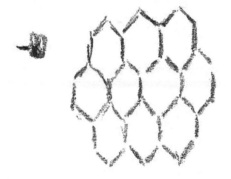

DANCE IN THE DAY

And so it was . . . As the Greyhound walked deeper into the Forest, she homed in on the familiar buzzing sound. The Forest was a lovely place in the Sun's light, and she raised her head to the sky, relishing the Sun's warm rays. She loved how the light appeared to dance on the Forest floor, trickling through the Trees whenever the wild wind would blow. It made her feel lighter. She gamboled every now and again as she danced with the light to the sound of birds chirping and leaves rustling in the Trees and clinking against one another as they floated to the ground.

The Greyhound recalled how, before or after a race, when the racers had been let outdoors briefly, she would lie on the kennel floor and absorb the Sun's radiant light. Her mind would empty of all its burdens and expectations as they melted into the concrete. Worry did not invade the times she relished in the embrace of the Sun's incandescence. It strengthened her well-being and renewed her energy. She could bask in the morning light for hours if only she had been allowed. That's when she felt calm, at peace. That's when the Mouse had kept her company.

Where is the Mouse? she thought. The Bee buzzed nearby.

These thoughts whisked the Greyhound back to her puppyhood. She remembered giggling when her sister used to tell her she must have been a plant in a former life, because she loved sitting in the Sun so much. She loved her sister deeply and would do everything in her power to protect her. Her sister was an amazing racer too. They often competed in races together, and even if one ranked higher in the standings for a time, jealousy never reared its ugly head. It tickled them when they once tied for the win. They always lifted one another's Spirits and steadfastly applauded and praised each other's strengths. Other racers were jealous of their closeness. Regardless, they remained lovingly loyal to one another. The Greyhound smiled, remembering the good times she and her sister had shared.

Out of the corner of her eye, the Greyhound thought she saw the Mouse scratching in the leaves. Perhaps she was mistaken. Her thoughts circled back to that last fateful race when she and her sister had been separated. She missed her sister so much. The pain of that loss was overwhelming. She wondered what had happened to her. Was she okay? Was she alive? Would she ever see her again? She hoped her sister was safe. She knew she probably was not still racing, for they had learned she was pregnant right before they raced that day. The bittersweet heaviness of that horrible day was unbearable. Darkness crept in now as clouds covered the Sun. Brooding a bit, she began to hear the sonorous sound of the Bee, amplifying with each step she took.

NATURE'S SWEET SPOTS

And so it was . . . Deeper into the Forest she went, and with her gaze cast downward by the weight of the disruptive memories of misfortune, she missed the enchantments the Forest offered. Her heart throbbed with loneliness as she pined for her former life. Dispirited, dark thoughts cast Shadows on her mood as the denseness of this part of the Forest grew thicker. It was difficult to maintain anything but the mist of melancholy that enveloped her most of the time now. She so wanted to be happy and to feel at peace with the world and with whom she was becoming since being forced from the Track. The desire to be loved and accepted, flaws and all, was what mattered most. But now she noticed only the clumps of deadening leaves crushed by animals who had trodden upon them and the broken branches severed in storms of seasons past that were strewn about the Forest floor. Due to the downward position of her head, she missed Nature's sweet spots.

Clouds covered the Sun, so its beams were no longer visible, but the dull amber light was just strong enough to penetrate the cloud cover and dimly light *the Way*. As she walked over the leaf litter, she noticed the crunching sound the dry leaves made. She didn't mind the sound, preferring it to the buzzing noise the Bee emitted. As soon as she thought of the Bee, as if out of the blue, there it was in front of her, flitting about. Round and round it flew above her head. She twitched her snout to keep it from landing on her nose. She never allowed it to touch her.

"There you are! It's about time you showed up!" buzzed the tiny thing loudly enough for a curious Squirrel, foraging for acorns, to pop its head out just above the leaf line. It looked skittishly at them, scurried partway up a Tree, then back down, and finally up again, this time out of sight. Its indecisiveness caught the Greyhound's attention.

"I've been waiting for you! I didn't think you actually had it in you to stay the course," said the Bee.

Before the Greyhound could even process its words, for they made her feel immediately uneasy, the Bee blurted, "It's time to go. There are others I want you to meet."

"Who are these others you want me to meet?" the Greyhound questioned.

The Bee whetted the Greyhound's curiosity with its mystique, but as usual, it did not answer her. She was annoyed the Bee didn't always provide her with the answers she sought. It could be quite stingy with information. She never stopped asking questions though. Curiosity was an integral part of her personality. Though she had no idea what lay before her, she believed the Bee when it said that she was free now. It was true—she had escaped the yard and was on her own, unleashed to go wherever she wished, but she couldn't help noticing there was nowhere to sprint in the denseness of the unfamiliar terrain. The Greyhound willingly followed the Bee even deeper into the Forest, hoping it would make good on its promises.

What are the odds of that happening? she had begun calculating, but the Bee buzzed in her ear, halting any statistical analysis.

PROMISES MEAN SOMETHING

And so it was . . . The Greyhound followed the Bee, hoping it would reveal a new life to her so she could begin again and finally be happy. After all, it had promised as much, if not more. The Bee continued to bombilate about how the Greyhound was now truly free—free from any human rules, regulations, or routines. It told her how she was miles away from anyone who had hurt her and explained there was no one she would have to worry about bumping into—not one, single person. The Bee promised the Greyhound she would be free to do whatever she pleased as soon as they reached their destination. It all sounded so perfect to the homesick Hound. All her hopes and dreams had been based on promises made emphatically and seemingly from the heart. The Bee had told her she was a trusting soul, always exposing her humble heart to the world, though it sounded more like condescension than a compliment. But she was who she was.

The Bee was right—there was no leash or Muzzle bound to her, no schedules to follow, no need to perform for anyone, and there wasn't a single reason to be on a strict diet to maintain the proper racing weight required for paddock inspections. There was no one to please here, no one to whom she had to answer. No longer was there a need to rise early or train all day to prepare for the next race. Absent now were the brutal training activities, and there was less of a risk of her getting hurt, since she wasn't racing. Many of her fellow racers had become horrifically injured and had died right in front her. Those images were indelibly etched in her mind's eye, never to be forgotten, but sometimes seen again in Night Terrors or when she was triggered or when they invaded a daydream.

Was this what freedom looked like? Eager to see what the Bee's plan entailed and semi-willing to give it a chance without calculating the cost of such a decision, the Greyhound walked with the Bee and listened to it intently. She didn't say much. It was difficult to utter even one word when the Bee was conjuring its tales and dirty deeds. They walked for hours into the bowels of the Forest. The thought of how she would find *the Way* out on her own crossed her mind, but it scattered into the gathering darkness. Her reliance on the Bee strengthened. Though tired, she kept telling herself, *I am free! I will find happiness. I will find a place I can call home.* She believed in promises. She wanted to believe in happy endings too.

THE WEASEL

And so it was . . . Westward they went, eventually coming across a wriggly animal rustling in the leaves ahead. The Greyhound had never come across such a critter.

"Don't you know what that is?" the Bee questioned haughtily.

She was beginning to realize that the purview of her life had been grossly limited, and she felt the sting of the Bee's words—words that reminded her of long ago, when she was told by a former racing mate, who had traveled over the Ocean to come to the Track, that she was not very worldly. She knew her own credentials surpassed his, but she wasn't mean and refused to throw it back in his face, even though the Bee had told her to. She was a racer and worked very hard at the only way of life she had ever known.

"That's the Weasel," said the Bee. "It's one of the clan members I want you to meet. It's a great hunter—perhaps an even better hunter than your kind."

Well aware of her lineage, she was able to ignore that sting. Her attention fixated on the creature in the leaves. It was dark brown with cute, rounded ears and looked harmless enough. The creature crawled closer and stared at the Greyhound. When their eyes locked, her stomach turned. Its beady, black eyes and the low vibration of its energy alarmed her.

The Bee provided a superficial introduction at best. "This is the Weasel. Weasel, this is the Hound."

"I'm a Greyhound," she said shyly, correcting the Bee.

The Weasel, not acknowledging the correction, explained to the Bee how it would take care of gathering some of the food for the group, while assuring the Greyhound there would be plenty for her too. She sensed the Weasel was only trying to curry favor with the Bee, but she thanked the Weasel in advance for its generosity anyway as the creature slinked off somewhere, looking for small mice to eat, according to the Bee. The thought of eating a mouse repulsed the Greyhound. The Weasel did not leave her with a very good feeling.

Where is the Mouse? she wondered.

"Ahem." The Bee cleared its throat. It particularly did not like it when the Greyhound thought of or spoke fondly of the Mouse. The Greyhound questioned the Bee's deliberate intention to divert her from such nostalgic thoughts or feelings, but the Bee deprived her of an answer.

"Don't dawdle. You must meet the Beaver."

A Beaver! the Greyhound thought. She had always wanted to meet a Beaver. When she was young, her Breeder had called her Bucky Beaver because her two front teeth protruded more than those of the other pups. The comment had made her self-conscious of her smile, so she did not dare do so very often.

THE BEAVER

And so it was . . . The Bee brought the Greyhound to a nearby Brook to meet the Beaver. The dark, russet-colored Beaver greeted them by flapping its flat black tail on the ground four times. The quantity of branches in its mouth prevented it from speaking outright. The Greyhound was impressed by the Beaver's strength and its powerful tail, which she calculated was about the length of the Beaver's body. Its girth grew from where the tail connected to the Beaver's backside up to its rounded end.

The Beaver dropped the Oak's heavy branches in the Brook, made sure they were secured with mud, then tucked its paddle-shaped tail underneath its body and perched upon its self-made seat.

That is so clever, the Greyhound thought. She noticed the creature's two unusually large front teeth and how they protruded a bit like hers. Now she understood why the reference to her teeth was so common when she was young, but she did not understand why someone would be so unkind as to make fun of her. *There's a difference,* she contemplated, *between curious comparisons and cruel comments.*

"Hello!" blurted the Beaver after it added another pile of branches onto the dam it was building.

"Hel—" the Greyhound began, but was interrupted by the Bee, too impatient for formal introductions.

"There's no need for pleasantries," said the Bee, quenching its insatiable thirst in the Brook.

The Greyhound realized she was parched, too, and asked the Beaver permission to drink from the Brook.

"Silly Hound, you don't need anyone's permission to do anything anymore. Remember?" gurgled the Bee, devoid of any propriety as it quenched its own thirst in a manner that mocked drowning. Etiquette and restraint were regarded as unnecessary concepts by the Bee.

Regardless, the Greyhound was especially thankful to both the Beaver and the beautiful Brook. The afternoon light shimmered on the water in the most pleasing way. The Sun's rays reached only this open part of the Forest where the Brook resided. The warmer light calmed the Greyhound's nerves, as did the babbling Brook. At that moment, she saw the Mouse out of the corner of her eye. It could have been her Mouse or one of the Weasel's. She wasn't certain and it had been a while since she and the Mouse last conversed.

The Greyhound concentrated on drinking. Her neck was so long that she had to be careful not to choke. First, she lowered her body, then, stretched her neck to reach the water.

"Why do you drink so daintily?" asked the Beaver. "Can't you just drink like the rest of us? You look like the Giraffe at the zoo. I can drink more than you and twice as fast." The Beaver continued to slurp as it spoke, and water spouted from between its gapped teeth. It choked a few times. This concerned the Greyhound, but the Bee never flinched.

"Well, my neck makes it impossible to gulp if the waterline is lower than my standing height. The water will travel to my lungs instead, causing me to choke, and I will not feel well if I rush the process."

"She's a lightweight," blurted the Bee, making the Greyhound's inability to drink in that position sound more like a fault than a necessity.

"And awkward," the Beaver added.

The Beaver laughed, then returned to its dam building. It didn't seem as though the Bee's bite bothered the Beaver one bit, but the Greyhound felt the sting of its insensitivity. She felt inferior and self-conscious when in it's vicinity. *Remember—I am free,* she kept repeating to herself so as not to sink into the bog of despair.

THE RAT

And so it was . . . The Greyhound, excited to be meeting new creatures, continued following the Bee. With every step, she left behind her old life and hoped the life the Bee offered would make her feel better. She hoped the sadness she still felt would melt into the cold ground. The Bee pointed out a pile of rotting wood in front of them. The Greyhound was surprised to learn it was a Rat's nest.

"The Rat tends to sleep all day and is not to be disturbed for any reason," the Bee warned. "Be sure never to wake a sleeping Rat!"

"Why not?" asked the Greyhound.

"Because it will turn on you in a fury. It will bite you without a second thought and devour you piece by piece," said the Bee, making sure it didn't buzz too loudly. "But you can trust it, otherwise."

"I'll be sure to remember that," responded the Greyhound, a bit confused by the duality of the warning.

"The Rat will join us tonight," said the Bee as they skirted around the Rat's nest.

THE SQUIRREL

And so it was . . . In the distance, the Greyhound spied a hearty, brown Squirrel circling the trunk of a humongous White Oak Tree. She wanted to see a Squirrel up close, so she sped off, leaving the Bee reeling in her wake. In a flash, the Greyhound was upon the Squirrel, who was floundering on the lowest branches of the great Oak, trying to reach the oaknuts that hung upon them. It was so busy stuffing oaknuts into its cheeks that it hadn't seen the Greyhound speeding towards it. A flurry of activity ensued when the Squirrel finally saw the giant Hound. It flew up the Tree to a higher, safer branch. As it was a mast year for the mighty Oak, bunches of oaknuts showered the ground. Some clocked the Greyhound on the head as she jumped as high as she could to try and get a better look at the Squirrel. When the Squirrel reached safety, it dropped a few more of the oaknuts on the Greyhound's head. The Greyhound snapped out of the trance and shook her head.

"I am so sorry," said the Greyhound, startled by her own behavior. "I don't know what came over me! I did not mean to frighten you. I'd never hurt you. It's just that when I saw you, the need to see you up close became overwhelming. I've seen so many of your kind, but never up close."

"My, my, my! You didn't startle me. Don't worry. Don't you worry. You would never be able to catch me anyway," mumbled the Squirrel, whose cheeks were chock-full of nuts. "I'm too nimble and quick. Nimble and quick, that's right and I have no intention of meeting my fate in such an undesirable way."

"What is it that you are doing?" asked the Greyhound.

"Gathering nuts, of course. One can never have enough of them. Never enough nuts! Never enough berries!" the Squirrel remarked, not stopping its frenetic task.

"What's going on here?" the Bee said upon its arrival at the scene.

"Nothing much," said the Squirrel, who finally came down the Oak Tree just out of the Greyhound's reach. An oaknut or two fell out of its mouth. One narrowly missed the Bee.

"I see the two of you have met," the Bee said with glee. "Now I don't have to waste time on introductions."

"We sure did! We sure did," the Squirrel said, its voice muffled by its full mouth. It was a challenge to understand what the Squirrel was saying, but the Greyhound half-smiled at the sight of the simply silly creature.

"You found your prey drive," said the Bee to the Greyhound.

"My what?" she asked, recalibrating her attention in the Bee's direction.

"Your desire to chase after things you think you can catch. It's the most basic of your instincts," stated the Bee with an air of cruelty guised as fact. "And how did you know it was a Squirrel?"

"I had no intention of catching the Squirrel," the Greyhound said defensively. She felt the sting of the Bee's words, though she tried ignoring the uncomfortable feeling in the pit of her stomach. She knew the small furry critter was a Squirrel because the Girl had taught her.

"Squirrels live in the yard, back ho–" she caught and corrected herself, "I mean, back in the JeepGirl's yard." It registered with the Greyhound that it was the first time she had called the Girl JeepGirl. She rather preferred the latter name to the starkness of the former.

"Remember, you belong with me now," the Bee said snidely.

The Greyhound's entire body shook as the Bee's baleful tone rained down upon her, drenching her true desire. Some of her fur flew into the doomy air, then floated to the ground.

"Time to go," said the Bee. "We will see you later, Squirrel. Don't dally."

THE BEE

And so it was . . . The Bee continued flying while the Greyhound walked by its side. The entire time it buzzed of great adventures and how wonderfully fulfilling the Greyhound's new life would be. In time, it told her, she would come to see the choice she had made as being the only one possible. The Bee convinced the Greyhound to stay in its world. Though her authentic Self was just below the surface of her doubt and insecurities, the Bee was able to keep her from realizing the power of her authenticity as it thwarted her confidence and self-worth. The lost Greyhound had become so vulnerable to the Bee's influence over her that it remained remarkable. The Bee juggled a delicate balance between keeping the Greyhound interested in its promises and the Greyhound's own desire to return to the JeepGirl. The Bee created a false reality she believed was attainable. Being a grand manipulator of thought, it could puff her up with feelings of worthiness, then diminish her self-confidence all in the same *breath*, which was enough for her to lose faith in her instincts and innate abilities and keep her from listening to those faithful pokes and nudges of truth she once counted on to guide her. The Bee had the knack of making the Greyhound question every decision, contrary to her own desire to make decisions deliberately. Its plan enabled it to stick around as long as both acknowledged its presence. The power of persuasion was the Bee's forte. It instilled in the Greyhound's mind that she was lost and no longer belonged with anyone but it. Her yearning to belong and to be loved benefited the Bee greatly and fueled its insatiable need to control her. When the bullying had begun, her anxieties emerged for the first time, and the tinnitus of the Bee heightened them. Keeping the Greyhound distracted with mindless banter was the Bee's finest talent. It hindered the Greyhound's ability to concentrate and focus on what she truly wanted from life. The Bee's constant buzz was a masterful tactic, which prevented the Greyhound from formulating her own belief system and left no room for her to even imagine changing the system imposed upon her early in life.

The Bee imbued her with negative thoughts. She truly believed no one could possibly want or love her, especially with all her quirks, flaws, Scars, and pain. Some external Scars were ugly representations of her internal wounds. Her wounds were the accumulation of years of being bullied, gaslighted, and lied to, on top of being emotionally and verbally abused. She only wished to be loved, to be at peace, and to feel joy again. At the very least, the Bee was company in the mist of her loneliness.

THE NOOK

And so it was . . . Dusk had fallen as they reached their final destination—a dark Nook in an obscure part of the Forest not too far from the Brook. There was nothing special about the Nook, other than it was cradled in an unnaturally deep, bowl-like depression in the ground. On the north side of the Nook, large boulders created a wall of protection for the odd group. The floor consisted of compacted leaves, rotten bits of food and some oaknut shells that had been cracked open, their contents partially consumed. A semicircle of Pine Trees gave harbor on the south side of the clearing, and the ground there was laden with soft pine needles. The Greyhound noticed that dense Trees blocked most of the light, which fought to permeate the space.

Perhaps, the Greyhound pondered, *if the wind would just blow the Trees enough so that the light of the gibbous Moon could shine through, it would be a pleasant enough Nook.*

Often, throughout her life, she did not feel as well or as safe when the Sunlight or Moonlight was hidden from her. It had always been that way. The Bee took advantage of the Greyhound's declining mood. Even though she wanted to rest, it had other plans.

THE NOOK BY NIGHT

And so it was . . . Night fell upon the Nook. The Beaver, the Squirrel, and the Weasel arrived three hours prior to the witching hour, as the Bee had instructed. They startled the exhausted Greyhound, who had closed her eyes for a moment. One of the only times she was allowed to rest her weary body and mind was when the Bee was busy pollen hunting or sleeping. The bustling entrance of the boisterous group renewed the Greyhound's energy a bit. Curiosity awakened her need to know what fun the Bee had in store for her on her first night in the Nook.

The Bee welcomed the group, which came laden with food and drink. They lined themselves against the boulders while the Greyhound remained on the small bed of pine needles, where she felt a kinship with the Pines. Not daring to presume she was welcome, she waited to be invited to join the clique. She knew better than to cross the Bee, for fear of being harangued by it, or worse—stung.

A party of sorts began. The Bee buzzed and whirred in the air. The Weasel whistled while the Beaver batted its tail on one of the boulders, keeping the beat. The Squirrel scampered up and down a nearby Oak Tree. Its rustling added another octave of sound below the Weasel's whistling but above the Beaver's drumming. The Squirrel enjoyed the reverie but continued looking for oaknuts as it did so. It stuffed them into its mouth only to spit them out into a hole it had dug beneath the Tree. It did this tirelessly. The Greyhound was impressed by its tenacity for the task but simultaneously appalled by its gluttonous stash. The Squirrel provided the show that accompanied the clan's song—the song of chaos. They all stuffed themselves with berries, bark, and bugs. The Greyhound watched and ate a few berries that had rolled close enough for her to reach them. A somewhat enjoyable feeling slowly overtook her. She was just about to join the festivities when a horrifyingly frightening creature catapulted from behind the boulders into the middle of the group, abruptly ending the song.

"Ah ha!" it said, rattling the night air. Its bristly fur was as black as a Starless night; its eyes were even blacker; its tail was hairless and spiraled. The Greyhound, who was caught off guard, vaulted into the air from her reposed position.

"Everything's fine," said the Bee as they all laughed at her overreaction. "That's the Rat I told you about earlier. Remember we passed by its nest?"

"Yes, hello. It's nice to make your acquaintance," said the Greyhound, composing herself, though remnants of fear lingered in her voice.

"What have we here?" asked the Rat in a drawn out, menacing tone. It eyed the Greyhound up and down as it crept closer. "You're an unusual one and so out of place. You're not from around here, are you?"

The Rat unraveled its tightly coiled tail with its stubby front arms and long claws. Its voice was low and grisly, and it elongated every word it uttered.

"No, I am not," the Greyhound responded, faltering a bit. "I came from the Southern Greyhound Racing Track, which is very, very far away from here."

The Rat turned abruptly to join the group, not really caring what the

Greyhound had said. It only cared about the little bits of fruit and berries it was scavenging from the others as it walked by each one of the distracted revelers. No one said a word about the Rat stealing food. If any one of them had, it would have attacked, and no one wanted to be bitten by a Rat famous for carrying contagions.

They all relished in one another's stories of stealing food from other Forest animals. Stories about the Hare who lived in the Meadow near the Farmer's barn were among their favorites. The Bee was the first to poke fun at the Hare, noting his silly long ears and penchant for hanging around Bluebirds. The wry Bee pointed out how similar the Greyhound's ears were to the Hare's, and the clan clamored with laughter.

"That's not very nice," said the Greyhound coolly. She had long ago learned not to react to bullies but to say at least something in her defense or in defense of another victim. She never let anyone see her cry. It was later, when she was alone, that she broke down in the wake of the humiliation.

"Oh, lighten up," railed the Rat with a maniacal look in its eyes that would frighten any living creature. "It was just a joke."

"Well, it's not funny. I don't find it amusing," the Greyhound replied, demurely maintaining her composure. The incident had triggered her. It reminded her of when other Greyhounds had made fun of her because she didn't think their jokes were funny. She didn't show it, but her throat was closing, making it difficult to speak as the laughter loudened.

"Well, everyone else is laughing!" the Rat said, riling the group.

The bunch of them guffawed, while the Greyhound resumed her position under the Pines. She wondered if these animals had special powers, like the Bee's, to know her thoughts and fears. She knew irking them would be unwise, so, as the rest of the rowdy bunch continued its boisterous laughter, she tried sleeping but failed. She could not sleep in the Nook. Her head pounded. She was so dizzy.

THE NOOK BY DAY

And so it was . . . The next two days swarmed with activity. Somehow, it had become her job to provide food and water for the group. The Weasel, a conniving trickster, had promised it would help her, but it never did. The Beaver had said it would help as well, but *it* never did. They all had lied to her. They only took care of themselves. The Bee, the grandest prevaricator among them, convinced the Greyhound that her efforts to provide for others was a worthy purpose. It said she would be an integral part of the clan if she gathered the food and water. Although she quietly refused to join in on their gossiping and devious behavior, she felt she could become part of their community. After all, where else was she going to go?

The Greyhound did not mind helping and felt somewhat useful at first, because they all went to her if they needed anything. She was told she was essential for her ability to find food more easily than the others, because of her keen eyesight. They praised her for how tall she was and often asked her to reach high up in an Oak Tree or stretch to grab some necessary item for their nests. She even collected water from the Brook whenever they were thirsty, which was most of the time. They took advantage of her superior hearing too. When the Rat scrounged for food, the Greyhound was the one who kept a lookout; it had become her job to alert the others if a predatory animal approached the Nook, though danger never came from outside the Nook—only from inside. After those first couple of days, she felt indentured, spending the days doing the bidding of others with barely a return on the effort she put forth. If only she could see the Moon.

FLOW LIKE WATER

And so it was . . . The Brook was a Magickal place situated sixteen strides north of the Nook where the Greyhound collected water for the clan. It ran west to east, in opposition to the Sun's path, though the Greyhound had not investigated how far in each direction it reached. She always kept the Brook on her right side when exploring and on her left when returning so she could find the Nook again, which was marked by the tips of the tall Pines visible from the Brook's bank. The Brook was her favorite place to go. It offered a much-needed respite from the Bee's persistent rants. Very much like the Bee, the Brook wasn't in the least bit quiet. It babbled constantly. But unlike the Bee, the Brook's sound was pleasant and mesmerizingly peaceful. The Greyhound enjoyed how its water flowed effortlessly over the stones and felled branches from the nearby Oaks and Pines. Bright-green moss covered some of the Tree trunks that had found the Brook to be their last resting place. *A most peaceful ending,* she thought.

The water was crystal clear and fresh and tasted delightful. With her thirst quenched, she admired the WaterStones that sheeted the Brook's bed. The WaterStones, as she liked to think of them, intrigued her. *How much time,* she wondered, *has it taken for them to become so rounded? Years? Decades? A lifetime? Millennia? I wonder how I can smooth out my rough edges?* The sight of the WaterStones soothed her, and they felt smooth when she ran her paw over the ones that skirted the Brook.

The air at the water's edge was crisp and whisked her *breath* away. She inhaled deeply. *Breathing* in the fresh air calmed her. Her body became lighter; her mind emptied itself of unwelcome, disturbing thoughts. When she visited the Brook, she did not think about the others. She did not think about routines or about the past or the future. She simply envisioned being one of the smooth, round WaterStones over which the water flowed with ease. She imagined submerging herself in the water and having it wash away her pain. The Greyhound stood there, solitary, in a moment of peace—one with the WaterStones and the Brook—one with her surroundings and the protective Trees—one with Nature.

SIX

—

THE CHALLENGE

THE UNEXPECTED
AND THE UNWANTED

And so it was . . . The Greyhound wandered to the Brook every available moment she had to herself. Times when the Bee left her alone were rare, so she took advantage of such opportunities. On the fourth day of her Forest stay—a particularly nice day—she saw a White-Tailed Doe in the distance, close to the Brook's edge. The Doe was feasting on some plump berries from a hearty green bush.

The Greyhound approached her with care, hoping not to frighten the beautiful creature.

"Excuse me. Hello," the Greyhound whispered.

The Doe abruptly postured at attention and cocked her head to the right. Their two sets of eyes locked. A twig with some burgundy berries draped out of the Doe's mouth. She stood perfectly still, as if frozen in time.

"Hello," said the Greyhound again, very softly. "I mean you no harm. I'm looking for friends. Do you want to be my friend?"

"Sure!" the White-Tailed Doe said agreeably. "I don't have many friends," she added as her tail twitched.

The Greyhound smiled. "Neither do I! It looks as though we have something in common already. I am a Greyhound."

"Oh, for a minute there, I mistook you for another Doe," the Doe said, gulping the berries. She continued munching on the twig.

The Greyhound noticed that some of the reddish berries had stained the white fur around the Doe's mouth, making it appear as though she had on lipstick similar in color to the one she had seen on the JeepGirl. She smiled again.

"No, but I can see how you could think that was true. We are the same height, and our body structure is similar."

The two creatures were indeed very much alike. Both had tall, skinny legs, long necks, and broad chests of white fur that cascaded and disappeared underneath. The tips of their tails were the same too. Even though the Doe had a fluffy short tail and the Greyhound a very long one, both had a white tip. The best feature they shared was their kind, golden-brown eyes. Their eyes revealed it was safe to be in one another's company, and they became instantaneous Spirit-Sisters!

The two walked slowly, side by side, close enough to feel the warmth of one another as the cool Autumn air cloaked the area. The Doe was a survivor. She taught the Greyhound which berries were safe to eat and which were poisonous, though pleasing to the eye. The Greyhound learned it was safe to eat all sorts of berries, from the Huckleberry and Chokeberry to the Mulberry and the Saskatoon Berry. Her favorite was the Blackberry. The Doe showed her the poisonous ones too—the Holly Berry on the bright-green bush with the pointed leaves, the red Mistletoe Berry, and finally, the Woody Nightshade Berry found on the Bittersweet plant. The Greyhound was very hungry, so she ate a few of the good berries, making sure to avoid the bad ones. She compared the berries to those in her life and came to the sad realization that there were more poisonous ones than good. They strolled along the Brook, for it was the brighter part of the Forest. All the while, the Greyhound was mindful of the Nook's location. She preferred not to get lost.

The two rested on a pile of leaves and chatted away the morning. While enjoying one another's company, the relaxed Greyhound saw a tiny black dot moving close to her front right toe. The insect crawled on top of her paw, and she tried to shoo it off, but it would not leave; she tried to push it off with her other paw, but it was stuck. It would not come off. It blatantly refused.

The Doe watched her. "Those buggers are difficult to remove once they latch on to you."

"I think it bit me. It won't come off!" exclaimed the confounded Greyhound.

"That's a Tick," the Doe explained dryly. "It probably fell from my fur. They like me, for some reason."

"What does it want with me? Why has it latched onto me?" questioned the Greyhound. "I wasn't bothering it. I mean it no harm."

The Greyhound couldn't understand how any species could hurt another.

"Oh, it is nothing you did or didn't do. It doesn't care whether you are a kind soul or a cruel one. It just wants to feed and satiate its needs," the Doe said nonchalantly.

"Really?" exclaimed the Greyhound. "How does it do that?"

"It's a bloodsucker! It adheres to your fur with its barbs, burrows into your skin, bites you, then sucks out your blood, sometimes without notice," said the Doe matter-of-factly. "Be careful! The nasty creatures carry diseases that can make you quite ill, much like Rats."

"Ick!" The Greyhound gasped, wondering why the creature would want to hurt her intentionally. Without hesitation, she used her front teeth, bit off the Tick, and spit it out. The Tick, which landed upright, quickly made its way through the leaves and reached the Doe, who simply blew away the leaf the Tick had been clinging to. The Tick busied off, most likely looking for its next victim.

"I will definitely keep an eye out for malignant bloodsuckers from now on," said the Greyhound.

"They come in all forms," said the Doe. "Be especially wary of energy vampires. They will drain you of all your energy, and you'll feel exhausted after being in their presence."

"I will. Thanks for telling me," said the Greyhound.

The Sun was overhead as morning moved melodiously into midday. The only time the Sun fully revealed herself was in this part of the Forest. The Greyhound and the Doe conversed for a while, but time was an impediment for the two. It was hunting season, a very dangerous time for the Doe. The Greyhound was mindful as well that she could easily be mistaken for a Doe and meet her demise.

"I best be on my way," the Doe said, rising from the leafy ground.

The Greyhound concurred. "Yes, it's getting late. I must go as well. The Bee is looking for me again. I still can hear it buzzing."

Both perked their ears. "I hope to see you again, my ForestFriend," said the Greyhound sincerely.

"That would be delightful," replied the Doe. "You'd be wise to avoid anything that has the capability to sting over and over again." She bowed, then lifted her head to the Sun as if she were waving good-bye.

The Greyhound mirrored the gesture. Then the two dear-hearted creatures walked in opposite directions, forever ForestFriends and Spirit-Sisters. The Greyhound smiled; her heart warmed. The feeling reminded her of when the Mouse told her she'd know something *by Heart*. Was she beginning to understand what her tiny companion meant? Something moved nearby, but she didn't have time to pay it any mind. Right now, she was pleased she had made a true friend but was afraid the Bee would discover her secret.

UNRELENTING ROUTINES

And so it was . . . Night overtook the Nook, and the raucous bunch began its ritual of drinking and eating to excess. It went on and on. Their behavior was foreign to the Greyhound. They flung food for fun and hurled insults, all the while laughing at one another's injuries and buffoonery, but she could not partake in their shenanigans. She just couldn't.

The outlier of the group, the Greyhound stayed on the edge of the Nook under one of the Pine Trees she had befriended. Lack of sleep wore at her tolerance. The motley crew cared the least bit if they disturbed the Greyhound's sleep. She couldn't understand their callousness. She desperately needed her sleep. They made fun of her for not having enough energy to play with them. Rest was imperative though, especially after all the work she had done gathering the sweetest of twigs and young bark for the Beaver, oaknuts for the Squirrel, and fruit for the Rat. She stood her ground when it concerned the Weasel's meal prep, though.

It profoundly saddened her to bear witness to such a horrible habit. Her refusal to assist in the gathering and demise of the tiny mice that were the Weasel's delicacy was met with much scrutiny from the bunch. They labeled her a coward and called her softhearted. She pretended to sleep whenever the Weasel joined the group. She could not help but note the resemblance of the helpless creatures it devoured to the long-lost Mouse she considered her friend.

Thoughts of the Mouse entered her mind from time to time, especially late at night when everyone finally retreated to their respective nests. She often wondered what had happened to the Mouse, but the scrutiny she would have endured was not worth allowing a single tear to fall. She couldn't shake the feeling she was being watched, so she lay awake thinking, *How is this fun for them? Are they truly as happy as they appear? Do they really enjoy hurting one another and making fun of others? I don't find it funny, but I guess I should be happy I am still free.*

BE AWARE OF
TANGENTIAL RESPONSES

And so it was . . . Every day and night was the same as the previous. The only evident change was the waxing gibbous Moon whose light had steadily increased since she had left the JeepGirl's yard. The Greyhound barely saw her Moon, for the dense Forest kept it from her. It was rare for her to catch a glimpse of him through the thick Trees. She longed to see him—to sneak away while the others slept—to visit the Brook where she knew her Moon would be visible. Per the Bee's instruction, she was not allowed to leave the Nook at night, and the noises of the night sounded as terrifying as the Bee described, so she didn't dare.

Routines ran their course. Daily she asked the Bee where the open field it had promised to show her was located, but it always gave her a tangential response and told her to be quiet. She had begun to believe that the Bee had lied to her. Her head hurt so much worse now than it had at the Shelter or the Track.

Part of her routine included learning how to collect the fermented nectar from fallen Crabapples for the Bee and the Squirrel, who preferred the nectar over the special berries that the Rat and the Weasel spent part of their days gathering for themselves. They relished in their unique collection of berries from the Rowan Tree. These were different from the berries the Doe had taught the Greyhound she could eat. The group consumed the apples and the aberrant berries in excess so they could become intoxicated.

The first night the Greyhound had seen them all in that state, she thought it was somewhat amusing, as the creatures stumbled on brush, slurred their words, sang off-key, and lost their place when they told a story. *There was no harm in that,* she thought. But as the week wore on, and the craziness continued unrelentingly, she started to question the pointlessness of such behavior.

Of course, she had tried a minuscule bite of one of the apples once, because apples were her favorite treat, but her skinny frame could not process the unique juice as the others could. She was not equipped to partake in the consumption of the nectar, and that saddened her somewhat, because she could not laugh uncontrollably as the others did, or feel the freedom and joy their behavior implied. Their mistreatment of her intensified when they were in that state. Regardless, she watched over them to be sure they didn't hurt themselves. One time, the Beaver had imbibed so much that it swayed and stumbled as it walked. The Greyhound caught its tail in her mouth just in time to stop it from smashing into the boulder, but the next day, to her surprise, the Beaver had absolutely no recollection of the event.

She examined how they were free to become someone else and lose themselves in the charade. Thus, she was left with only herself and the Trees as company, and right now, she did not like herself. She did not like what she saw, what she heard, how she felt. She didn't like being made fun of either. Everything fell victim to her doubt. Had she really been an excellent racer? Would she ever get that nudging feeling again, like she had when the Mouse was around? Since meeting the Doe, she questioned if she had ever really had any true friends. During these moments, she missed the Mouse and the JeepGirl. She also doubted if she had ever really belonged anywhere. The Greyhound longed for a place to call her own.

THE SKUNK

And so it was . . . As dusk fell, marking the end of the sixth day, the Greyhound nestled on the pine needles for a brief nap. Rest was crucial before the others arrived for the festivities. Just as she was about to close her eyes, a very funky animal meandered into the Nook.

"Hi there, LittleOne," said the Greyhound quietly, so as not to startle the black-and-white furred creature. The Skunk peeked out from behind one of the boulders and sniffed in the direction of the Greyhound.

"Hello," the Greyhound said, making sure she sounded friendly.

The Skunk cautiously moved forward a step, but not so far as to expose himself to danger. The Greyhound sensed his caution.

"Greetings," said the Skunk.

"I've never met anyone like you before," the Greyhound said, hoping she didn't sound judgmental.

"I have never seen *you* in the Forest before," replied the Skunk.

"You are right about that. I've never been in any Forest before this visit. It has only been . . . hmmm . . . I don't know how long it has been since I made my way here," explained the Greyhound. "The days and nights are blending. They all seem the same." She wondered how much time had passed. *It must be about a week,* she calculated from what she could see by the light of the Moon that was discernible through the Pines.

"Would you care to stay for the festivities? The others will be arriving momentarily, but I must warn you, they have a bad habit of gossiping about everyone—and be sure not to get caught in their debauchery."

"That is quite gracious of you," replied the Skunk. "I don't often receive invitations."

"Why not?" asked the Greyhound innocently.

The Skunk didn't have the chance to answer. The gang arrived with thunderous laughter.

"What is a Skunk doing here?" the Weasel wailed at the Greyhound.

"What's a Skunk doing in our Nook?" the Beaver blurted as bits of bark blew out of its mouth in every direction.

Before the Greyhound could answer, the Rat and the Bee showed up with the Squirrel lagging behind them.

"Why is that Skunk trespassing?" said the two in unison, in a tone that had a dark timbre to it.

The Greyhound stepped in front of the Skunk and said, "I invited him to stay for dinner. He is my guest."

She was careful not to sound too commandeering. She knew *she* was still a guest as well and did not wish to offend any of them.

"He can stay, right?" she asked timidly, hoping the answer would be yes.

"The Skunk may stay for a brief stint," replied the Bee, begrudgingly granting the Greyhound's request. "But no funny business with that tail of yours, Skunk!"

"Of course not," the Skunk replied. "I wouldn't dream of it."

The Greyhound did not understand the reference to the Skunk's appendage. Regardless, the party started. The group, minus the Greyhound and the Skunk, drank the sweet nectar and engorged their bellies. The Greyhound had become quite hungry, so she asked the Squirrel if she could have a few of the nonintoxicating berries. A large stockpile of them was centered in front of the animal.

The Squirrel squawked, "Why no! Absolutely not! Absolutely not. You can't have any of my berries. These are mine! One can never have enough berries! Never enough!"

"But you couldn't possibly eat all of those tonight," the Greyhound said, not understanding why the creature would not share the food the Greyhound herself had gathered for it. "Won't you share some, please?"

"No, no, no! One can never have enough of anything," squeaked the Squirrel as it shoved more and more berries into its ballooning cheeks.

The Rat overheard the conversation and slinked closer to the Greyhound. Whispering slowly, in an ominous tone, it said, "If you are hungry, just go over there and take the food. The others won't care. It's yours by right."

"It's not mine to take," the Greyhound said meekly. An odd pang in her gut told her it was wrong to take what didn't belong to her.

"Then I'll go steal the berries for you," replied the Rat.

"No. They're not yours to take either," said the Greyhound earnestly. She did not like the Rat. It made the fur on the back of her neck stand up straight.

The Rat continued as it chomped away on a large piece of cheese it had stolen from the Farmer who lived beyond on the edge of the Forest. "I take whatever I desire, whenever I desire it."

"I do not feel comfortable doing that," the Greyhound replied.

"You are a fool, Hound!" the Rat railed loudly. "You are too nice! You will not survive in this world without taking what you need or desire!"

"She will survive just fine," the Skunk chimed in. "She is a kindhearted creature and not in need of the influence of those who wish to change her true Nature. Leave her alone."

The commotion caught the attention of the Bee and the Weasel, who had been pretending they weren't listening, though it was clear to the Greyhound they had been. She knew the Bee was always listening to her.

"Rat, are you going to take that from a Skunk?" the Bee asked, which provoked the Rat to take action.

"Yeah! Are you going to let that smelly black-and-white creature speak to you that way?" hollered the Weasel.

"You're an odd one, aren't you, Skunk?" asked the Rat, who was now perturbed by the Skunk's presence. "What is with that ugly, white stripe that plagues the top of your body and runs from the tip of your puny, pink nose to the tip of your smelly tail?"

The Rat and the Weasel encroached on the Skunk's space. The Greyhound sensed they were going to attack and hurt him. An unusual heat emanated from inside of her, and something nudged her just as it had the day she defended the Yorkie. Her head pounded. Lightheadedness overtook her. Without hesitation, she leapt in front of the Skunk, protecting it from the hostile group.

"Enough!" shouted the Greyhound.

"You really think you can stop us, Hound?" the Rat asked rhetorically. "Ha! I dare you to try!"

The Rat lowered its front legs to the ground as its backside rose. Its wiry tail stood erect, pointing at the dark sky. It slowly crept closer to the Greyhound as if stalking its prey. Recognizing the Rat's menacing stance and observing the Skunk who readied itself for battle as well, the Greyhound, alert to the danger, wondered if she would be able to jump high enough to get out of the reach of the Rat's bite.

She did not have to wonder very long. Before the Rat took one more step, the Skunk shot underneath the Greyhound's tall legs, stood in front of her, scratched at the ground, stomped his two front paws with a thud, turned his backside to the group of bullies, and lifted his white-striped tail straight towards the Tree tops. He looked up at the Greyhound and winked as if to say, *Watch this!* then sprayed the Rat and Weasel directly in their eyes. The mist was powerful enough to reach the Beaver by the boulder, and the Squirrel, who had been laughing at the spectacle from a low-lying limb. A single drop hit the Bee too. It flapped its wings wildly. They all ranted as they ran fuming into the night, eager to wash off the Skunk's secret weapon.

"Are you okay?" the Skunk asked the Greyhound.

"I think so," she replied. "Are you?"

"Yes," said the Skunk as he lowered and readjusted his tail that was still twitching in its defensive position.

"That's a mighty powerful natural defense system you've got there! Thank you for saving me," the Greyhound said, relieved the confrontation had ended without injury to herself or the Skunk.

"You are very welcome, my friend. You have been kind to me. You accepted me as I am and are not repulsed by my scent as the rest of the Forest animals are," said the Skunk.

"It does not bother me," said the Greyhound. "I somewhat care for the scent, though I admit, it was quite pungent upon release."

"It sure is. I must go now, but I hope you choose not to stay here. You don't belong here. These creatures are not nice. They do not appreciate you or know you *by Heart*," the Skunk said genuinely.

"But I have nowhere to go," the Greyhound said. Her voice cracked.

"The truth is, DearOne, you can go home." The Skunk nose-bumped the Greyhound with fondness and scampered away.

"Good-bye, my friend," said the Greyhound as she watched another friend disappear into the void.

CHANGE COMES IN ALL FORMS

And so it was . . . The Greyhound spent the next few hours lying beneath the Pines, contemplating the Skunk's gentle words and the clan's mean-spiritedness. Confrontations were not her favorite, though she did not shrink in their presence. When someone was being hurt, made fun of, or being judged harshly, the tension created a sick feeling in the space just below the Greyhound's heart. Overcome by a feeling similar to the one she had experienced on the harrowing ride that brought her to the cold, corner Cage, the Greyhound could not ignore the introspection. Deep inside, she felt a shift.

What is this feeling? Why am I always so sad? she wondered. *Why, just when I begin to enjoy myself, must all things fall apart? I am so tired. It's true what the Skunk said—I don't belong here. But where do I belong?*

Just then, the Bee's entourage returned to the Nook and without missing a beat, the rave continued to the horror of the Greyhound, who stayed curled up, tightly huddled beneath the Pines. The Skunk's scent still lingered in the Nook.

VOICES CARRY

And so it was . . . Later that night, the Greyhound, who had challenged the clan's authority earlier, became the target for the evening as the clan mounted an assault against the Greyhound. The nefarious Rat was the first to begin the battering; it's animus towards the Greyhound was palpable to all.

"Why are you still here?" the Rat said. "You are not wanted here. If I were you, I couldn't be in a place where I am not wanted!"

"I thought you were my friends," the Greyhound said to the clan as she looked directly at the Bee. "You told me this is where I would find freedom. You made a promise. You told me I would be happy here."

"Look at you!" The Rat grew nastier. "You are so thin-skinned!"

"Literally and figuratively," added the Weasel.

The rancor of the Rat and the Weasel was venomous.

"So what if I am?" barked the Greyhound. "I have no choice. I have to stay fit. Any extra weight would add to my race time. We Greyhounds are thin by nature. I have to be if I am to race again someday."

"Race?" blurted the Bee. "Hmph! You are no longer a racer. Your Owner sent you away! No one wants you. You're a has-been. You are nothing but a failure. You've failed at everything you've ever done! You failed at racing, at friendships, and at love!"

"I am *not* a failure," the Greyhound barked back. "Enough! Leave me, Bee!" Her bark was so loud that it blew the Bee to the other side of the Nook. The Bee, flailing, landed on the flat tail of the Beaver whose instinctual reaction was to swat it off, sending the Bee tumbling through the air where it finally landed on one of the boulders. The brooding Bee flapped its wings wildly, and flew directly at the Greyhound, facing-off as if it were about to sting. But it was injured. As it flew into the night, retreating to its nest, it announced it was retiring for the evening. The gathering ended abruptly.

Stunned by the strength of the Greyhound's bark, the rest of the group slithered silently and quickly to their respective nests. The Squirrel ran high up the Tree and disappeared amid the oaknuts. The Weasel burrowed down an escape route between the boulders. The Beaver scurried back home to the west bank of the Brook, and the Rat ran off, blending into the darkness most likely in search of more scraps of food to steal.

The Greyhound stood statuesque. She did not know from what depths of her being that bark had originated. She felt empowered that she had stood her ground, but she needed to inspect this new voice she rarely exercised. The Rat had gone too far. The Greyhound had reached her limit. She couldn't stand being bullied one more time. She had had enough! The clan's obstreperous behavior and the Nook's negative energy enveloped her. It crushed her Spirit. It depleted her of emotional stability. It consumed her. She felt dizzy. The Nook was changing her, and she did not like who she was becoming. Angry with herself for staying as long as she had with such horrible creatures who cared for no one but themselves, and doubly upset for thinking they actually cared about her, she questioned how she could have been so gullible. But self-reflection would not be further explored tonight. Her energy was spent.

She consumed the bits of food that remained, and from her bed of needles, for the first time since arriving in the Nook, she saw through the Trees the luminiferous beams of the gibbous Moon, though the Moon himself remained hidden above the Treetops. It was as if the Moon's magnetic pull was dragging her away from the Nook—his effect on her profound.

"I have to leave this place," she howled to the sky. "But where do I go? How will I ever find *the Way* out of this darkness?" She howled for the past. She howled for the pain. She howled for the Harvest Moon to save her. She howled and howled without fear of retribution. She howled because she had to. She howled because she wanted to.

SEVEN

—

THE CHOICE

PANIC ATTACKS

And so it was . . . The Greyhound had never howled before, and it felt good to embrace her basic instinct. *How can I possibly get myself out of this situation?* she thought. *This is my only chance.*

To be detected by the clan would be catastrophic. The Bee continually calculated her whereabouts and constantly monitored what she was doing, how she was feeling, what she was thinking, and why. The Greyhound could not figure out how the Bee accomplished this, but it did. Getting as far away from the Nook as possible was paramount. The disheartened Greyhound slipped away from the band of bandits, snoring loudly in their respective nests.

Surreptitiously, she exited the confines of the Nook. With each careful step, she made her way towards the Brook as memories of her past came crashing down in excruciating waves. She fought back the tears as the darkness turned darker still. She wondered why the Trees were hiding the Moon's light. Her anxiety surged, her head pounded, and the painful undulations heightened her sense of doom. She could not *breathe*. Panic enveloped her. She felt ill. Her *breathing* became more labored.

What is happening to me? She reeled. *My head feels like it's going to explode! I feel like I've been hit by a Mack Truck! Am I dying? Is this how my life will end, in the blackness of the night, in the middle of nowhere, lost and alone? At least at the Track, I could have died in a familiar place.*

How could she be happy with all the buzzing in her head and the dizziness? She thought about how the Bee had buzzed more frantically in her ear when she had pleasant thoughts of returning to the JeepGirl, or had regained an iota of confidence in her abilities, or had begun to hear her own thoughts again. The Bee's constant badgering continuously reminded her of her flaws. Too often, it had threatened to sting her and the Mouse, and that fear paralyzed her. The Bee said it would kill them if it chose to sting them multiple times. The buzzing that was imbedded in her brain confused her. It smothered the tender words the Mouse used to say that gave her comfort. The pain in her head was excruciating. She needed help desperately.

Who would help a lost Greyhound with so many Scars? she thought.

STOP RUNNING

And so it was . . . The forlorn Greyhound wished never to return to the Nook, but in order to continue the Journey out of the Forest, she had to pass the Bee's nest. The thought of awakening the thing made her shudder. A few hairs fell. She envisioned the Bee asleep and concentrated on that thought alone. She needed a miracle. Slowly and cautiously, she made her way to the Bee's nest and looked up at a particular section of the Linden Tree's intersecting branches where the Bee's nest lay. The Bee loved the Linden Tree. Its fruit was a source of food for the bugger, and it emitted an entrancing elixir that caused the Bee to sleep deeply. The Greyhound nosed over the branches to see the Bee finally resting. Its wings were bruised, and the Greyhound felt remorseful that she had caused the trauma. The Greyhound was confounded by the fact that she could still hear the sleeping Bee's buzzing in her head. The irony that the Bee was nestled in a protective cluster of heart-shaped leaves was not lost on the Greyhound. She wondered if the Bee actually had a heart. It could be so cruel.

The thick leaves of the Linden Tree didn't allow the light of the Moon to penetrate, so any movement went undetected. It was her only chance to sneak away, Sighthound unseen. She knew she must go. She was gone in a flash, making the second great escape of her life! Once again, she found herself running away alone. The darkness and her concern for her own safety prohibited her from galloping, so only a trot (not an optimal velocity for a critical exit) was possible.

A thousand questions rambled through her mind as she made her way. Being far enough away from the Nook, the Greyhound stopped to rest and stood disillusioned under a Sugar Maple Tree that was clinging to the last of its leaves in defiance of Autumn's will.

Why am I always running? Is this the only way I'll be happy? But I'm not happy. What else is there? I don't really belong with these creatures. Is this what it's like to have friends? This isn't who I am. I don't know who

I want to be. Should I go back to the JeepGirl? Should I leave the Mouse and everyone else behind as the Bee suggested? Should I continue in this life alone? Should I continue in this life at all?

THERE ARE ONLY DECISIONS

And so it was . . . The confidence she had gained, before the nightmare of her extraction from the Track had begun, was now diminishing, exhausted by the drama and chaos of her week in the Nook, notwithstanding the events of the night. She needed rest desperately. In the distance, she saw a triad of Pine Trees she hoped would offer her protection until the morning. The Pines had been kind to her thus far. When she reached them, she asked permission for their protection. They gifted it to her readily and gladly. She curled up tightly in the middle of the Pines, covered herself with pine needles as best she could, and rested her weary body, though there was not much rest for her mind.

"Why is it so difficult for me to make a decision? I'm like the Squirrel who couldn't decide whether to go up or down the Tree!" she quietly asked the Pines.

The Greyhound remained silent, expecting the Pines to respond. Instead, an old Snowy White Owl hooted an unsolicited response. "Hoo, hoo. Perhaps it's because you are afraid."

The Greyhound followed the deep, gravelly voice and found the Snowy White Owl easily seen in the invisible Moon's growing light. The Snowy White Owl was just to her right, across the Brook, perched on a pile of felled Cherry and Elm Trees that skirted that particular section.

"Afraid?" the Greyhound asked, wondering what the stately creature meant. "Afraid of what?"

"Of *hoo* you are. You are desperately afraid of making decisions," the Snowy White Owl whistled as it flew closer to the Greyhound and settled on a large Cherry Tree branch that jutted over the Brook.

"But I don't want to make the wrong decision," the Greyhound confessed. Defending herself was an everyday occurrence, something she had done since the bullying had begun. She was very aware of this particular flaw, but it was something she had learned to do to survive the backlash she received when voicing her honest opinion. No matter what opinion she shared, friends, family, Owners, Trainers, other racers, and those she loved continually questioned her, the facts she knew she knew, or the way she chose to tackle a task or problem. They all had labeled the Greyhound a *highly sensitive soul* and not in a complimentary manner.

One particular friend, back at the Track, incessantly questioned her capabilities and her knowledge regarding racing and life in general. On one occasion, she explained to her misinformed friend that the Sun was actually a Star, but the fellow racer insisted it was really a planet. It was another racer who stepped in and corrected the friend for the Greyhound. A subsequent conversation included a debate about whether the Big Dipper in the night sky was also called the Plough. The Greyhound knew it was, but to her dismay, her friend doubted her once again. She had long ago lost that friend without a word as to why.

As she thought about her friendship with the Doe and how gently and lovingly the Doe had treated her, the Greyhound wondered again if those she had once considered friends had ever truly been friends. In her core, she knew the Nook rogues were not her friends. She so desperately had wanted to fit in and belong someplace or with someone that she had compromised her own integrity by being in the Nook. She knew that now. Forfeiting her integrity would not happen again. Having integrity was one of the qualities she actually liked about herself.

The White Owl continued, but in a delicate fashion. "True. *Hoo, hoo,* but you categorize those decisions, correct?"

"Yes, I believe there are good decisions and bad decisions. There are right decisions and wrong decisions that can be made too," the Greyhound stated confidently, without being haughty. She did not know how to be obnoxious, but she surely recognized the trait in others who had crossed her path, so she tried to avoid being so.

"*Hoo.* There are no wrong decisions, DearOne—only decisions. *Hoo, hoo,*" said the wise White Owl.

"Hmmm. That sounds plausible," said the Greyhound, processing the White Owl's words. "Perhaps that *is* true. If you would please excuse me, I would love to continue our conversation, but I am truly quite tired and unable to give you the full and proper attention you deserve. I must depart before they find me. What do you call yourself?"

"*Hoo.* I am a Snowy White Owl. *Hoo,*" answered the Owl.

"Thank you for conversing with me, Snowy White Owl," said the Greyhound.

"Anytime, DearOne."

The White Owl's wisdom struck a chord in her heart. He made sense. It was information the Greyhound would need to hold close and revisit. She felt moved to look up to see the clouds had parted during their discussion.

"Those Stars have been keeping watch over you at the Moon's behest," the Snowy White Owl whistled insightfully.

"They have?" she asked with wonderment. I haven't been able to see any of them from the Nook.

"Yes, DearOne. They are always with you. They remain devoted even when you can't see them," the Snowy White Owl solemnly offered, attempting to comfort her.

It comforted her indeed, so much so, that she nodded off for a few minutes.

Awaking abruptly, unaware of the moment sleep had overcome her, she raised her head to see the Snowy White Owl taking flight. His wingspan was the length of her body, and his grace and beauty were equally inspiring. She gazed upon him in amazement as he soared among the Stars. She wished she could fly—fly far, far away from this place. She'd fly right over the Moon to live among the Stars and never come back. The thought soothed her. *What a wondrous life it would be to live among the Stars,* she thought.

The Greyhound, revisiting her choices, pondered her position on each, and came to a decision—she would not return to the Nook. She walked on, gazing upward every now and then to see if she could still spy the Snowy White Owl who had enlightened her.

The night was so black, but as she continued on her Journey, the clouds dissolved, and the water reflected the Stars' light just enough so she would not injure herself on obstacles strewn about the ground along the Brook's edge. The Greyhound decided to follow the Brook eastward instead of her usual westbound route. She had never explored this end of the Forest, but *the Way* she chose felt right. As she trotted with the flow of the Brook, she began to see more of the Star-adorned sky and a radiant light far off in the distance. It felt good to be one with the Brook and to be running in the night light. Aside from the evening she left the JeepGirl, she had always run with other racers, and only ever during the day. This was different. She felt freer without the Bee's constant hum, which had been drowning out not only her own thoughts but the Crickets, the Nightingales, and the other sounds of the Forest.

Another shift in her energy fueled her anxieties. She wasn't yet able to hold on to the peacefulness of heart for very long. The soothing sounds of the Brook had become muffled by the sound of her own heartbeat. That familiar fear fell fast and furiously upon her, forcing the exuberance of the escape to wane. Her gait slowed. She stopped.

Desperate in thought, the Greyhound looked up at the night sky, *What am I doing? This is futile. Where am I going? How can I do this alone? I need help! Someone, please help me!*

You asked for help? The voice was familiar. It whispered, "You are not alone, DearOne."

Something tickled her toe. Looking down, she saw the Mouse.

Where did you come from? How did you get here? How did you hear me? She was sure she hadn't spoken out loud for fear the Shadows would overhear her and report back to the Bee. Despite her questions, she was grateful the Mouse was with her.

I didn't think I'd ever see you again, thought the Greyhound. Her inner voice trembled. Tears welled in her eyes, but none fell. The Greyhound couldn't even muster a smile. Her mood was still quite dim.

I am always with you, communicated the Mouse. *One day, you will learn to recognize the brave energy within you. Know now that you are never alone.*

The Greyhound nodded. Not lingering too long, they made sure to drink from the Brook and eat a few tasty berries the Doe had deemed safe. They avoided the tart berries that were not so pleasing to the palate. She missed her ForestFriend deeply. The Mouse climbed on the Greyhound's back. It held on to the soft scruff of her neck and whispered, "Let's go home." Then the Greyhound and the Mouse trotted off, far away from the darkness of the Nook, towards the light.

EIGHT

—

THE STARS

TEARS MAY FALL

And so it was . . . In the deeper recesses of the Forest, the air had lacked movement. It was only by the Brook's side where the Greyhound had felt even the slightest breeze. A shift in the flow of the Forest air heightened the Greyhound's senses. A zephyr caressed her as it passed by, causing her to reflexively *breathe* in the cleaner air.

An airier part of the Forest would be a welcome change. I think there's a clearing up ahead, thought the Greyhound tentatively.

There certainly is, DearOne. Keep relying on your gifts more and more, communicated the Mouse.

What gifts? the Greyhound asked.

"Don't lose sight now, DearOne. Keep looking ahead," squeaked the tiny Mouse.

The two came to a place where the Forest burst open, revealing the bottom of a series of rocky Knolls.

Afraid her voice would carry on the wind and awaken the Bee, the Greyhound continued communicating through thought vibrations, *It is so bright up there!*

The Mouse agreed, *Yes, it is quite special! Go on. It's okay.*

The Greyhound wondered for a moment how the Mouse knew she wanted to trek up the Knoll alone.

Yes, I will wait for you until you need me. The loyal creature nodded back, tapping the leg of the curious Greyhound.

And so the Greyhound sped towards the top of the Knoll to discover the source of the brilliant light. Her heart raced, not out of fear but out of the growing anticipation. Reaching the top, she could see clearly now. There he was—her magnificent emerging Moon with his fullness majestically displayed before her in wondrous beams of light that lit up the Valley below. She felt as though she could jump up and sit beside him in the vast space of the night sky as if she were a great Phoenix who remembered it had wings to rise from the flames and ashes of its former life. Instead, the Greyhound sat down in what is considered a sitting position for Greyhounds. She was told long ago that when all four legs faced forward, with only her undercarriage grazing the ground, she looked like the great Egyptian Sphinx. So she sat, Sphinxlike, gazing at the Moon like an old love. For the first time in her young life, she saw the whole of the Moon, and he was brilliant! The unbearable weight she had been carrying on her Journey lightened and moved her to tears as thousands of shimmering Stars surrounded the Moon. A band of pure white light encircled the Moon and the space in between filled with an indescribable, radiant energy. It was Magickal!

"I've never seen anything like this," whispered the Greyhound to the Stars. "I am overwhelmed by the light, your shining brilliance, and the full Moon's magnificence."

"Then why are you crying?" asked a little Star that twinkled when it spoke.

"I don't know why. I just can't keep the tears from falling," whimpered the Greyhound.

"We fall too," said one bright Star.

"You do?" the Greyhound asked, astounded.

"Why yes, we fall all the time, and if you make a genuine wish while we are falling, your wish will come true," blinked a Star, coming even closer to her than the last.

"What's a wish?" she inquired humbly.

"It's something you desire in your heart, something good you want dearly to happen," said a smaller Star, sailing by the Knoll.

"I'm too sad to make a wish right now," the Greyhound said honestly as tears continued to fall.

"It's okay to be sad, but remember to be happy later," a sister Star said, trying to console the Greyhound.

An enlightened Star that had existed for billions of years spoke up, "DearOne, know that every moment of life is like a bubble that bursts into a new beginning. That new beginning has the power to manifest into anything imaginable. Use your imagination to assemble the life you've hoped for—the one you store deep in your HeartBox. And if that choice doesn't bear the outcome you desire, you can rest assured the next moment will usher in another new beginning, and the chance to choose again will present itself. New beginnings are infinite like us."

"I am humbled by your sage advice, but I'm confused. How would I know what I want if I don't even know where I belong or who I am?" she cried as tears trickled off her snout and splashed upon a stone underfoot.

NINE

—

THE MOON

JUST BREATHE

And so it was . . . A gentle voice, in a much deeper tone than those of the Stars, spoke. "Surely you remember who you are, DearHeart." It was the Moon, growing brighter and brighter as he came closer and closer to the precipice where the Greyhound sat.

"Truly I don't, dear Moon," said the Greyhound with deep humility.

"Just *breathe*," said the Moon.

The Greyhound's body resisted at first. She was quite winded from the sprint up the Knoll and from crying so much, both of which drained her energy, but she did as the majestic Moon instructed: she took a deep, deep *breath*.

"Close your eyes, DearHeart," said the Moon. "*Breathe*. Concentrate on becoming calm, on becoming one with your surroundings. *Breathe*, slowly, in and out—in and out. *Breathe*. Take your time. Listen to and feel the rhythm of your heartbeat. *Breathe* in and out. *Breathe* in the sweetness of the love that surrounds you. Exhale the pain and the grief of the past, for thoughts of the past cannot hurt you any longer and will never serve you well."

The Greyhound closed her eyes and focused on the beating of her heart. She *breathed* in *the Way* as shone. Soon, a sense of calm caressed her, and she noticed the noises of the night again—the Snowy White Owl hooting in the distance, the flutter of a Bat's wings as it passed by, the Crickets chirping underfoot, and the Elm and Pine Trees rustling in the Valley below her. What a pleasant euphony. It was euphoric!

For the first time in a long time, she wasn't afraid. She was protected by the Moon's healing beams, and the special connection that was birthing between her and the Stars provided additional healing light. Upon opening her eyes, she saw the Treetops below glowing like a sea of emeralds in the Moonlight. They swayed back and forth in union with her *breathing*, each a part of the oneness of the universe.

Is this what it feels like to be well? she thought. *I haven't felt well in a long time. Too long.*

"Just breathe," the Moon whispered. "Allow your thought-loops to quiet. Expel them into the ether. Now, DearHeart, what do you know, and what do you not know?"

"I know that I do not wish to go back to the Nook."

A deep *breath* escaped naturally.

"What else?" spurred the Moon.

The Greyhound didn't answer right away. She was processing old wounds and newly discovered feelings. She stared at the sky and watched the Stars gleaming. Finally, she spoke.

"I know I can't ever go back to the Track, even though parts of me linger there and I still miss it so," said the Greyhound, unexpectedly tearful. The way in which she had perceived her life had defined her up until this moment, and now that perception was shifting and morphing into a new way of seeing the world.

"This is true. It would be wise to look ahead and not to allow past hardships and the pathos of life to impede your progress or your tomorrows," the Moon gently advised.

"But I don't know where to go now. I am utterly lost. I don't even have a proper name," the Greyhound said as a few tears trickled down her cheek, lost forever in the rocky ground.

"DearHeart, you are not lost. I assure you. You know exactly where you belong, and you know *the Way*." He comforted her anxious heart and surrounded her in beams of healing light. The Greyhound, shrouded by his powerful Moonbeams, appeared Starlike herself and shone so bright on the edge of Nirvana.

"I do?" questioned the Greyhound, whose tears had dampened the fine fur of her paw.

"Yes, you do, DearHeart."

MAGICK

And so it was . . . The Moon instructed the Stars that had been dancing in the Moonlight to tell the Greyhound the origin of her name. They were honored and delighted to do so.

"You see," said the Stars in loving unison, "we have been around for eons and have witnessed the evolution of Earth and human language. The name your ancestors bestowed upon you is rich and dates back to the ancient Egyptians who called you *greihundr*, which means dog-hunter."

That made perfect sense to the Greyhound, who knew she was from a distinguished line of hunters. She had seen the Handlers in the Shelter looking at paintings and etchings of Greyhounds in ancient Egyptian hieroglyphs. History lessons enthralled her.

The Stars continued their dissertation. "Another meaning of your name, *g'her*, means to shine, or to twinkle, like we do! And another ancient spelling of your name, *gryjandi*, signifies morning twilight or brightness." The Stars became brighter and brighter as they explained the etymology of her name. "Your name also means Sun," they sang sweetly.

Now it was clear why she loved the Sun so much. Astonished not only by the purity of the light the Stars and the Moon emanated, but also by the significance of what she had just been told, the Greyhound stood up and leaned over the edge. She gazed at the Moon, who made his way closer to her.

"My name means all they say it does?"

Yes. The Moon nodded. "Just as the Stars twinkle and shine in the night sky to guide you whenever you lose *the Way*, you, too, DearHeart, have an incredible light within you. Believe in its Magickal healing properties, and it will light *the Way*."

"I see now what the White Fox meant when it said the light within has Magickal powers!"

The full Moon nodded again.

"I am humbled to share some of the Stars' special characteristics," said the Greyhound, bowing her head in reverence to the light. "But what is Magick? I forgot to ask the White Fox. What if I can't access this Magick when I must?"

The Moon beamed, invoking the Stars to answer the Greyhound.

"Magick is as old as time," said one of the largest Stars. "It is when life happens effortlessly and just *is*. Magick is the secret ingredient for those seemingly impossible occurrences to serendipitously blossom and unfold into amazing moments and miracles."

A Star close by sparkled and added, "That Magick is within *you*—it is within all of us. It surrounds you. It follows you wherever you go. It makes you truly magnificent."

"Magick is that knowing you feel in your HeartBox," another Star said, whizzing by her. "It is your guide, and in turn, it will serve as a guide for others, because they will see your Magick, your inner light shining ever so brightly, glimmering and sparkling like we do and like the morning Star—our glorious Sun."

"Your Magick will grow and radiate the more firmly you believe in its power—in yourself!" said the tiniest Star among them.

"Where does it get its power?" the Greyhound asked curiously.

"You ask questions to which you already know the answers, DearHeart," replied the Moon.

"Our gifts give it power?" asked the Greyhound, trying to understand all she was being taught. She was a good student, though out of practice. She had not needed to learn something new in a long time. Life at the Track had become rote. The rituals of racing and the grueling schedule had left no room for much else. The Greyhound was fascinated by all that existed beyond the life she had been forced to live.

"Yes," answered a group of Stars positioned above the Greyhound. "When you share your Magick and innate gifts with the world, others will see your brilliance, your brightness, and be forever touched by your light. Everyone possesses a unique light, but some don't recognize their own Magick and forget the truth of who they are. You must remember this Magick is kept deep within your heart and can never be extinguished, though trying times might dim it," explained the Moon.

"How do I know what gifts I possess?"

"You will know, DearHeart," the patient Moon told her. "Listen *by Heart*, and if you are as quiet as a Mouse, you will be able to recognize your Magick and use it for good. Avail yourself of that feeling of knowing when it rises within you, tried and true."

"But no one will love me with all my Scars. I am ugly and broken, and I have lost so many pieces of myself along *the Way*!"

She hung her head. Her nose grazed the ground. A gush of tears came and could not be stopped. She relinquished control over them. Oh, those tears! Something on the ground tickled the side of her snout tenderly, but she couldn't see anything through the tears.

"We don't mind your Scars at all," relayed the Stars.

The Moon knew the Greyhound had deeper wounds beneath all the

Scars—the unseen ones—the ones not yet shared with the rest of the world, and he knew how utterly debilitating they were. The Moon moved closer to the poor Greyhound. "You have a choice, DearHeart. You can carry your Scars as broken bits and parts of yourself that become deeper and heavier with time and neglect, but by choosing to carry this load, your Scars will attempt to snuff out your light, your gifts, your dreams, your Magick. Your thoughts will consume your days and your nights. They will blind you to the beauty of life and keep you hostage to the Shadows. Or, you can choose to see your Scars as the Stars do—as orbs filled with healing golden and white light that shine and reveal *the Way*. As brightness is your namesake, your Scars can help you heal when you transform them into Stardust—healing light energy, a gift garnished with Magick. Others, who suffer Scars of their own, will be able to see your light and the Magick you share with the world, and they will discover they, too, are able to lighten the burden of their own darkness. What you have been searching for is not out there, for it cannot be seen. It is right here, DearHeart—within you."

The Moon touched the Greyhound's heart.

"What you said sounds so poetic, but I don't know how to do what you say. I've tried and tried," the Greyhound said softly. "I really wish to learn, but I don't know how."

"Just *be*," said the Moon tenderly. "Be patient for answers that will come to you in time and in the form of new beginnings. Be kind to your Self. Be as gentle and loving with your Self as you are with others. Be mindful of what the Stars shared with you when you arrived—they gift their Magick when the last of their bright light turns into Stardust as they fall from the night sky and become one with the universe."

Maybe I will be lucky enough to see a falling Star, thought the Greyhound, recalling what the Stars had told her about wishes.

BE PATIENT

And so it was . . . It was about this time that the Greyhound's tears abated enough for her to see the Mouse.

"Did you find what you were searching for?" the Mouse whispered, gently prodding her.

"I'm not sure, but I think so. I do know that I must find a shooting Star," she said.

"I'm sure you will," said the Mouse.

Some doubt, though dulled, lingered in the air around the Greyhound. The two sat silently and still on that sacred ground.

"What if we don't see one?" asked the Greyhound.

The Moon smiled when he heard her use of the word *I* had become *we*. It was a good thing—progress. She was beginning to understand that *the Way* to attain peace included accepting all the parts of her Self, one of which was the Mouse.

"We will," assured the Mouse.

"What if we don't?" insisted the Greyhound.

A consoling voice floated on the crisp air, *"Breathe*, DearHeart. *Breathe* as the Stars do. When you *breathe* deeply enough, that energy becomes like water and flows through you and all things. Be patient. There is time."

WISH WELL AND WISELY

And so it was . . . The Greyhound and the Mouse watched the night sky, and every now and again, the Moon gently reminded the Greyhound to *breathe*, and she did. She searched and searched the sky until her *breathing* became calmer and more rhythmic, and she could hear her heart beat in rhythm with the Mouse's. Beyond the Trees and Hills, beyond the mighty River that meandered through the Valley below, beyond the majesty of Nature and the Cosmos before her, the Greyhound saw farther and felt more deeply than she had ever known was possible. She remained transfixed by the expansiveness of the scene and how it affected her soul.

There's a whole world beyond what I could ever have fathomed. I understand that now. So many places and possibilities exist out there. It's overwhelming and wondrous, Magickal and mysterious all at once, and I want to see more of it, she thought.

You will. Anything is possible, the Mouse responded.

The Greyhound searched and searched the sky, looking for the slightest variance of light in the atmosphere. She spotted a particularly radiant Star. She watched as the Star took a deep *breath*, then shot across the sky.

"Make a wish!" sang the Stars. "Do make a wish!"

"I wish . . ."

She didn't dare say her wish out loud for fear its echo would float down the Knoll and be heard by the Bee. It was safe and sound in her HeartBox.

She and the Mouse watched as the Star glided gleefully, sprinkling its Magickal Stardust across the sky above them.

Sensational! She wanted to shout.

The light lingered for some time, then softly faded as the Star's light appeared to extinguish.

"What happened to the Star?" the Greyhound asked sadly.

"Its light has been relinquished. It has become one with All," the Moon chimed.

Fighting back the tears again, she asked, "But why did it have to lose its spectacular light?"

The Moon knew her *by Heart* and knew she was a highly sensitive soul with empathy not limited to Earthly things so, with great tenderness, he explained, "It didn't wholly extinguish. It chose to metamorphose and become part of your light, DearHeart."

"The Star did that for me?" the Greyhound asked, absolutely humbled by the gesture.

"Yes, that was its gift. It chose to share its Magickal Stardust with you. That is how your wish will come true," the Moon explained.

The Greyhound's gaze was riveted to the sky where the Star had fallen, and she lost herself in its truth and in her own. The past was fading with the light too. The invasive thoughts of the Track, the disturbing energy of the Nook and the Bee subsided in waves. The Greyhound felt an unusual feeling in and around her heart. She looked down at the Mouse, who smiled at her.

I feel safe—at peace. I've only ever felt this sensation when I was a young puppy. No. Wait. She thought of the JeepGirl. *I felt the same way when the JeepGirl hugged me and when she told me I was safe. Now I know what she meant.*

What you feel is love, the Mouse communicated. *It's a powerful emotion with miraculous, healing energy.*

"Indeed," the Moon concurred. "That Mouse of yours is a Magickal little thing too. It is a reliable Spirit you can always trust. It knows you completely—all your faults and strengths, all your quirks and eccentricities, all your insecurities and Scars, and all your hopes and dreams. It knows you as I know you. It is always with you, DearHeart."

GRATITUDE BEGETS GRACE

And so it was . . . The Greyhound looked at the Mouse with renewed gratitude. She felt like they had been together forever and that a lifetime had passed since their Journey had begun. Had they been together forever? She thought back as far as she could remember, but it was time to say good-bye to the Stars and her Moon.

Good-bye Stars, thought the Greyhound, mindful of how barking good-bye could awaken the Bee.

Good-bye, good-bye, good-bye! the Stars glimmered and glowed.

Good-bye, Moon. I will miss you so much, the Greyhound said, admiring the Moon in all his sublimity. It was unclear if she would ever see the full Moon again, but she would not cry this time. She was safe and felt the peace of the present moment showering over her like the Stardust had.

There is no need for good-byes, DearHeart. I am always here for you, though not always visible. I may change somewhat, for I am a shapeshifter, and you may not see all of me, but just know—I Am. Remember the light of love you witnessed tonight and that sense of knowing deep inside you and how it felt, and you will always be okay, however you are in that moment.

"But what about during the day?" the Greyhound whispered. "What if I need help when the Sun is shining?"

The Moon answered, "The Great Star, is the grandmaster of all the Stars, and the gatekeeper of the day, as I am of the night. I am always near, only hidden sometimes by the brilliance of her rays. If I am on the far side, guiding others, I will return upon completion of my synchronous rotation. Just because you can't see me doesn't mean I am not with you, DearHeart. I am always with you."

Funny, the Greyhound thought. *The Mouse has said those last few words to me so many times.*

The Moon continued to slide silently across the sky—a most mesmerizing and majestic sight to behold. He continued, "In that light, the Sun may also offer you counsel. You can ask for her guidance. In the meantime, if you are unable to wait for me, seek out the Mouse. The Mouse is your true guide—your compass. It will never disappoint you, hurt you, or lead you astray. It will not judge you as others have judged you, or as you judge yourself. The Mouse will love you always—just the way you are."

"Scars and all?"

"Yes, DearHeart, Scars and all. The Mouse is part of the Magick inside you!"

The Moon paused, then said, "It is time for me to go for now, DearHeart."

The Mouse is like Stardust too?

"Yes," answered the Moon tenderly.

I will forever remember this night and all you have taught me, Moon, thought the Greyhound with pure love in her heart.

The Greyhound observed a change in the night sky as the Moon sank below the Earth. He left a solitary line of dazzling white light, marking the horizon where the Earth and Space met. The Greyhound understood that the Moon would return to her, and the light that made him shine would make him visible to her once again. As the Moon gifted his own light back to the Sun, the Mouse and the Greyhound knew it was time to continue their Journey. Still wrapped in a cocoon of healing Stardust and Moonbeams, and with reverent love in her heart, the Greyhound tapped the side of the Mouse, who then scurried up the long leg of the extraordinarily tall Hound.

"Hold on tight!" the Greyhound told the Mouse. "I don't want to lose you again."

The Mouse held on to a tuft of fur on the nape of the Greyhound's neck as they ambled down the Knoll.

TEN

—

THE ACTION

FORGIVENESS

And so it was . . . The Greyhound remained solemn and introspective during the descent of the Knoll. Her silence served as the Mouse's cue that she needed some quiet time to absorb all the lessons she had learned from her CelestialFriends. There was so much to consider, so much to embrace. The Greyhound reflected on the spectacle she had witnessed, and words were kept in her HeartBox for the time being. For now, the Mouse held on tightly, and the Greyhound was content enough that the Mouse was with her.

Every now and then, she smiled when she thought about how the celestial encounter had enlightened her. Still in awe of the Star's story of her name, she was unable to share with the Mouse how she felt, but part of her sensed the Mouse already knew. Thoughts about who she really was beyond the superficial Scars and the wounds that festered below meandered through her mind. She thought about who she had been, who she wanted to be, and who she would become as she healed.

Could I really be happy? Could I help others by sharing my light? In my heart, I know I cannot return to my old life, and I know I must never return to the Nook. But where do I go now? I must be gentler with myself, just as the Moon said. I guess I haven't ever been that way towards myself. I've always been worried about pleasing everyone else. I must be patient. I know for sure I haven't been very successful at being that either. I want to be loved and to love again.

The Mouse let sufficient time pass and finally engaged the Greyhound in conversation. *May I ask you something, DearOne?*

Of course, the Greyhound communicated.

Where do you wish you could go now? Where do you know of a pleasant place to live out the rest of your days? I know you made a wish upon that Star. It's time to believe in that wish. It can come true you know.

I wished I could be with the JeepGirl, thought the Greyhound, who preferred communicating this way.

That's a fine wish, confirmed the Mouse.

How can I go back? asked the Greyhound. *I hurt her deeply. What if she doesn't want me anymore and won't welcome me back?*

"Forgiveness!" a brassy, baritone voice broke through the distillation of the Greyhound's questioning.

It was not the Mouse's voice that she heard in her heart. The voice was just ahead of them at the entrance to the Forest, where the Sun shone fully now upon the leafy ground. The Greyhound saw an interesting Tree towering above them, appearing as though it were a part of the sky.

"Was it you who said that?" asked the Greyhound of the Tree.

"Forgiveness," repeated the Tree. "When you ask her, your JeepGirl will forgive you."

"What is Forgiveness?" the Greyhound inquired.

"Forgiveness is only recognized *by Heart,*" the Tree replied. "It is when you are truly sorry for a hurtful word said or misdeed done. It matters not if it was intentional or unintentional. You must feel remorseful from the bottom of your heart. Forgiveness is releasing another from the chaos that is created in the wake of discord and conflict. It does not mean that we condone or excuse the person's wrongdoing or ever truly forget the offense, but we release the person or our Self from the blame and the guilt that weighs heavily upon us. In doing so, we cut the cords that bind us to resentment and pain so we are able to move forward with our life in love, light and peace."

The Greyhound nodded, indicating she understood, then asked, "What kind of Tree are you, if I may inquire? How did you learn so much about Forgiveness?"

"I am an Almond Tree. My history reaches back centuries. I was taught the gift of Forgiveness by my ancestors."

"You, too, have ancestors," said the Mouse to the Greyhound.

"Wherever you're going, remember to ask Forgiveness of those you have hurt. It is important to offer Forgiveness to anyone who may have hurt you as well. And forgiving your Self, DearOne, is the most precious of all gifts. Forgiveness will free your troubled heart. You will feel better. You will heal. I promise, and I am not one who makes promises lightly."

"Thank you so much for your ancient wisdom. May we rest a moment under your canopy?"

"Aye, you may," said the Almond Tree.

The Almond Tree offered them some of its seeds to eat. The Greyhound loved their flavor.

WHAT WOULD YOU DO
IF YOU WEREN'T AFRAID?

And so it was . . . The Mouse slid down the Greyhound's neck and the two rested a while. They enjoyed the almonds, and then took a short nap despite the cool shift in temperature. The Greyhound dreamt of being with the JeepGirl. She envisioned the tiny yard that overlooked the Ballfield and imagined how happy she'd feel living in harmony with the JeepGirl and the Mouse.

When the Mouse awakened the Greyhound, it was time to make another decision.

"We must go soon," said the Mouse. "Do you care to discuss your dream?"

"It was a delightful dream, unlike the Night Terrors that usually torture me. I wasn't afraid. I felt at peace, like I had when we were overlooking the Valley on top of the Knoll."

"Can you recall its details?" inquired the Mouse.

"I was with the JeepGirl in her home. It was warm inside and smelled of cinnamon spice. It was heavenly. Cozy blankets and delicious apples were waiting for me. Afterward, I snuggled against her as we sat in silence. I dreamt the air changed, and soon the Sun was close enough to the small yard to warm me. The JeepGirl took me places I had never been. We led a simple life, but I was happy. The Westie and the Yorkie were there. And you—you were there too! So were the Stars. And of course, the Moon!"

"That is a wonderful dream, DearOne," the Mouse said. "I guess you found your answer."

Hmph, I guess I have, thought the Greyhound. She cocked her head sideways. Her ear flopped over her left eye. *The Mouse is always right,* she thought.

"What would you do if you weren't afraid?" the Mouse asked.

If I weren't afraid? I would run right back to the JeepGirl.

"You're listening *by Heart*. Now, let's find *the Way*," said the Mouse.

The healing interaction with the Moon and the Stars had begun to take effect. Small parts of the Greyhound—her indecision being one of them, her fear being another—showed signs of repair. Twisted feelings of unworthiness began unraveling. So much more healing needed to happen, but for now, she and the Mouse would walk together clad in Stardust.

AWARENESS

And so it was . . . With her decision made, the two said good-bye to the Almond Tree. They took great care not to garner any attention as they traveled, but they needed to reenter the Forest briefly in order to continue eastbound. The Greyhound remembered that the back of the Girl's house faced the eastern sky, where the Sun rose in the morning and cast its light on her hind legs in the tiny yard but fell upon her face at dusk as she looked westward, towards the Ballfield. She believed she would be able to find the Brook again with relative ease if she concentrated on the flow and quality of the air. The air was becoming denser, the day darker too, but she was not as afraid as she had been. The Mouse was with her and now she knew she had guardians in the sky that kept watch ever long.

It was her superior sighthound senses that aided her in finding *the Way*. She ran at a steady pace, jumping high enough over felled Trees so as not to become injured. She smiled, at times, as she listened to Birds calling one another. Could it be that she was enjoying herself?

Could it be that this is what it feels like to make a decision with confidence, knowing it was made by Heart? She wondered.

All her senses heightened and the Brook was found with little difficulty. She sailed over WaterStones and Waterlogs on the Brook's edge. When they stopped to take a drink, the fresh water somehow tasted better than it had before. Because she could not run after drinking a lot of water, the two walked in the same direction as the water flowed. That, too, had a soothing effect on her and helped her to remain present.

PERCEPTION IS EVERYTHING

And so it was . . . As the Greyhound and the Mouse walked along the Brook, she noticed how the Forest's appearance differed from the day she had arrived in the Nook.

What has changed? she thought. *The Pine Trees seem greener, their scent more energizing, and the HollyBerries are a brighter shade of red than I remember.*

Some animals were drinking from the Brook, so she smiled and nodded to each as she passed by on the opposite bank. She spied tiny scarlet ladybugs crawling in some leaf litter nearby, as caterpillars inched up Trees, and cute chipmunks played tag around one of the Oaks. The Forest seemed fresh and alive as if it, too, had been replenished by the light of the full Moon and marked by the Star's Magickal dust. Leaves fell like raindrops now, and a few even fell on her, tickling her nose. And helicopter seeds fell every which way from the Maple Trees. She blew them off and smiled.

What was once a mishmash of sounds was now a symphony of discernible and variable ones. She could actually hear the moment when the stem of a leaf broke its hold from the twig that had secured it in place, and when it made contact with the ground—a fate which had befallen those who preceded it.

To lose a part of one's Self is not easy to accept, she thought, empathizing with both the leaf and the twig. Colorful leaves crunched beneath her paws, and the crackling sound made her want to prance. Birds of varying kinds harmonized a sweet song. She wished she could sing with them, but dared not, for she still feared the Bee would hear her. Geese clucking high above the Treetops, headed south. A chipmunk told her they were flying south for the Winter. She remembered Winter was coming, his *breath* grew colder, but she did not dwell on the warning the Doe and the Hydrangeas had made. She felt too alive to contemplate the danger.

They walked for some time, and as they did, the Greyhound thought she could hear the cackling of the clan far off in the deeper woods. Some of her fur fell as she quivered with fear, which interrupted her quiet, internal peace. Clouds moved in, as if conjured by her negative thoughts of the Bee, and cast a pall over her mood. The Greyhound began to feel more melancholic. She did not know why this happened, but it did. Melancholy had a habit of crushing the Greyhound's cheerier moods. More clouds hovered above as her fear mounted.

She noticed the Mouse's silence, and how the Brook had disappeared somewhere into the Forest floor. Just then, the sky unleashed a thunderous clap. Frightened by the bang which reminded her of the gunshot that killed her friend, the Greyhound took off, darting around boulders and Trees. The memories that resurfaced unbalanced her. She ran as though her own life were in the line of fire. In the distance, she saw white pillars standing tall and ran towards the White Angels until she found a cluster of White-Barked Birches commanding the area. Their long branches laced with silvery leaves hung gracefully, and their white-papered trunks lightened the space, but she still felt danger in the air.

ELEVEN

—

THE ANGELS

ANGELS WILL PROTECT ME

And so it was . . . The White-Barked Birches towered above the Greyhound and offered shelter from the impending storm. The Greyhound curled her body beneath their canopy. Special among the Trees, the White-Barked Birches told her their branches had the unique ability to bend and not break when storms raged. This was of great comfort to her. She was thankful for some shelter from the cold rain and wind that approached. The Birches told her their white bark had healing powers that helped ease depression and anxiety in those who sought their assistance. She was thunderstruck!

Perhaps they can help heal me, she thought.

As she continued listening, she became more relaxed and the more relaxed, the safer she felt. A few deep *breaths* accompanied the feeling. The White Birches shared how they symbolized divine feminine fertility, grace, and protection. By simply meeting the beautiful Trees and experiencing the protection they gifted her, she knew this to be true. Tales were told of how witches used their white branches to make *besoms*, or broomsticks, and how these were also used by shamans during their powerful, revelatory Journeys. The Greyhound loved learning about their lore. It made her forget the impending storm and the Bee. The Greyhound told the White Birches a little about her own Journey, and they, in turn, listened. She shared how she would not need a fertility ritual because the ability to have pups of her own had been cruelly ripped from her innards when she was at the Shelter without her knowledge or consent. It saddened her so to think of how she'd never have pups or a family of her own.

"Can you help heal me?" she pleaded.

Just then, the Mouse arrived. The Greyhound smiled. She didn't know where the Mouse had gone, but she would sleep this night, knowing she was protected by her White Angels and that her tiny friend was safe too. The White Birches accepted the title and kept watch over the exhausted Greyhound.

"You must learn to control your volleying thoughts and emotions through the tension and relaxation of your *breathing*," they explained. "Bend like our branches whenever you feel turmoil bubbling within you. It will take time and patience, but most of all, practice in order to become more flexible like us."

"I will. I will practice," she promised.

The band of White Birches beckoned her to rest to allow for healing. The White Angels kept watch as she slept beside the Mouse.

BEND INSTEAD OF BREAKING

And so it was . . . The Greyhound slept so deeply that upon waking, she realized the storm had passed over them. Its remnants were strewn about the ground. As the sky brightened, she could see large branches of nearby Elms and Maples scattered everywhere, but the branches of the White Birch Trees had not broken during the storm. Some had bent as the White Angels had foretold. Amazed by their strength, the lesson touched her deeply and was one she would remember. She truly craved the ability to bend and not break anymore than she had already broken.

She searched the sky for a rainbow. She thought it might have made an appearance in the only visible sliver of sky that was still being pressed on each side by two dark-gray storm clouds that were fighting to remain in the area, but she couldn't find one. Rainbows were one of her favorite things, and the Greyhound, believing they were Mother Nature's gift of hope to those who had survived a storm, always sought them out after a rain.

The Greyhound's heart skipped a beat as she searched for the Mouse, who she thought had been taken by the storm. When she finally found the Mouse, resting in a tiny crevice at the base of the White Birch's trunk, the Greyhound was glad her supposition had been incorrect. Relieved they both had been spared injury, the Greyhound bowed to her White Angels in thanks. The two unlikely companions moved on towards the rising Sun. Looking back to nod another good-bye, a great Circle comprised of branches and twigs came into her sight line. She could see a great Circle surrounding the Tree they had slept under. In full view of the scene, her gratefulness expanded. A shower of Sunshine shone through the clouds that morning, and the air, fresh and cleansed by the rain, delighted her.

IT'S OKAY TO ASK FOR HELP SOMETIMES

And so it was . . . The path on which they had been traveling for the better part of the morning was unfamiliar. Fear snaked its way back into her mind for a moment. The Greyhound was disquieted by her inability to know *the Way* clearly and sustainably. This feeling of uncertainty had not been part of her life at the Track, when she had been assured of her abilities and confident in her preparation for and execution of a race. Her frustration had fomented only after her last three years of racing when she was unable to satisfy her new Trainer and Owner. That's when the bullying was aflame.

"I've lost *the Way!*" she said to the Mouse.

"It's okay. You will find it," the Mouse replied certainly.

"How can I find it when I don't know where it is?" questioned the Greyhound with labored *breath.*

"You are so hard on yourself, DearOne. So in your head. Be gentle with your Self," said the Mouse. "You did a marvelous job finding *the Way* out of the dark part of the Forest, and of finding the Moon and the shooting Star. You often forget your accomplishments, and if and when you do remember them, you do not pay tribute to yourself or the effort and energy you afforded them. You do not always have to do everything so perfectly or all on your own. It is okay to ask your Angels for help, as you did with the Birch Trees. Angels come in many forms. Some are considered Earth Angels, some we meet on our Journey through life, and some we may never see, but we know they are with us, helping us. Remember, all the Magick you require to find *the Way* lies within you. You'll know it *by Heart.*"

The Greyhound decided she must trust the Mouse, as the Moon had urged. She knew the Mouse spoke the truth, but she was so desperate for nourishment and warmth that she didn't have enough energy to concentrate.

"I need help. I am lost!" she barked softly.

"A little louder," squeaked the Mouse.

She raised her head to the Sun and howled, "Angels? Please, I need help!"

With the Trees behind her, fear froze her throat closed. She prayed the howl had not been heard by the Rat or the Weasel, for they would surely report back to the Bee. Motionless, she listened and held her *breath* involuntarily. There was a much larger animal in their midst, rustling in the leaves.

"Use your gifts," the Mouse encouraged.

Sniffing, the Greyhound got a whiff of the animal's scent, then exhaled with relief. It was the Doe, who had recognized her voice.

"It's you! I can't believe it's really you!" said the Doe. Her tail vibrated with excitement as she approached.

"I can't believe it's *you*!" the Greyhound replied with the same fancy tail wag.

They stood nose to nose and entwined their long necks in a loving embrace. The Greyhound composed herself.

"We need help, Spirit-Sister. The Brook retreated into the ground a ways back, and I don't know *the Way* now that we have left the dense Forest. It was a dark night when I first arrived, and now I do not recognize anything."

"Do not fret, my fine ForestFriend. I think I may know who can help you," the Doe said reassuringly. "If you follow those tall grasses in the distance, you will come to a wooden, split-rail Fence. There you will find the Hare. I'm sure he won't mind helping you both. He has the time to help."

Could that be the same Hare the Nook gang was making fun of a couple of nights ago? the Greyhound wondered.

The Doe couldn't help but notice the adorable Mouse standing on the Greyhound's left foot.

"I'm sorry," said the Greyhound, "This is the Mouse, my DearFriend."

"Hello, LittleOne! Any friend of this sweet Spirit is a friend of mine," the Doe said, lowering her head to meet the Mouse.

"The pleasure is mine," returned the Mouse, touching the Doe's nose with its tiny hand.

The Doe's nose twitched.

"I wish we could spend the day dallying, but there's no time to catch up now. I saw the Bee buzzing about in the Nook this morning. It seemed quite frantic. It is most likely searching for you. It seems to have some kind of mad connection with you, as you had mentioned."

"That can't be good," the Greyhound whispered.

"One of its wings appears to be injured," the Doe added.

"Oh, yes, it was injured during the encounter with the Skunk—a story I hope to tell you someday," the Greyhound said. "I really must go, though I do not wish to leave you again."

"You must go. Fate has brought us twice together, and perhaps it shall look upon us kindly again someday," the Doe said. "Go! You have to go! Don't say good-bye, just say we will meet again soon. Now go, DearOne."

"Soon," said the Greyhound.

She did not care for good-byes herself. They reminded her of the good-byes of the past that had left their Scars upon her sensitive soul. She saw nothing good about them at all really. She did not dare look back this time. It would have broken her heart. The Mouse was already atop the Greyhound as she sprinted towards the tall grasses directly in her sight line.

SOMETIMES SITUATIONS ARE NOT AS THEY SEEM

And so it was . . . Eventually, the Greyhound came upon the split-rail Fence just as the Doe had described. The Greyhound and the Mouse continued walking alongside it for some time, then rested in a patch of flowers that were preparing for Winter. The Doe had called the funny flowers Dandelions. A few of them were a dulled yellow, but most had a translucent appearance, and their feathery seeds floated away when the Mouse, who was closest to the ground, *breathed* on them. The Greyhound sat down to watch the Dandelions swaying back and forth blissfully in the breeze as the Mouse frolicked in their golden glow.

The Greyhound was learning that her gift of literally being able to see behind her often came in handy. She saw an animal approaching them before the creature tapped her on her hind leg. This fellow's fur was light brown and streaked with white stripes, much like the stripes on her own fur, though hers were black. Its ears were longer than her own, and she could see that the animal's hind legs were mighty and powerful. Its feet were longish too, and its tail was fluffier than the fur that covered its body. She turned her head to see the animal looking up at her with a puzzled expression.

Maybe this is the Hare, but he doesn't fit the clan's cruel description, she thought as she glanced at the Mouse, who nodded.

"Excuse me, have you got the time?" the Hare asked.

"Have I got time?"

"The time. Have you the time?" the Hare asked again.

"I think it's almost midday," said the Greyhound, looking up at the Sun's position in the open sky above the field.

"No, no," the Hare said, a bit amused that the Greyhound had misunderstood his concept of time. "By time, I mean can you spare some time to help me find the time I lost. It's round, a tad heavy, and it has numbers on it. The Rat stole it a while back."

"There it is," said the Mouse, pointing to a broken watch imbedded in the ground, half covered by Dandelion feathers.

"Much obliged," the Hare said, retrieving the timepiece. "It belongs to my brother. I must return it to him."

"Pardon me, sir. Are you the Hare? The Doe sent us. We are lost," the Greyhound declared.

Still looking at the timepiece in his hand, the Hare nodded, "Uh, yup, I sure am. That Doe is a kind one. She sure is. Beautiful inside and out that one there. How do you know you're lost? If you have time, you are not lost. There is always time enough so one never need be lost."

"I *am* lost," the Greyhound said, confused. "I need to find *the Way* to the JeepGirl's house next to the Ballfield.

"Well, I'm not familiar with that place, but I have the time to help you find *the Way*," answered the Hare.

The Greyhound glanced at the open field and became entangled in a daydream about racing. As the Hare continued chatting about time, the Greyhound's anticipation grew. She had a pressing question that was itching to be asked of the Hare.

"Excuse me, sir. I heard long ago that Hares can run as swift as the wind. Is it true?"

"A-ffirmative! You appear to be a racer yourself," the Hare said admiringly. "Your legs are lean and long, and your streamlined musculature is marvelous for racing. Let's have us a race! Shall we?"

The Greyhound was not used to being complimented. It was a pleasant enough feeling. It had been stated in a tone dissimilar to the one used by those who had bullied her. She marveled at how the tone someone chose to use made such a difference in the meaning of the words spoken.

"I wish I had the time to race, but we have to be going," the Greyhound said disappointedly.

"My, my! You *are* in quite a rush. You are missing key moments in time. I will share my time with you. I have the time. So do you," said the Hare. He sounded pretty sure of himself.

The Greyhound looked at the Mouse, who had crawled on top of the Fence post and sat next to a Bluebird, who had been sitting there the whole time.

The Mouse nodded. "Remember what the Moon taught you: You must learn patience. All things will reveal themselves, in time, DearOne. Go, enjoy racing again. Isn't it exactly what you've been longing to do?"

The Greyhound took a full *breath* and smiled at the Mouse. She sprang over the split-rail Fence with ease, dispersing Dandelion seeds as she landed in the tall grass. The Hare ducked underneath the bottom rail of the Fence, and together they strolled to the far side of the Meadow. All the while, the Hare relayed an eloquent dissertation he had named "The Irrelevance of Time".

Reaching the far side of the Meadow, the Greyhound stretched back and forth to prime her muscles. The two masters of racing stood, side by side. The Mouse shouted words all too familiar to the Greyhound.

"Ready!"

The Greyhound's heart pounded with excitement. She set her sight on the Mouse and the Bluebird in the distance. She was ready!

"Set!"

The Greyhound leaned all her weight onto her strong, hind legs as she prepared for the release.

"Go!"

The Greyhound sprinted off the mark before the Hare even flinched. She ran like lightning etched across a stormy sky. She ran without fear— without any great expectations. The wind blew across her body without resistance. The extreme flexibility of her spine enabled her to lift all her legs off the ground at once while her body outstretched fully, and once again when her legs were tucked beneath her. She was flying. It was a sight to be seen! She was born to run. Her large heart pumped blood to her muscles as her speed increased. Her heart was larger than any other breed of dog, allowing for optimum oxygenation of her muscles. Running connected her to her Spirit. She was free!

Soon the Hare caught up and passed her on the right. The Greyhound did not fault herself for coming up short. She knew if she waited long enough, the Hare would tire before she did. She waited. He did tire. She bolted past him towards the Mouse.

"That was incredible!" said the Mouse. "You exercised your patience, and it rewarded you."

The Greyhound could not yet speak. Catching her *breath* was of paramount importance. The Hare joined them within seconds and rested on his back among the Dandelions. The Bluebird chirped and whistled with delight, bursting into song while the two recuperated.

After a few minutes, the Hare spoke. "You are a born leader, my friend, not a follower. It takes great courage to run the way you do. You have incredible instincts and speed control."

He looked at the Mouse. "She runs *by Heart* that one there. Doesn't she?"

The Mouse nodded.

"If in life we all could be as surefooted as she, what possibilities there would be!" the Hare remarked.

The Hare's observation gave the Greyhound great pause. *What if I was as surefooted in my life as I am when I am racing? Why am I not?* She wondered what prevented the transference of that assuredness she experienced, when training and racing, to everyday life. The Greyhound's self-assessment had to wait.

"It is time!" exclaimed the Hare. "The Bluebird and I will walk with you part of *the Way*. The Bluebird is able to see above and beyond our limited position, and she will fly high over the Forest and Valley. She will find the house overlooking the Ballfield you described and return to us. Don't worry, the Bluebird will point us in the right direction."

"That is very kind of her. Thank you so much," the Greyhound replied. "And thank you for running with me. You are impressive in every way."

The Hare nodded, and the three continued walking east. The Bluebird, embraced by the clear blue sky, took flight.

I AM SURROUNDED
BY EARTH ANGELS

And so it was . . . In the light of the afternoon, the Bluebird returned with news.

"Chirp, chirp, whistle, chirp," said the Bluebird.

The Hare interpreted for her. "She says the house you described lies a stone's throw away from the mighty Merrimack River. When we find the River, we'll find the house."

The Bluebird continued chirping excitedly.

"She says the River is not too far away. We must follow the Meadow until it ends. It's there that a sizable Hill sits with a great Circle in its center."

"I know that Hill!" exclaimed the Greyhound gleefully. "I've been there with the JeepGirl. I came by way of it that night. I must have missed seeing the River in the darkness, but I saw it when we were on top of the Knoll."

"Which night?" asked the Hare, but the Greyhound refused to speak of it.

Mindful of the Greyhound's sudden shift in mood, the Hare added, "Time isn't waiting for us. We best be moving on. It's getting dark. "

The Moon, still in full light, rose, greeting them and illuminating *the Way*. The Bluebird led them to a most welcoming family of Weeping Willow Trees. There they could rest from the race and the excitement of the day. Before becoming too tired, the Hare, with the Greyhound's help, dug a shallow impression in the ground under one of the Weeping Willows. It would serve as his bed. The Greyhound and the Hare were both very skilled diggers so the job was not taxing at all. The Willow told them where to dig a second hole beneath its trunk. A plentiful bounty of water bubbled up from the ground. They were all grateful for the Willow's gracious offering.

The Bluebird, who had flown far that day, nested in the branches high above them and was the first to fall fast asleep cradled in the warmth of her own wings. The Bluebird's vocal cords vibrated as it slept. *What a pleasant sound,* thought the Greyhound. She had a nagging feeling she knew the Bluebird from somewhere, but couldn't remember where.

The Hare followed suit in sleep as it furrowed into the fertile ground. The Mouse slipped under the Hare's belly to keep warm. The Mouse had discerned by the look on the Greyhound's face that she needed to be on her own. There was much to contemplate, so she went to lie down alone under one of the other Willows. The Greyhound quietly tiptoed away from the trio, but not too far.

TWELVE

—

THE SCARS

WEEPING AND WILLOWS

And so it was . . . The Greyhound wandered among the family of Weeping Willows and stopped beneath the largest one, in awe of its size. Clearly, it was the eldest. This particular Weeping Willow towered above the others, and the Greyhound learned later that it had long ago earned the respect of the colossal Eastern White Pines she was so fond of—the only Trees that surpassed the grandeur of its height. The Greyhound wondered if the Birds found it difficult to maneuver over the giant Tree. The Willow's canopy stretched almost as wide as it was tall; its branches gently kissed the ground. The very tips of its leaves glistened in the Moonlight.

"Under here," the Weeping Willow whispered to the exhausted Greyhound. "You can rest under here. I will shelter you from the storm, WillowyOne."

"Thank you kindly, oh GreatTree, but I do not sense a storm brewing," the Greyhound said. "I see the Stars clearly, but I do need to rest."

The Willow clarified, "The storm that rages within, DearOne."

The old Willow was wise. The compassion and empathy of its kind enabled it to feel the emotional turmoil and pain that whirled within the Greyhound's heart, much like the Greyhound felt when *she* witnessed anyone in pain.

The Greyhound choked up, knowing what the Willow meant. It was the storm that had amassed in the months—perhaps years—prior, lurking just below the surface of her daily life, churning now like the turbulent water she had seen accumulate at the base of the Beaver's dam. She crawled under the branches that caressed the ground and hid her weary body and her heavy heart from the rest of the world. To keep warm, she curled her legs in tightly as the White Fox had taught her, and she was relieved the Willow's low-lying branches blocked the cold breeze from reaching her.

She was overcome with emotion. The traumatic events of the past two weeks and years of bullying had taken their toll on her. Too physically and emotionally drained to restrain the barrage of tears that surfaced, she wept. The Greyhound could not stop herself from crying this time, and there was no reason left to hold back. She cried and cried and cried.

"I'm sorry. I don't want to cry, but I can't help it. I'm so sorry. The tears come without warning and I can't stop them."

"It's okay to cry, WillowyOne," whispered the Willow Tree. "It is no small feat to come as far as you have. It is wholly healing to weep. There is never any reason to be sorry for weeping, WillowyOne. Never. Healing requires feeling. Tears are a natural release of all the negative energy the body and mind mistakenly house. But remember, cry gently, WillowyOne."

So she did.

MEASURE LIFE BY MOMENTS

And so it was . . . The poor creature let the tears come quietly, for she did not wish to disturb the slumber of the others. Thoughts of her distant, and not so distant past fell like raindrops. She cried to the Willow. Or was it to the Moon? Maybe it was to her own Spirit. She could not tell which. She cried about how she had lost everything in an onslaught of traumatizing events. Everything in her life had disappeared in a single moment—her career, her stellar reputation, her racing buddies, her love, the place she had called home, her strength, her health, her Self—all of it! Everything she had ever known was gone in a torrent of unrelenting disbelief, pain, and despair. Her world had crumbled before her very eyes in one dizzying, destructive blow. The pain of her life flashed before her now. Gutted, she wept.

The events of her former life and the bullying she had endured had done irreparable harm. Life had shown her only snapshots of joy, but still, it had been her life. The Bee had gained its power over her in the aftermath of that physical and psychological pain. Its dreadful din convinced her that a new kind of love would only bring her heartache and more pain. There was no reason to believe that the JeepGirl could ever love her for who she had become—one who was wounded—one with so many Scars, one who cried beneath the Stars, one who cried under the Willow Tree. How could anyone ever love her now? Her Scars had made her so unattractive. Maybe the Bee was right. No one wanted her.

There were a few fond memories of winning races and falling in love a couple of times, but it always had ended in heartache. When she loved, she loved so incredibly deep and with every fiber of her being, but in the end, as everything must end, she was the one left picking up the pieces of her shattered heart and remnants of the life she had built with another, while they moved on unaffected. In her experience, love arrived as knowing. It happened in an instant, bursting her heart open like fireworks exploding in the sky, filling it with spectacular colors. It was something so Magickal! She loved love. But the kind of love she experienced always morphed into a dense air of apathy, indifference, or nonchalance. Excuses for inaction abounded, and the unwillingness to put forth the effort, commitment, compassion, and attention necessary to nurture love had been consistently absent. Life had been woven around those she loved, but they had refused to do the same for her, or at least meet her halfway. Nonetheless, she persisted in loving, for a time. She just wanted to be accepted with all her quirks and particularities. Abandoned in the end, either through betrayal, indifference, a forced departure, or through some other horrible fate, that's where she always found herself.

She told the Willow she believed the Bee was right—not even her Owner had loved her. How could she have, when she forced the Greyhound to experience the painful tattooing of each of her ears, which branded, numbered, and categorized her, leaving her unnamed. The Owner had also turned a blind eye to the other young Greyhounds that bullied her. They called her names and barked that she was too skinny, that her jaw protruded farther than theirs, that her nose was too long—like a witch's. They labeled her as different—a misfit. She had grown faster than most other pups, which gave them more fodder because she was taller than they, and even though she liked being tall, they made fun of that quality too. She was even bullied because the pupil in her left eye was larger than the right, a condition called Adie's pupil, the Track doctor had said. She also had trouble with that left eye they labeled lazy, though she tried desperately to keep it straight. Tilting her head slightly to the left, partially covering it with her long ear so others could only see her right eye, had become a habitual tic. The eye pain surged as unrelenting as the bullying and the Bee's earsplitting buzzing. There was no respite from the pain of any of it.

The Greyhound explained to the Willow Tree that her handsome Companion used to say the bullying and the pain she felt as a result was her own fault. She remembered days when he barked at her for sharing with him the most unpleasant encounters she had had or the injustices they both had witnessed or suffered together. Her head would hurt in the long days that followed any such discord. It was so uncomfortable and alarming to be spoken to so intensely. He had the habit of dismissing her concerns. She never understood how the Hound could be so caring one minute and so cruel the next. How had she let herself care about him for as long as she did or allow anyone to treat her less than? She questioned why she accepted less than for so long from those to whom she had given her heart. They had loved one another, she and her Companion. She knew that. They had shared so many Magickal times. She had to believe that was the reason why they had remained together for so long. They had tried their best at loving one another the only way each knew how. How it had ended was all so complicated, confusing, and heartbreaking.

Another painful memory surfaced as she continued sharing her past with the Willow. The incident had occurred after she had raced exactly how her Trainer had instructed—right down to the smallest detail of leading with her left paw when the lure was released. She had done everything to perfection—or so she thought. She had even won, but when she came off the Track, the Trainer screamed that she had come out of the gate with the incorrect paw. It was supposed to have been the right paw the Trainer insisted. The Trainer's anger was palpable. It took her by surprise, as did the gaslighting.

But how could that be? she thought at the time. No mistake had been made on her part. She had been told to lead with the left. She was always so confused and never knew how to please her Trainer. The gaslighting was relentless. Her performance was one of the best around, but the Trainer reminded her that she had only placed in the top four fifty-seven times out of the eighty-seven races run. Denigrated in front of all the other racers and friends, a single tear had trickled down her cheek that day. Her Owner stepped between her and her Trainer. The Greyhound thought she would be defended and praised for her consistent hard work, instead, the Owner chided her, saying it was a sign of weakness to be so emotional. Subsequently, the Owner, in cahoots with the Trainer, locked her up in her Cage without allowing her to stretch as was customary after a race. She

156

recalled the grave discomfort.

I thought all beings spoke the truth, but I'm wrong—they don't, the Greyhound thought.

"Unfortunately not all are truth sayers, but there are many still left in the world," the Willow said. "You can recognize them *by Heart.*"

The Greyhound had experienced so many incidents of a tragic nature. There was the time an opposing teammate cut her off on the turn, causing her to stumble and tumble terribly. She had gotten up almost immediately and continued running despite all the cuts, bruises, and blood. Still she placed in the top four, but she knew that wouldn't be good enough. Once off the Track, the Trainer screamed at her again, telling her how inept she was, and blamed her for not anticipating the other racer's strategy. Her Trainer sent her to her Cage immediately, without attending to her bloody cuts and scrapes. Other racers were given medical attention and time to recover from their injuries and were even prohibited from racing until they were fully healed, and she believed she would be shown the same care. She was dead wrong! The very next day, the Trainer pulled her out of her Cage, put on her numbered racing vest and Muzzle, and said, "If you don't place in the top three today, you will never race again! Do you hear me, Hound?"

She knew well enough not to respond or look directly in her Trainer's eyes. The words rattled her to the core. Not race? What would she do with the rest of her life if she could not race? She only knew how to race. She would be lost. Summoning the little strength that lingered inside her tired and broken body, she had raced that day and won, but not without consequence. Some of her wounds had reopened and others were not healing well. She *had* won, but it did not matter, because her body had failed her—she passed out.

That night, following the race, she had been led into the pitch-black truck. It was the darkest of places, where crates were stacked one on top of the other. She and other racers were packed so tightly they could barely *breathe.* Even now, beneath the Willow Tree, she could still hear the doors of the truck slam shut, leaving her and the others in blackness. The wailing of her fellow racers tore at her heartstrings. They were all frightened. They were all hungry and thirsty. In the past, stories of retired racers being sent away had been tossed around, but none matched the reality that confronted her. The stench during that ride was unforgettable. More than anything, she remembered the fear that consumed her—the fear of a future unknown.

She shared with the Willow Tree how she feared she was going to be killed at the end of that ride, afraid they all would disappear. The Greyhound had already lost so many loved ones throughout the years—so many aunts and uncles, grandparents, cousins, and friends. Once, she had even witnessed a puppy die. The image of the tiny one was burned in her brain. Her own father had died a few months before she had been taken from the Track. Throughout her life, his positive Nature had given her hope that better days were ahead, but his death changed her forever. The darkness of the truck reminded her of the unbearable loss. The ride had seemed endless. Even the blood from her injuries had dried on her fur by the time she had reached the cold corner Cage.

The Greyhound explained how she had been muzzled and measured her entire life. Everything had been measured, not only for the inspections in the paddock before every race, but also in every aspect of her life—her height, her weight, how much she ate and drank, the length of her tail, her sight, her speed, her agility, her successes and failures, her daily schedule, how fast she came out of the gate, her accuracy on the turn, the time it took to finish a race, how well she trained and executed orders, how well she interacted with other racers. Every single facet of her life—measured. No wonder she thought she had to be perfect. She had been conditioned to accept nothing less than perfection.

With the years of performance came exhaustion; with the abuse and bullying, disillusionment; with the loss of her cherished racing career, despair. It all crept in so methodically and unnoticed, until its weight crushed her, wreaking havoc on her body and pulverizing her Spirit. Melancholy, flashbacks, and panic attacks plagued her, day and night— symptoms of a deeper malaise.

Under the Willow Tree, she cried! She cried out for all of it! She cried to the Willow and to the Moon. She cried out to her Spirit, which had left her long ago. She cried out for its return.

DOUBLE VISION

And so it was . . . The Willow Tree listened to every word the Greyhound shared as she unburdened her soul. The Tree's empathy allowed her to lay down those burdens without restraint. She even told the Willow her deepest secret, sharing how she truly saw the world through a double lens. She had never told any living creature she literally saw double. Her eyes had been broken since birth. They did not work like everyone else's. Whenever she looked at anything, she saw two images. Two! Two of everything! Even her beloved Moon appeared as two orbs in the sky. Every day of her life the pain in her eyes, the pain of seeing, overwhelmed her, but she made sure she never, ever, complained. That's why she strove for perfection, ever to excel at every task set before her. She didn't want to be pitied, because anyone who found out that she saw double might label her as different or defective. The fear she would be forced to stop racing had forever been a source of overwhelm. Being the best at everything she did was the only option. The quest for perfection had cost her though. She wanted the pain to be miraculously catapulted into the Cosmos so it could be consumed by the Sun. She desired quiet, internal peace and was desperate for a quiet mind and a pain-free body.

Sharing, for the Greyhound, was like walking off the edge of a cliff. In the past, others pretended to care, but her vulnerability, the information she shared, and her true feelings had always been dismissed or used against her later to intentionally hurt and wound her. She still suffered from the shrapnel of that emotional torture.

The Willow's soft branches caressed the fragile Greyhound as she sought to stop the sad litany of tears.

MY TRUTH IS MY VOICE

And so it was . . . Through her tears, the Greyhound saw the Mouse sitting next to her at the base of the Willow's trunk. She was not ashamed the Mouse had overheard her deepest secrets. It was a relief and a comfort to her that someone other than the Moon finally knew her secret pain. Thankful for the release and for no longer having to hold the secrets hostage, she let the ground beneath her absorb the heavy energy.

The Mouse witnessed the Greyhound struggling to take any kind of meaningful *breath*.

"*Breathe*, DearOne," whispered the Mouse. "*Breathe* as the Moon guided you to do."

She took a deep *breath*, in and out—in and out—in and out.

The Willow added lovingly, "I am profoundly sorry for the enormity of the loss you have experienced. Earth Angels and Spirits, people, friends, material things, and emotions come and go with the wind. Each teaches us something about ourselves that we were unwilling to recognize on our own. When their influence wanes they move on, leaving us with new opportunities, new choices, new awakenings, and they make room for new beginnings and experiences we otherwise would not have had had they remained. In life, there is loss, but there is also living, and, WillowyOne, you have not been living. You've only been existing. And they are not the same. So much healing happened tonight, WillowyOne. You released a great deal of the pain you held within the depths of your body and mind. You confronted your Scars and their truth, and you have found your own voice. This surrendering has made room in your HeartSpace to help your authentic Self find the strength it needs to fully heal and emerge. Now you need to sleep, for it is in sleeping that you will continue healing. You must sleep to awaken."

The grateful Greyhound respectfully thanked the Willow for listening. The Willow encouraged her to close her weary eyes. With the Mouse by her side and the Moon looming above, the Greyhound, unburdened, felt safe enough to drift off into a deep, healing slumber.

THIRTEEN

—

THE KISMET

THE SUN ALWAYS SHINES

And so it was . . . The morning was blanketed in a crisp mid-Autumn chill. In the coming month, Autumn would make his exit so Winter could take his place. Gracing them with her presence, the Sun softly awakened the slumbering friends. Each of them greeted the Sun uniquely. The Greyhound stretched her nose to the amber sky, followed by a downward position, then shook to warm herself. The Mouse outstretched its front arms towards the Sun, while the Hare hopped in place to get his blood pumping, and the Bluebird flapped her wings as she sang a song in unison with the sound of the Sunshine. The Greyhound, profoundly grateful to the Sun, who had warmed the ground by day, knew she would not have survived the cold night without her help.

The Greyhound also thanked the Weeping Willow for its sweet sympathy and safe harbor.

"I will not forget the compassion you afforded me last night, dearest Willow. Nor will I forget the generous time you spent listening to me. I will never forget you Willow Tree," said the Greyhound.

"Our time together will not be forgotten. There will always be a safe place for you here, WillowyOne." As a grand gesture to the Greyhound, the Willow shook its cascading canopy as the friends departed.

LISTEN BY HEART

And so it was . . . The friends continued traveling and enjoying their time together. They laughed when the Hare told a funny tale. They clapped when the Bluebird flew directly towards the ground, grazing it before it flew straight towards the sky, where it flipped upside down, then soared right side up. The Bluebird taught them how to sing, and the Greyhound loved it. Singing made her heart glad. Her new friends told her she had a remarkable voice when she rooed. When she sang, she noticed all her worries and troubles stayed away and only the melody filled the space in her troubled mind. At midday, the Bluebird whistled she was off in search of the best ground route to the JeepGirl's house, one the Greyhound could traverse.

The friends walked east for a while and took a nap beneath a Pine Tree they befriended while they waited for the return of the Bluebird.

As afternoon approached, the Greyhound was able to find moments when she felt glad to be with her new friends. Whenever she felt a bit anxious, she would practice *breathing* deeply. When thoughts of all the traumatizing experiences surfaced—all the hurt, the loss, the pain, the sadness—she noticed, if she accepted the tortured parts of the past and released them into the Cosmos and left them there, glimpses of a more peaceful countenance glowed in her heart.

The Mouse taught her about self-reliance and how to remain confident in her innate abilities. The Mouse was a masterful teacher and a patient one. It told her to remember all the lessons she had learned from her time in the Forest. The Mouse continued offering instruction on how to listen *by Heart*, and how to rely on that deep feeling—that nudge—that gentle poke, that inner calm that showed her *the Way* to a truer knowing and way of being.

"To listen *by Heart* is to listen with Spirit. To listen with Spirit is to know the truth of one's Self. To know the truth of one's Self is to recognize love. Choose love. Always choose love. That's when the real knowing occurs. Then you will have a peaceful heart," said the Mouse.

The Greyhound listened intently that afternoon. The Hare did as well. The Mouse assured the Greyhound she could trust that feeling without fear of failure. The Greyhound was learning she could trust the Mouse too. The Moon had told her so. With time and practice, she wondered if she would learn how to make decisions more easily, based on that tickle of inner truth. The Mouse told the Greyhound she could live a purposeful and meaningful life again the more she exercised that awareness. Just as the Stars had foretold, she would come to know her Magick and the gifts she could offer to the world. The Mouse reminded her of this.

SERENDIPITY

And so it was . . . Dusk ushered in the Bluebird's arrival; it was time for the Bluebird and the Hare to return to the Farm. They had traveled a great distance to help the Greyhound.

"Tweet, tweet, chirp, whistle!" The Bluebird announced she had a parting gift for the Greyhound.

While combing the land for *the Way* to the mighty Merrimack River, the Bluebird had come across a friend. He told the Bluebird he knew of the Greyhound well enough to know that she was a brave soul and a defender of the underdog. The Bluebird chirped excitedly as this friend approached.

"Hellooo, DearFriend! I knew we would meet again," shouted the Skunk from far away.

The Greyhound was the first to spot the Skunk. "What are you doing here?" she asked, happy to see her loyal friend again.

The Skunk, now close enough for the others to see and smell him, heartily explained, "This beautiful Bluebird here told me about a brindled Greyhound that was lost and needed to find *the Way* home. It just so happens that I live along the banks of your mighty Merrimack River, and I know exactly which house is yours. I've lived in that area my entire life."

"How do you know where the JeepGirl lives?" the Greyhound asked. She cocked her head to the side.

"I saw you!" The Skunk smiled. "I saw you the night your Jeepgirl let you out, and you jumped the chain-link Fence. You were quite distraught and in such a hurry that you did not notice me in the dark. I did not tell you this in the Nook, because I did not know you wished to return to the one you call the JeepGirl."

"Serendipity!" proclaimed the Hare. "Time sure does have a way of surprising us."

The Greyhound didn't even have to ask the question when the Hare burst into an explanation of the term. "Serendipity is that miraculous moment when something you desire or need to happen simply appears before you Magickally. If one is open to such occurrences, they happen quite frequently; if one is closed to the Magick, serendipity only happens once in a blue Moon."

A blue Moon? thought the Greyhound. *Now that would be Magickal or sad, depending on how one looks at it.*

"GentleGiant, you'll be okay with the Skunk and the Mouse by your side," added the Hare. "I'd like to stay and have proper exchanges with your loyal friend here, but it's time. I surely will remember you, and I won't ever forget our race, Hound." Turning to the Mouse, the Hare continued, "Mouse, thank you for finding the time."

The Mouse nodded.

"Good-bye, DearFriend. I will remember you *by Heart*," said the Greyhound. She was learning.

Turning to the Bluebird, the Greyhound said, "I know you from somewhere. It will come to me. Anyway, thank you so much for finding my DearFriend, and thanks for all your help. I appreciate it very much."

The Bluebird fluttered its wings in acknowledgment.

The unusual friendship that had emerged between the Greyhound and the Skunk was a unique bond. Both were outcasts—scarred by bullies that had crossed their paths, and both had special gifts. The Skunk would surely bring her the rest of *the Way*.

THE MIGHTY MERRIMACK

And so it was . . . The Skunk led the Greyhound and the Mouse to the banks of the mighty Merrimack River. At one point, they took the time to stop and witness the Sun, who showcased a sky bedazzled with colors that seemed to have been intentionally blended as they would on an artist's palette for a particular effect. The wispy clouds reflected the Sun's last light and cast a dark sapphire-and-magenta haze that hovered just above the horizon, silhouetting the Trees that defined the bank of the mighty River. And the dark waters of the River Magickally transformed into sparkling WaterStars that flitted on its surface.

"Isn't it gorgeous?" commented the Skunk.

"Yes, yes it is—quite," replied the Greyhound. "The WaterStars remind me of the Stars I met on the Knoll. The ones that keep the Moon company. Just when I think I have seen Nature at her finest, she surprises me once again and surpasses her own beauty in spectacular fashion. It takes my *breath* away every time."

"I agree," said the Skunk. "I am bewitched on a daily basis by the power and beauty of Mother Nature. I have the utmost respect for her."

As they continued along the bank, the chilly Autumn wind howled, and the Greyhound became increasingly concerned for her well-being as the air bit her thin skin. The absence of fur on her underbelly and hindquarters, from living a life primarily reposed on concrete flooring, and the fine coat of fur that happened to clad portions of her muscular body failed to provide her warmth in this harsh environment. Unlike the thick fur of the Skunk and the Hare, or the protective feathers of the Bluebird, the Greyhound had little to keep her warm. She needed to find the JeepGirl's house before she was overcome by the elements.

The Mouse hung on in its usual riding place as the Greyhound kept pace with the Skunk. There was a particular point where the mighty Merrimack and the highway intersected. The Greyhound clearly recalled the distance between the highway and the JeepGirl's house based on the ride home from the Shelter, a day that seemed like a lifetime ago. It was there the Greyhound and the Skunk stopped to catch their *breath* again. The Mouse slid down the Greyhound's leg.

They were getting closer. The Greyhound felt her heart skip a beat. The whizzing of cars and the rumbling of heavy trucks passing overhead reminded her of how the sound had helped lull her to sleep her first night in the basement of the JeepGirl's house. As the Greyhound *breathed* deeply, her keen sense of smell homed in on a pleasant, familiar scent—the redolent scent of vanilla bean and bergamot. She loved that sweet orange smell, and knew it well. Her nose twitched.

"It's the JeepGirl!" she barked out loud. "It's the JeepGirl! I'd know her scent anywhere."

"Where?" asked the Skunk. "I don't see anyone."

"She's nearby. I know it!" The Greyhound barked with so much hope her voice tremored.

It was a strange, exhilarating sensation. Without the Bee buzzing about, she was more mindful of her surroundings than she had ever been.

"She's above us! I hear her Jeep, and I recognize her scent. I wonder if she's been searching for me ever since I jumped the Fence?" exclaimed the Greyhound.

Without warning, the Greyhound darted up the embankment and took off headlong into the dark night. Spotting the little black Jeep up ahead, she locked it in her sights, keeping her focus on the tire cover and the yin-yang flower design. The danger the vehicles posed was dire, but her only concern was reaching the JeepGirl. She kept close to the guardrail on her right. Images of the Track, which had similar rails on both sides, flashed before her. She dared not stray to the left or she'd be met with the same fate as one of the racers the year before. She imagined herself passing racers on the far right side of the Track closest to the spectators.

Though she galloped as fast as she could for some time, she was unable to catch up to the Jeep, which had sped off into the darkness; its unique taillights no longer visible. Weary from exhaustion, she stopped cold in her tracks. She was done. No matter how desperately she desired to continue running, it was impossible for her to sustain the pace. Every ounce of stored energy and strength had been used to try to reach the JeepGirl. Before she had the chance to jump the guardrail to safety, a vehicle pulled over, stopping in front of her. An occupant jumped out, grabbed her, and put her in the truck. She did not know the person, but there she was, in the backseat of a stranger's truck with no energy to fight for her freedom and unaware of where she was being taken. Would she ever see her friends again? Would she die here? There was no choice but to accept her fate. Hope faded as she slipped out of consciousness.

HOPE FLOATS

And so it was . . . The Greyhound awoke in a panic, frozen in fear. She studied her surroundings.

Sniff, sniff.

Acclimating, she knew where she was and sighed, defeated by the scent. The Shelter's familiar smells surrounded her—the cleaning products the Handlers used, the Husky still in his Cage, and the musty Cage where she lay just the week before. Once again, she was overcome with despair. She allowed herself to groan.

The pain her body bore was too much for her to handle. The tarred surface of the highway and the debris that riddled the road had taken their toll on her paws and underbelly. New abrasions, cuts, and gashes oozed blood. Her lower legs were wrapped in gauze. She cried unabashedly, but no one came to rescue her. Most of the dogs whimpered, grunted, or barked for attention, but staff was limited, and though they tried, they could not immediately help every dog. The Greyhound had come so far, yet here she was again, in a Cage on a cold, concrete floor just where her Journey had begun. Had her tiresome Journey been for nothing?

I can't believe I'm back here, alone again. Naturally, the lone Greyhound took a deep *breath*, and another, and another after that one. *Is this the end of my story? Is this my punishment—the price I must pay for wanting freedom and peace? That's what the Bee would tell me.* She took another deep *breath. No! No. I don't want it to be the end. I can't place any credence in what the Bee says. I want more from life. So much more.*

She wondered what made her so vulnerable to the Bee's ostensible assurances. Why had its false promises appealed to her so much, and why had she believed every word it said? All its pandering rambled through her brain—*I'll take care of you,* the Bee had claimed. *I can show you what freedom is really like. You can trust me.* Why had she believed it when it professed—*I will be the only one you'll ever need. You don't need anyone else but me. I will give you all you desire. I promise.* Why had she risked everything for its false promises?

Why did I trust the Bee's wheedling? she thought. *Why did I give up the possibility of a good life with the JeepGirl? I even had a yard with a Pine Tree.*

She had not given herself a chance to be happy and believed the blame rested solely on herself. How could she have been so naive as to believe the Bee was sincere in any way, shape, or form? Had she really been so desperate for love that she ignored all the warning signs that literally buzzed about her? She was an intelligent creature. How had the Bee broken through her defenses? She knew in her heart, shortly after meeting the Bee, that it was not good for her. She knew it had lied to her over and over again, but she had chosen to disregard the red flags and the chaos that adhered to it and her when it was near. She knew the Bee could never give her what she needed or the life she had imagined in her dreams. The Bee had no dreams of its own, for it didn't know how to dream or love. It just did all it knew how to do—exist for its own sake, sting, and leave destruction in the wake of its din.

SHADOWS

And so it was . . . Although the waning gibbous Moon brightened the courtyard when she was let out the second night in the Shelter, the Greyhound was still overcome by the exhaustion of her Journey. Unlike former Shelter nights, she fell asleep, dead to the world around her, wishing never to wake up.

The dark Shadows returned, but this time it was her own Shadow that frightened her. In the dream, she was back in the Forest and could see a flickering light dancing amid the Trees. At first, she felt her heart pounding in her head as the Shadows came closer, but they did not completely enshroud her Spirit. A radiant spectre bedighted in Moonlight surrounded the Shadows. It spoke without words. The Angelic being assured her that fear was not present in this place. The Angel's message reminded her of the White Arctic Fox's wisdom regarding fear—*Nothing can hurt you.* In her dream, she took a deep *breath* in and out.

The Angel spoke to her through comforting oscillations. *Shadows simply reveal the power of the light, DearestOne. Without the light, there can be no Shadows. Shadows exist because of the light. You, too, have a Shadow, and you fear it not.*

The Greyhound acknowledged the revelation. *True. I don't fear my own Shadow. I've seen it so many times too; it shapeshifts like the Moon; it follows me wherever I go. I guess my Shadow is truly a part of me.*

You are correct, DearOne. Your Shadow is a part of you, and there is no need to fear other Shadows, for they, too, are made both of the light and the darkness. Without both, there would be a great void—no Sun, no day, no Moon, no night, and no Stars to sail the galaxy. There would be no way to discern the truth of things without light. Believe in the power of the light. Fear not when the Shadows visit you, simply wrap them in Stardust when they approach, and soon they will leave in peace as they are absorbed by the light and become enlightened. They cannot subsist in Stardust, for Stardust is Magickal.

In her dream, the Greyhound thanked the Angel for her profound insight.

When the Greyhound awoke, she took several deep *breaths*, pondering the dream and recalling the Angel who had gingerly prompted her to remember the lessons she had been taught. She remembered that the Stars and her Moon were made of light. They had told her she, too, harbored a light within her, and she needed only to have faith in her own light in order to heal. She realized her Journey had forever changed her for the better. Whatever fate she succumbed to, she would never be alone. Not surprised by what she saw, she took another deep *breath.*

FORGIVENESS IS A GIFT

And so it was . . . As the Greyhound mindfully inhaled and exhaled, the Mouse popped its head out from beneath the bristly, burlap blanket.

"I see you are learning the Angel's lesson of the Shadows and the Light. Remember it well, and it will serve you well. Now, you must eat to regain your strength for what lies ahead," advised the Mouse. "Please, take a sip of water and a morsel of food. The control of that power—the choice to fight or die—is yours, DearOne. No one can make that choice for you."

The Greyhound's sinking Spirit was evidenced by her declining health, but the Mouse made sense. Before heeding the Mouse's counsel, the Greyhound asked with a heavy heart, "Why do you care if I live or die? Why do you still want to be with me?"

She knew the Mouse would speak the truth.

"Because I love you—unconditionally!" the Mouse replied. "I love all the parts of you, even those parts you feel lack in some way. Even those parts you have yet to forgive."

The Greyhound had longed to hear those words her whole life. She remembered what the Almond Tree had said.

She replied, "I am so sorry if I hurt you. I never meant to abandon you as others have abandoned me. I did not realize that listening to the Bee would cause me to lose you." She paused. Her jaw chattered—a telltale sign of her heart's affection. "I love you too!" she cooed.

The Mouse blinked slowly in acceptance of the Greyhound's sincere apology. It reminded the Greyhound more of what the Almond Tree had taught her about Forgiveness.

"I will always forgive you," the Mouse said compassionately, "but now it is time to forgive not only those who hurt you profoundly, but also to forgive your Self, DearOne. The longer you wait the more easily you will succumb to the Bee's guile, and the longer your wounds will fester."

The Greyhound took another deep *breath*. She knew it was true. It was time to forgive and free herself from the pain of the past she had been carrying as though she were Atlas himself. The Greyhound bowed her head in adoration as the Mouse touched her tear-drenched snout endearingly. The Greyhound forced herself to drink a few sips of water and nibble a couple of bites of the unappealing food in the stainless steel bowls. If she was going to choose to live and create a new life, she would need all the nourishment and brave energy she could summon. The Mouse glanced up at the Greyhound. The Greyhound's head was cocked to the left, her ears touched at attention. Her nose twitched.

THERE IS ALWAYS A CHOICE

And so it was . . . The Greyhound decided wholeheartedly that she would try one more time to reach the JeepGirl. That was where she wanted to be. That was where she hoped she belonged. A plan was devised to act swiftly so as not to be noticed by any of the Handlers or visitors. She would wait until late afternoon, when the dogs were released into the courtyard, to make her next great escape. This plan would be on her own terms, unfettered by any extraneous influence. She waited patiently as her anticipation heightened.

I know what I want, she thought. *I want to be mindful of my desires and intentions, and I want clarity of purpose. I want to be sure of my own decisions and steadfast in their execution. I want fear to fade and fall away forever from my being. I want to sleep without my Cage door closed or without being caged at all. I want to be free. I want to run free without restraints. I want a reciprocal love—a love, that when nurtured, grows exponentially. I want quiet on all fronts—mind, body, Spirit—I want quiet, internal peace.*

The Greyhound felt a fiery energy deep within her ignite. She would be ready.

WHEN THE TIME IS RIGHT,
ALL WILL APPEAR EFFORTLESS

And so it was . . . Like clockwork, the dogs were released into the courtyard following dinner. The Greyhound studied the Fence before her, not with fear in her belly but with fearlessness. The other dogs busied themselves playing with the various balls scattered about the ground and argued over thick ropes they tried to pull out of one another's mouths. All the while, the Greyhound calculated how many strides it would take to scale the Fence.

The Mouse touched her paw and pointed its nose downward so that the Greyhound would look at the base of the Fence. There was a Skunk. It was *the* Skunk, her Skunk, her LoyalFriend. There was no mistaking him. The thick tuft of long, scruffy, white fur on the top of his head and his unusually fluffy tail were uniquely his signature. She was astonished.

How did the Skunk find me? she thought.

A familiar, sweet sound came from above. It was the Bluebird chirping feverishly as it did loops in the air above the courtyard, trying to capture her attention.

"Oh, my goodness! My LoyalFriend," she said to the Skunk, "what are you doing here? How did you find me?" the Greyhound whispered.

"It was all the Bluebird's doing," the Skunk humbly acknowledged. "She never left us. The Hare had to return to the Farm to give his brother the timepiece, but the Bluebird stayed and kept watch over us from high above. She followed you when you bolted. She flew with you as you ran along the guardrail, and she witnessed the person in the truck swoop you off the highway, so she accompanied you to the Shelter, then returned to the River to guide me here to help rescue you."

"I'm so happy to see you both!" said the Greyhound. Something about the specific sound of the Bluebird's chirp caused the Greyhound to look at it with a feeling of knowing in her belly. "Now I remember you," said the Greyhound to the Bluebird. "You were here—right here, during that first week when I arrived in this place. That was you, right?"

The Bluebird twittered.

The Greyhound's heart expanded with joy, but she maintained control of her emotions so they would not attract any attention.

"I saw the look on your face as I approached. You are going to jump this Fence, aren't you?" asked the Skunk.

"Yes. I am," said the Greyhound. "DearFriend, would you mind distracting the others so they don't notice me?"

"Indubitably!" The Skunk accepted the mission with alacrity. "I'll strut along the Fence line away from you and stomp here and there and make a show of it. Oh, and I'll raise my tail, but in jest only. That should create a sufficient distraction."

"That's perfect." The Greyhound took a deep *breath.* "Okay, I'm ready. I've got this," the Greyhound exclaimed with a newfound confidence.

The Skunk sauntered along the Fence, garnering immediate attention. Ropes dropped and balls bounced as the dogs howled and barked when they noticed him. He stomped his front feet every now and again and turned his rear to the pack to rile them. The staff noticed all the commotion, then noticed the Skunk. A frenzy ensued. The minute the Skunk stomped his back paws and lifted his Magickal tail straight up to the heavens, the Handlers screamed and everyone scattered.

The Skunk performed brilliantly! Dogs jumped on the Fence trying to reach him as the Handlers corralled the rowdy dogs back into the building. The last image the Greyhound saw was the bouncing balls of confusion behind her. She took a deep *breath* and, in two strides, was airborne! The Mouse held on tight as the Greyhound sailed over the Fence as if she had sprouted wings of her own. No one even noticed her. For the first time, she was grateful no one had.

Once over the Fence, the Greyhound didn't look back. Her sight was aimed at the Bluebird fluttering above the buildings. She ran as fast as she could, following the Bluebird. Ignoring the pain in her legs, she trotted and darted around parked cars, cantered across streets, passing rows of houses as her mind raced. It dawned on her that she wasn't running away from something, but rather towards something—something so good. One drop of doubt hovered in the air.

Fear is nothing, she repeated to herself. *Drench it in Stardust.*

She acknowledged the fear, then let it flow right over her as though she was one of those WaterStones in the Brook. She released it into the Autumnal air, where it evaporated. She was growing more mindful and was learning to control her usual flux of emotion.

NOT EVERY JOURNEY HAS A DESTINATION

And so it was . . . The Bluebird led *the Way.* The Greyhound put all her faith and trust in the tiny, blue speck flying high above her in the clear blue sky. A few times the Greyhound lost sight of the Bluebird when it became cloaked by the clouds, but she feared not, knowing that if the afternoon Sun was still behind those clouds, so, too, was the Bluebird.

"We are getting closer!" the Greyhound rooed to the Bluebird.

The familiar scents of the Ballfield and the Trees surrounding it wafted in her direction. As the Bluebird flew over the highway and she raced under it, the Ballfield came into her sight line. Her heart pounded audibly. The Bluebird landed on a sturdy branch in one of the Pine Trees on the outskirts of the Ballfield. The Greyhound, seconds behind, came to a halt under the Pine. She panted hard and focused on slowing her *breath.* The Mouse patted the Greyhound's neck and slid down her leg to the ground. They waited together under the Pine's lopping branches, hidden from the occasional passerby, until the Skunk arrived. Twilight also came, as did the calmer rhythms of the Greyhound's *breathing.* She was the first to spot the Skunk scampering towards them.

"He made it!" the Greyhound exclaimed with glee. "DearFriends, how can I thank you enough for all the help you've given me? I am forever indebted to you both."

"Tweet, tweet, tweet!" the Bluebird blurted, signaling no such debt existed among friends.

"The Bluebird speaks truthfully," added the Skunk. "That's what friends do for one another. Friendship does not come at a cost, and no mental tallies are kept of who has helped whom. We help one another in times of need, whether great or small, against foe or the tumult of a tough day. We will always be here for you. We know you would come to our aid, too, without hesitation, for that is who *you* are."

The Greyhound thought about past friendships and compared them to the friendships that had newly blossomed. *What the Skunk said was true. No judgment exists when hearts are joined in the true bond of ForeverFriends. Its endurance depends on trust and unconditional love just like any other kind of love.*

"Thank you so much for being my ForeverFriends. I've never had truer ones. I appreciate you and am grateful our paths crossed." The words sounded a bit garbled through her sniffles.

"It's time to go home now," the Mouse gingerly added.

"I smell vanilla bean and bergamot!" the Greyhound said.

The fear that her joy would summon the Bee hovered just below the Tree. Her demeanor shifted as thoughts of being turned away by the JeepGirl surfaced.

But what if she doesn't want me? What if, when she discovers the Scars of my life, she rejects me and abandons me as I abandoned her? She looked at the Mouse for guidance.

"What-ifs are your fears surfacing. Be mindful of the lessons you've learned along this most revelatory Journey. Maintain control of that power within you, DearOne," said the Mouse.

"You mean like the lesson of the White Arctic Fox?" the Greyhound asked. The Fox's lesson had become a prevalent one on her Journey.

"Yes. You have a choice, DearOne. There is always a choice. You can absolutely turn right around and make your way in this life on your own, or you can take a step forward into the unknown and take another chance on the life only you can imagine for yourself. You alone know what is the best path for your highest good. You know—"

"—*by Heart*," the Greyhound finished the Mouse's sentence. She took a deep *breath* and exhaled the fear.

The Mouse smiled. The Bluebird twittered. The Skunk thumped his front paws. There were no good-byes exchanged under the emerging Moon's waning quarter light. The Greyhound instead told her friends she would see them soon. She pranced across the Ballfield, towards the JeepGirl's yard with her head high and the white heart outlined in her fur visible to the Shadows of the night. She rooed softly enough for the JeepGirl to hear her.

No more than a moment had passed when the Greyhound saw the JeepGirl peer out of the second-story window, her smile visible in the Moonlight. The Greyhound leapt over the chain-link Fence with ease just as the JeepGirl ran through the Cedar gate. The JeepGirl sprang across the driveway and entered the enclosure, dropped to her knees and greeted the Greyhound with a loving embrace. The Greyhound felt relieved by the JeepGirl's welcoming hug. Another deep *breath* was released. The

Greyhound could see the Skunk and the Bluebird watching the Magickal reunion from behind the trunk of the neighbor's Lignum Tree. Still entwined with the JeepGirl, the Greyhound could only blink her eyes in acknowledgment of their presence and her gratitude.

"It's you! You're alive!" the JeepGirl said as tears of relief and joy welled in her eyes. "Thank the Stars above you are okay! I missed you so much! I've been looking for you day and night. Please don't ever leave me again." Tears fell from her hazel eyes as she continued hugging the Greyhound.

She cries tears too, thought the Greyhound as she leaned into the JeepGirl's embrace.

Everyone does, sometimes, DearOne, added the Mouse, making its way through one of the links in the metal Fence.

The JeepGirl looked up at the Moon. "Thank you, thank you!"

The Greyhound cocked her head in amazement that the JeepGirl was talking to the Moon. Casting her eyes downward, the JeepGirl said to the Greyhound, "I thought you were gone forever! I don't know where you went or what may have happened to you, but I am beyond happy you found *the Way* home. Come on, Girl, let's go inside!"

Her words were Magick. Never taking her hand off the Greyhound's back, the JeepGirl led her to the familiar red-hued door and into the sweet smelling, warm home.

ONE STEP AT A TIME

And so it was . . . The JeepGirl's tears cloaked the presence of the Mouse from her. The Mouse scurried up the stairs and hid behind the broomstick in the corner of the landing. The Greyhound wondered why the Mouse had chosen to go up the stairs instead of into the basement where she expected the JeepGirl to take her. She had made peace with that reality. It was better to be there than in the Shelter or the Nook.

"We aren't going that way," said the JeepGirl, pointing at the staircase.

The Greyhound, with a tilted glance, looked at the JeepGirl, flummoxed. Her nose twitched.

"We are going upstairs this time," the JeepGirl said invitingly.

"Your belly was recuperating from surgery when you were here last. The veterinarian told me I shouldn't force you to climb stairs until you were healed. But you're ready now, I see. After all you must have been through, I bet you'll be able to conquer these stairs quickly."

Gently, the JeepGirl guided the Greyhound to the staircase, which the Greyhound had forgotten about and which now loomed before her. The JeepGirl lifted the Greyhound's front left paw and placed it on the first step, then the right. The Greyhound trembled as the JeepGirl lifted her back paws. She coaxed the Greyhound while holding firmly to her body.

"I've gotcha, Girl. I won't let go. You are safe. I've gotcha."

The JeepGirl guided the Greyhound's every step—first one, then the next, then the next, until they both reached the top of the staircase quite exhausted. In unison, they both sighed with relief.

THERE'S NO PLACE LIKE A HOME

And so it was . . . The JeepGirl directed the Greyhound to the narrow galley kitchen. Straightaway, she gave the Greyhound water and some fresh food with apples. The Greyhound was grateful for the meal. Not only had it been a very long day but also a taxing Journey.

"This is your home now," the JeepGirl whispered.

It was a very modest home. There were four rooms in all, but the larger room had two couches in it. The JeepGirl led the Greyhound around the home. The Greyhound sniffed here and there, and the aroma of cinnamon spice simmering on the stove combined with the vanilla bean and bergamot the JeepGirl wore pleased her.

"This is your couch," the JeepGirl said, pointing to a wrought iron couch that had a thick cloth cushion on it.

Mine? What do you mean? the Greyhound asked with a puzzled look.

"You can get up on it," the JeepGirl motioned with her hand as she patted the couch a few times. "Up. Up. It's okay. Come on up."

The Greyhound understood the JeepGirl's hand motion and the command "Up," so she leapt up and settled down next to the JeepGirl. She laid her head on the JeepGirl's leg and welcomed her gentle touch. The Greyhound was in awe of her good fortune, though still skeptical of how long it would last. Betrayal had marked her life. Despite the resurgence of doubt darkening her mind, she remained focused on the goodness that surrounded her, closed her eyes, and relished the loving attention. As she became more comfortable and drowsy, her body leaned into the back of the couch, then she twisted upside down with all four legs sticking straight up, towards the ceiling. It had been years since she had felt relaxed enough to be in a roached position. There had not been enough room in previous Cages for this most comfortable position. She fell fast asleep.

SOMETIMES IT IS AS IT SEEMS

And so it was . . . After some time, the JeepGirl woke the Greyhound so she could tend to the cuts and scrapes the Greyhound had sustained on her Journey. Dried blood covered her leg, and the Greyhound flinched when the JeepGirl touched the area. The Greyhound hadn't even noticed the new gouge on her leg.

"It's okay, Girl. I won't hurt you. I'll be gentle," the JeepGirl said reassuringly.

But it wasn't the JeepGirl's touch that worried the Greyhound or caused her to jerk away; it was the fact that the JeepGirl would see all the Scars she bore all over her body.

I have to trust her, she thought. *I must.*

She felt the Mouse's presence nearby.

Yes, DearOne, you do. You can. By trusting the Doe, the Hare, the Bluebird, and the Skunk, you've learned that not only does true friendship exist, but in trusting yourself you found the Way *here. As you already know, you can trust this Earth Angel if you just give her a chance, as you have been given another chance by her.*

The Greyhound took a deep *breath* and recognized that feeling of knowing, signaling it was okay. *She* would be okay. She took a chance and relaxed into the moment as the JeepGirl tended to her wounds.

The JeepGirl cleaned and dressed all the Greyhound's visible wounds. "That's it, Girl, you are safe. Let me help you," said the JeepGirl in a whisper. "It looks like you've been through a lot," the JeepGirl acknowledged. "I can't imagine the pain you've felt from the infliction of each cut. You have so many Scars, DearOne—so many. All those races you've run. All the places you've been in the last week. I can't even imagine where you went on your Journey. But I can promise you that all these wounds will heal, and those Scars will fade with time. You *will* heal. We all have Scars we bear, inside and out. I have one on my belly too. I had the same operation you did. I am no longer able to have children of my own, and I am so sorry you will not be able to have puppies of your own. It's not easy to hear that news or live with that reality, though others may think it is simple. Sometimes it's unbearable."

The Greyhound looked up at the JeepGirl in amazement. *How could she know so much about me by only looking at my Scars?* she thought.

The Mouse answered, *Because she has been marked with Scars of her own. Her sincere understanding of the anguish that accompanies having Scars and deep wounds allows her to know you* by Heart. *It's called empathy. It's that same feeling you've had before when you felt badly for the Yorkie or the Skunk. That's empathy—the compassionate understanding of what someone is going through or feeling. Not everyone has it, but you possess the gift of empathy just like the Trees do.*

The Greyhound understood the Mouse and thought, *Perhaps that's why I am so sensitive. I feel too much sometimes. Sometimes it's just too much. Is that why I feel so much all the time?*

It is, communicated the Mouse.

The JeepGirl finished tending to the Greyhound's wounds, then led her to the stairs. The Greyhound began to shake again. The staircase was terribly frightening, more from this vantage point than from the bottom, looking up. It was so steep. She didn't think she could ever get down.

This is more difficult than winning a race or jumping a Fence, she thought.

The JeepGirl was a patient teacher. She didn't give up on the Greyhound and continued to reassure her. "You're doing a great job, Girl. I know it's overwhelming, but you can do it! It will get easier each time. Don't worry! I've got you. I won't let you fall. I promise."

I must keep trusting her. I must conquer these stairs! Okay, step by step. Hold steady.

She wanted to be with the sweet Girl and hoped the feeling was mutual. The Greyhound worked hard to reach the red-hued door on her own, but she relied on the JeepGirl who stayed in front of her during the descent in case she slipped. The challenge was met with success. They reached the bottom without incident, and the JeepGirl let the Greyhound out into the yard without a leash this time.

"Go on. I know you know *the Way*. Go ahead, but please, please come back when you're done. Okay?"

I will. I promise. The Greyhound nodded. She knew how heavy promises made could become, but this promise would be easy to keep.

She was shocked that she didn't have a leash attached to her collar. Was the JeepGirl really trusting her not to leave again? The Greyhound was confounded that the JeepGirl actually wanted her to come back. Her heart filled with love. She felt it in every fiber of her being. She looked back at the JeepGirl just as she was about to go through the space behind the garage. A few tears fell from the JeepGirl's hazel eyes. She quickly did what she needed to do, turned around, and shot out from behind the garage as if she had been catapulted through the air by some invisible force. The entire scene had been spotlighted by the Moon.

"Wow!" said the JeepGirl. "That was amazing! It looked like you were flying. Come on, let's go to sleep. You can show me more of who you really are tomorrow."

The JeepGirl led the Greyhound up the staircase again. This time, the Greyhound was not afraid. She was learning. Once upstairs, the JeepGirl showed the Greyhound her very own place to sleep. It was a different kind of Cage, more cave-like, covered and encased with a soft fabric, inside and out. There was no door, and she didn't have to jump up over another Cage to reach it—the Girl had made her a step. She didn't have to sleep on concrete, torn paper or a gnarly burlap blanket. In this Cage, the bottom was cushy and comfortable like the couch. It didn't hurt her aching muscles or her bony frame. There was even a soft, puffy pillow. She loved the pillow best. The JeepGirl covered her with the same soft, blue blanket as she had done before and kissed the top of her head gently.

"Sleep. You are safe now. I love you," said the JeepGirl, who pet the Greyhound at length. The Greyhound's heart was glad.

A NAMING

And so it was . . . The JeepGirl paused petting the Greyhound. "You need a name," she whispered. "You left before I could give you one."

The Greyhound's right ear perked up, the left one folded over itself, partially hiding that lazy left eye of hers. She couldn't believe what she was hearing.

"Woof, woof," the Greyhound softly signaled her approval.

"Yup, that's right. You need a name," said the JeepGirl. "Let's see. The name the spectators saw on their brochure was Mars, but that's not personal enough, though I love the red planet in general. Well, you do have gorgeous brindle fur. Hmmm."

The JeepGirl looked up to the right, like the Greyhound did when she was contemplating something.

"What about BrindleMars! Yes. That's it! BrindleMars! Do you like it?"

"Roo, roo, roo!" *Yes, yes! I love it very much! Thank you. Thank you. I have a name! Mouse! I have a name!* Elated and overcome with joy, she rooed a few more times so the JeepGirl understood her appreciation.

"Oooo. I've never heard a dog roo before, but I read that your breed roos. You sound like a wolf howling in the wild. I love it! I'm so glad you approve of your name," said the JeepGirl.

"Can I call you JeepGirl?" the Greyhound rooed. "It suits you."

The JeepGirl stroked the Greyhound. "Now we are a family. I love you so much, BrindleMars."

"Ditto, JeepGirl!" purred the Greyhound.

Soon she slumbered with the Mouse snuggled beneath the blankets.

TRUE FRIENDS
ARE FOREVER FRIENDS

And so it was . . . The following day was a special one. The JeepGirl was home all day. She led the Greyhound outside, but not for the usual reason.

"Go ahead, Girl, you can walk around. I know there isn't enough room to run, but you can explore the yard."

The Greyhound stood statuesque in awe of her freedom. While the JeepGirl prepared the yard for Winter, the Greyhound sniffed around its perimeter and familiarized herself with her new environment, smiling as she did so. She loved being free to roam at her leisure. She and the JeepGirl both enjoyed being close to Nature. The JeepGirl educated the Greyhound and taught her the proper terminology of objects and things she had never seen before. There were the paving stones that led to the path behind the garage that the Greyhound had missed seeing because it was nighttime when she had left. There were also wooden flower boxes that bordered the back of the garage, from which the JeepGirl was removing fallen leaves. There were no flowers in them yet, only remnants of Gerbera Daisies, sun worshipers that had shriveled in the cold. The JeepGirl explained that Gerbera Daisies can ease one's sorrow and lighten the Spirit. The JeepGirl continued planting various bulbs that would sprout when Spring arrived. The Greyhound had no idea what Spring was, but she cared much for flowers and knew Winter was going to arrive first. There was the miniature Weeping Cherry Tree in the corner that reminded the Greyhound of the Weeping Willow Trees that had offered her solace. She was sure to make its acquaintance. There was so much to explore in her new life. She felt her heart opening.

The next day, while the JeepGirl raked more leaves, the Greyhound took a stroll to the smaller yard and watched the activity in the Ballfield. She noticed a tiny dog with one of the families.

"Are my eyes deceiving me?" the Greyhound exclaimed to the Mouse, who was more often by her side than not.

"Your eyes may deceive you, but your heart never will. It *is* the Yorkie!" said the Mouse.

The Greyhound began rooing happily to get the dog's attention. "Yorkie! Yorkie!"

The family noticed the Greyhound behind the Fence and came up the incline to say hello.

"I knew it was you!" exclaimed the Greyhound as her tiny friend nosed her through the chain-link Fence.

They were both so happy to see one another again. Their tails wagged with excitement. The JeepGirl joined her to say hello to the family. It was obvious she loved Yorkshire Terriers too. She squatted down and poked her fingers through the Fence and petted the Yorkie's head.

"Hi, LittleOne," she said. "You are so adorable!"

Another couple joined them, and their dog was none other than the West Highland White Terrier. The three friends were jumping, rooing, and woofing jubilantly while the humans chatted about human things. The humans' conversation revealed that the Yorkie lived close by in the brick house across the Ballfield, and the Westie lived in the white house directly behind the Greyhound's new home. They couldn't believe their good fortune.

"I thought I saw you run past my house the other night. You were with a Bluebird and a Skunk," said the Yorkie.

The Westie wagged its stumpy tail in agreement.

The Yorkie translated for the Westie. "I believe she saw you behind the garage on the pathway last night, but she was inside her house and could not reach you."

The Greyhound understood the Westie without words, but thanked the Yorkie for his kind interpretive skills. The Greyhound was happy to hear the confidence in the Yorkie's voice.

"Serendipity! I've missed you both!" exclaimed the Greyhound. She knew the Hare would be proud of her for using his word.

As the humans chatted away, the three shared some of their adventures since their Shelter days. The trio was so happy they were neighbors and would be able to see each other often. The Westie and the Greyhound were especially giddy that they would be able to see each other and chat through the chain-link Fence behind the garage.

At one point during the conversation, the Greyhound turned to the Mouse who was hiding behind the young Pine Tree. She wondered what details she should share with the others about her Journey.

I feel most details would best be saved for another day or not shared at all. Thoughts?

The Mouse agreed.

"Hey," said the Yorkie. "I just overheard my Owner tell both of yours that they are going to make a plan so the three of us can meet in the Ballfield and run around."

"What do you mean, *Owner*?" asked the Greyhound, uncertain she wanted to hear the answer.

"Our Owners," repeated the Yorkie. "The people. They are our

Owners, and we belong to them—or they belong to us, depending on how you look at it. We belong to each other. Our Owners are our caretakers. They love us, and we love them."

The Yorkie sounded sincere. The Greyhound couldn't believe this tiny dog had just healed a small part of her by shifting her perspective of what the word *Owner* could signify. The connection between her Owner at the Track and the JeepGirl had never crossed her mind. Calmness caressed her like a gentle breeze. Redirecting her attention to her friends, she relished the moment.

THE SCHEDULE

And so it was . . . The Greyhound and the Mouse followed the JeepGirl's daily schedule. They awoke at dawn to the warbling of Birds as light gleamed into the space. The pleasant sound never startled the Greyhound out of sleep, but rather replaced her sleepiness with a sweet tingling awareness that she had found a home.

Each morning, the Greyhound and the JeepGirl welcomed in the day with a series of stretches.

"Strrretchh," the JeepGirl told the Greyhound.

The Greyhound walked her front legs far beyond their normal standing position, and with her head held high, stretched so far forward that only her back toes remained grounded. Then, leaning back with her hindquarters high in the air, she bowed her head until her nose just about touched the floor, The JeepGirl called this the downward dog, which the Greyhound found amusing.

Mornings were one of the Greyhound's favorite times. After stretching and tackling the steep steps, she was allowed to run to the enclosure, where she sniffed around and lounged in the grass as she listened to the Birds sing. The JeepGirl had given the Greyhound a lightweight coat that staved off the chill in the air enough so the Greyhound could linger outside and enjoy the commotion in the Ballfield. The Squirrels, high up in the Trees, leapt from limb to limb as they looked at her. They were always watching her. They made fun of her and how she looked, just like others had done throughout her life. She ignored them mostly.

Following the brief yard stay, it was up the stairs for a tasty breakfast. It had taken her only a couple of days to tackle the stairs. She realized she learned some things faster than others.

When it was time to say good-bye, the JeepGirl kissed her on her head and gave her a huge hug. The Greyhound loved the hugs! She had never been hugged so much. It felt warm and safe. She believed she would never tire of hugs. The Greyhound watched the JeepGirl from the side window as she climbed into her Jeep and drove away to work.

The Greyhound enjoyed her time alone until one of the neighborhood kids came by to take her for a walk. He would take her down the different neighborhood streets, and sometimes he'd walk her along the outskirts of the Ballfield. She liked the Boy. He was a kind soul and was good to her and always gave her a treat before he left. After the walk, she slept deeply and dreamt of growing old with all her faithful friends and, of course, with the JeepGirl.

Most days, when the JeepGirl returned from a job called teaching, she promptly took the Greyhound out, and the two of them played in the yard for a while. The Greyhound felt free when she played with the JeepGirl. It was a different way of viewing freedom. The meaning of freedom had transformed into something different for the Greyhound. She didn't limit it to simply running. She was beginning to realize that freedom was something felt deep inside, and the confines of a Fence or a Cage weren't enough to inhibit it.

Her favorite time was naptime, because she was able to jump on the JeepGirl's bed and snuggle. The Greyhound loved it when the JeepGirl stroked her head and neck. It was a serene time. Here, too, the Greyhound noticed a shift in her sleep habits. During the first few days with the JeepGirl, she was able to sleep deeply and restfully when she napped, but the Night Terrors and the Shadows still lurked around every few nights or so. She was used them, though she wished she could rid herself of them forever.

The Greyhound looked forward to dinnertime. The JeepGirl added fresh vegetables, some chicken, and some warm water that made a delicious broth in the kibble. At the Track, she mainly had cold, dry, bland food. Sometimes the racers had been given raw meat for which she had never developed a palete.

Following dinner, the JeepGirl was gone again to some place called martial arts. The Greyhound slept again until she returned and the two either hung out together on the other couch, the cozy leather one, or she listened to the JeepGirl sing. The Greyhound would just stare at the JeepGirl while she sang all sorts of songs. She had never heard such a sweet sound other than the Bluebird's song. In the past, it wasn't often that she heard Birds chirping, because the Track was so far removed from anything that remotely resembled Nature. But in this pretty place, the Greyhound heard all kinds of Birds singing in the Trees and awoke from her naps to their song, and that always lifted her Spirit.

Before bedtime, the Greyhound was allowed to linger longer in the yard. Nighttime was when she and the Moon met. She gazed at the Stars and had conversations with them too. She noticed as the week waned so, too, did her Moon. His quarter light was waning the last few nights and only a sliver of him appeared as a crescent against the midnight blue sky. She feared he would lose his light forever. The foreboding feeling she had experienced in the Forest hadn't quite left her. She needed her Moon. He soothed her soul.

The JeepGirl gazed at the Moon most nights too. Together they peered out the window in the JeepGirl's bedroom and looked fixedly at the celestial body. His light comforted them. The ritual of conversing with the Moon was shared by both of them too. The Greyhound learned how the JeepGirl was having trouble at the school where she taught. She overheard the JeepGirl talking to the Moon or on the phone to friends, explaining how she was being bullied by her boss on a daily basis. It was a tragic tale. Maybe someday, the Greyhound would share the JeepGirl's story with her new friends. For now, she would keep it in her HeartBox. The Greyhound was empathetic to the JeepGirl's woes and knew her friends would be empathetic, too, for they had been bullied as well and understood its traumatic effects.

The schedule was similar to the routine at the Track, but there were remarkable differences, namely the JeepGirl's affection and the warmth and calm energy of her home.

I could get used to this, thought the Greyhound.

Though the Mouse wasn't beside her, she could hear it foraging for leftovers in her bowl. The bowl was perched about two feet above the floor so the Greyhound would not choke. The Greyhound purposely left some food in her bowl or dropped a few bits on the floor for the Mouse each night. She got a kick out of watching the Mouse move the morsels one by one into the other room. They were huge in comparison to the Mouse's minuscule size. The Mouse then crawled into the baby-blue leather recliner positioned in the corner, facing the large, old floor-to-ceiling window and hid the food deep within the underbelly of the recliner, protected for future consumption. The food remained undetected by the JeepGirl. It made the Greyhound giggle. She was amazed by how much strength the tiny thing possessed. Was *she* that strong? She still didn't think so.

EPHEMERAL AND EFFERVESCENCE

And so it was . . . The JeepGirl and the Greyhound lived in harmony that first week, and their love grew exponentially, day-by-day. There was one day the JeepGirl labeled a special day. She neatly packed the Jeep with snacks, water, and the cozy, blue blanket. The Greyhound, clad in her new, lightweight coat, watched in suspense from the second-story window. She didn't know where they were going, but she couldn't contain her excitement as the JeepGirl brought her to the main yard. The Greyhound twirled round and round, doing zoomies, as the JeepGirl giggled. Then the JeepGirl led the Greyhound to the driveway, and up went the window of the Jeep as the rear gate opened. The Greyhound hopped into the Jeep without difficulty. They were off on an adventure!

As soon as the JeepGirl made the second right-hand turn, the Greyhound's anticipation amplified. She rooed. She knew exactly where they were headed—to the Hill! The JeepGirl parked the Jeep under an Oak Tree and opened the hatch.

"Okay, Girl, okay. Hold on, I'll getcha," said the JeepGirl reassuringly as she clipped the black leash onto the coordinating collar. The clicking sound did not bother the Greyhound this time.

"Hurry," the Greyhound purred. "Hurry!"

The JeepGirl led the Greyhound a different way than she had their first time at the Hill. "This is *the Way*, BrindleMars," the JeepGirl instructed.

The Greyhound followed, sticking close to the JeepGirl's right side. They walked together on the old cobblestone pathway the Greyhound had seen during their last visit. As they strolled, they passed hundreds of stone structures of varying shapes and sizes that jutted up from the ground.

What is this place? the Greyhound thought, letting out a little grunt.

"This is a graveyard," the JeepGirl explained. "Other people call it a cemetery, but I like calling it a graveyard because that's what it literally is. It is the place where people lay their family members to rest when those loved ones die. Each one of these headstones has up to three people beneath it buried deep in the ground. I think it's a beautiful, mysterious place. Each grave is a marker for a story just waiting to be told. Think about it, Girl, every person who has died led a life full of adventure, struggle, loss, and, hopefully, love. We all have our unique story we write for ourselves, then enact. There is so much lore here. I find it fascinating."

The Greyhound listened intently to the JeepGirl's graveyard tale.

"Let's go over there. I want to show you something," the JeepGirl said, pointing to a short stone wall just ahead of them. "Here is where my great-grandfather and great-grandmother are buried, as well as my grandfather and grandmother, and a few cousins. Next to them, my dearest uncle lies with his baby son, and just over there, a childhood friend is buried. There are so many of my family members buried here—so many. When people we love die, it's heartbreaking, and we miss them tremendously. Our bodies are ephemeral and bound to the Earth, but our Spirits effervesce and endure forever beyond the limits of time and space. That's what I believe. What helps me cope with the pain of such loss is the sweet grace of knowing that we are all connected. Often I feel the presence of a dog I used to have—Brittany. She was a great watchdog. And sometimes, I feel my nano is with me. I feel his essence around me when I need help, especially when I am doing house projects or, if I need to figure out why something isn't working, I call upon him to guide me. By trade he was a plumber, but he also tinkered with time—timepieces I mean."

The Greyhound thought about the Hare. She missed her friends.

The JeepGirl continued, "He fixed old watches and clocks. I don't feel my dad's presence very often. He passed two years ago. I imagine he's off visiting others or exploring the universe. He loved anything related to space and dedicated his life to projects that involved space exploration. I have no doubt you have had your share of loss, and I want you to know that you are not alone. The heaviness of a broken heart can be unbearable; it helps to know someone understands your sorrow."

The JeepGirl paused, sighed, and said, "Okay, I think it's best we go now. I do not wish to cry." But one teardrop traced her high cheekbone and fell on the headstone.

The Greyhound could feel the JeepGirl's heart breaking a little. She was empathetic to that feeling. She had lost so many family members and friends throughout her short life too. While she remained solemn and close to the JeepGirl's side, the Greyhound wondered if any of her own ancestors were buried in a graveyard near the Track.

The JeepGirl led the Greyhound down the familiar paved pathway that opened to the Hill. The two walked up the Hill, and the JeepGirl picked a perfect spot under a Dogwood Tree that had lost all its leaves and had begun sprouting tiny cherry-colored berries.

Looking down the JeepGirl said, "Oh look. I found another HeartStone!"

She put this one in her pocket, then she unraveled the blue blanket, unpacked the picnic lunch and poured water into a paper bowl. The Greyhound thought it was uncanny how the JeepGirl had found yet another HeartStone and equally glad she had been handed a tasty treat. The Birds sang a soothing tune, while the Sun smiled. The Greyhound allowed the peaceful feeling to wash over her, like the Brook had washed over the rounded stones.

It was a perfect and unseasonably warm Autumn day. The spot overlooked the delightful Montauk Daisies they had seen during their first visit here, though most of their beauty had long since departed. All that remained were their pointed leaves and their fallen stems, which had gone limp between the blades of grass. The Greyhound felt conflicted by the loss of their beauty.

A Dogwood Tree interrupted the Greyhound's contemplation of why beauty faded.

Well, hello.

Hello, the Greyhound answered.

Are you enjoying your time here? asked the Dogwood.

Why, yes I am, very much so, the Greyhound said politely.

You are so very strong, DearOne. I hope you realize that, the sincere Dogwood said.

I don't feel that I am strong, the Greyhound replied.

I know you are. I've heard the TreeTalk and the tales of a brave Greyhound and her Magickal Journey through the Forest. You are well known among the Trees, and I'm here to tell you, not only does my kind exude strength, but we also help others to find their own. I am certain of your strength, and I have no doubt you will continue to recognize it. It will grow with the reflection of Self as you heal. Be sure to give yourself some credit for the difficult experiences you've had and all you've learned as a result. It all has taken a brave heart and great strength of Spirit to survive and arrive at this moment as you have. There is power in your pain. You can harness that power and transform the pain energy into Magick. As you learn to tap into that Magick, you may surprise yourself and be amazed at all you can accomplish if you just believe in the Magick and in yourself, DearOne. You will come to know that your Magick can help heal others too.

Thank you for your kindness and your offering of strength, the Greyhound said. *I needed to hear all you have said. It reminds me of what someone dear to me said not long ago. I will keep your wise words in mind.*

Treasure these moments, the Tree added.

I will, answered the Greyhound.

Lunch and the pleasant exchange ended. The JeepGirl walked with the Greyhound to a section of the grounds where the Circle of Hydrangeas resided. The Greyhound recognized them immediately. Standing in the light of the afternoon Sun, the Greyhound, in awe of their mammoth size, noticed the Circle had retained most of its splendor, though the bunches of bright white petals had blushed.

Hello, DearOne! It's wonderful to see you again, the Circle communicated.

Hello! It's wonderful to see you all again too, the Greyhound said.

That's a fine-looking coat you are wearing, said the Circle.

Thank you! The JeepGirl gave it to me. It keeps me toasty, said the Greyhound. *And thank you for your prescient words regarding Winter. I kept them in mind throughout my harrowing Journey. They played a crucial role in my survival.* The Greyhound hesitated. Her desire to run around the Circle burned in her belly, but she was afraid the Hydrangeas and the JeepGirl would say no. After a few seconds, she summoned the courage to ask, *Would it be okay if I run within your Circle?*

That would be just fine, the Hydrangeas answered in unison.

The Greyhound exhaled, bowed, and said, *Thank you so much.*

The Greyhound grunted to catch the JeepGirl's attention. She knew what she wanted.

"This is a wonderful place to run! Please, please let me run free. Let me loose. This is the perfect spot. There is plenty of space for me to canter."

She was beginning to exude confidence. The Greyhound tugged lightly on the leash as she pulled the JeepGirl into the Circle.

"You want to run, Girl? Is that what you want? Okay, but you must promise to stay within the Circle. Okay? Please. I cringe at the thought of losing you again."

The Greyhound looked up at the JeepGirl with sincerity.

"I will! I promise!" she rooed. She kept her promises.

The JeepGirl unleashed her and said, "Come on, let's run!"

It was actually going to happen. The Greyhound felt a landslide of joy as she ran beside the JeepGirl to the halfway point, then took off alone, cantering to the far end of the Circle and back again. The Greyhound did more zoomies and leaped blithely into the sky. She leaped as high as the JeepGirl's hip then ran around the outskirts of the Circle.

"Impressive!" the JeepGirl shouted.

The Greyhound just wasn't sure how long the warm, wonderful feeling would last. Round and round the Circle she ran. The Hydrangeas swayed as they cheered. When she exhausted all her energy, she rejoined the JeepGirl in the center of the Circle and sat down to rest beside her. *Click.* The Greyhound heard the click but didn't mind, for it did not prohibit her from enjoying the moment with the JeepGirl and Nature. She was content.

FOURTEEN

—

THE KISS

INTENTIONS

And so it was . . . That evening was unlike the rest—the JeepGirl told the Greyhound she had been inspired by the Moon. "Tonight there is a new Moon. It is the perfect time to set our intentions for the coming days and month. We will repeat this again when the Moon is at his fullest."

"Ruff." The Greyhound was tickled by the fact that she and the JeepGirl shared an affinity for the Moon.

Gathering the necessary healing implements—a Quartz Crystal for cleansing, a Moonstone to pay homage to its namesake, and a white candle for purity and intention—the JeepGirl placed the items on a blue metal table at the foot of the bed. This was where she performed healing rituals for herself and those in her life. The Greyhound had hopped onto the small bed so she could get a better look. She was intrigued and loved when the JeepGirl showed her new things. Every day she was learning something new and fascinating.

"Intentions?" asked the Greyhound, tilting her head to the left and looking up quizzically. Her left ear flopped over her lazy eye.

When the Greyhound did this it made the JeepGirl smile.

"Intentions," the JeepGirl explained, "are our aspirations or what we aim to create in our life that is good and true for our Spirit—our higher Self. Think about what you want to manifest, then release it into the universe where kismet will do its work. I like to give mine to the Moon for safekeeping." She looked at the Greyhound whose nose was level with the tabletop.

The Greyhound pushed the JeepGirl's hand so the JeepGirl would continue with the ritual. The JeepGirl wrote her intentions on a piece of parchment and covered the paper with the Quartz Crystal. The Greyhound recognized that the crystal was the same as the crystals in the White Arctic Fox's Cave in her dream.

Serendipity! The Hare came to mind, The Greyhound smiled.

"Now it's your turn," the JeepGirl said. "Think of what you want to manifest and ask your Angels to help you. Know your intentions *by Heart*. Imagine them coming true, like little daily miracles. You'll see, BrindleMars, those that are meant to enhance your higher good will come to fruition whether by kismet or serendipity."

So much of what the JeepGirl said echoed what the Greyhound had learned on her Journey, and the Greyhound remained keenly aware of the lessons imbedded in such echoes. The Greyhound replied by licking the JeepGirl's hand. She loved it when the JeepGirl called her by name. They both smiled at one another while the new Moon watched over them. So the Greyhound set her intention to be present in each moment and to focus on her new life, not her old one. It would be challenging at times, this she knew, but it was a new beginning. She *breathed* the intention into her HeartBox.

The Moon communicated to the Greyhound that he had heard the favor asked of him and would surely and gladly aid the Greyhound in manifesting her intentions. The Greyhound knew that even though he was not visible to her, he was there with her. She could feel him. She knew he would always be there for her no matter what she felt or thought, whether she smiled or wept. She would wait for the time when the Moon reunited with the light that made him visible to the Earth. He would forever be her truest companion, her confidant, her protector, and she would forever be beholden to him. Her all-encompassing love for him had grown since the night atop the Knoll. Now she was sure the Moon felt the same about her.

BE ONE WITH NATURE

And so it was . . . A few days and nights had passed since the new Moon ritual and the JeepGirl and the Trees explained to the Greyhound all about Winter and what to expect when he arrived come the solstice in December. She couldn't imagine all they said regarding snow, ice, and the cold, but she had no reason to doubt the Trees, for they had never led her astray. Winter, the Trees assured her, would be as mighty as described.

Ballgames ended, and children, wrapped in their Fall sweaters and jackets, played on the swings, laughing and giggling with glee. Infectious giggles were one of the most enjoyable sounds the Greyhound had ever heard. She, too, had been given a coat to wear, which she loved, because it covered her back and underbelly where fur had not yet grown. None of her fur had fallen off since the Nook, and some time would be saved for further analysis. The coat was milk-chocolate brown and was dressed with all sorts of fun pink and white flowers, the tiniest of which reminded her of her celestial StarFriends. She was rather fond of the coat. It kept her warm indeed and made it much more bearable to be outside.

The Greyhound kept her close connection with Nature fluid. One morning, inspired by the peacefulness of heart she was experiencing, she gave the young White Pine Tree in the yard a hug. The Greyhound had watched the JeepGirl hug Trees many times. The JeepGirl had said that Nature possessed the power to heal, and the Greyhound knew it to be true. Listening to the powerful feeling inside her heart, she hugged the Tree in her own way, by leaning against it. It felt good. It felt right to express her true feelings without fear of an aggressive backlash.

"Purrr! Purrrr," said the Greyhound affectionately.

"I see you found *the Way*, DearOne. The White Forest Pines and the Pine that lives in the courtyard at the Shelter told me about you. They said you were a kind Spirit who thought she was lost," the Pine bellowed.

The Greyhound noticed a puffy-cheeked Squirrel smirking at her from high up in the bare branches of the White Oak. The Greyhound quickly brought her attention back to the Pine Tree and said, "I remember the White Pines of the Forest with much fondness, though I did not have much of a chance to spend time with the Pine Tree at the Shelter." *Wow,* she thought. *Trees can communicate with one another from afar? That is extraordinary!*

"We promised we would watch over you, for as long as you are here, DearOne," said the Pine and Oak in unison.

Not understanding the prophetic words they uttered, she simply bowed to both. The Greyhound recalled the JeepGirl explaining the healing capabilities of the Lignum Tree that resided in the neighbor's yard. As the days continued, the Lignum Tree would offer the Greyhound emotional strength. She also learned from the Pine Tree that she would require this strength, for it was there, in the Lignum Tree, where the Bee would reside come late Spring. News of the Bee made her shiver—she couldn't help it. A few hairs dislodged and were whisked away by a gentle breeze. The

Greyhound took a deep *breath,* which aided her in remaining focused on the good feeling within her heart.

BELIEVE IN HEALING

And so it was . . . Another week ticked towards the end of Autumn. The Greyhound had not completely healed, but she was making steady progress. Mindful of how various situations triggered her, she was getting better at dealing with her emotions by accepting the feelings that surfaced and allowing them to flow right over her like water and out into the universe, where the Stars could catch and consume them and transform them into Magickal Stardust. There they could no longer hurt her. The trauma she had endured had scarred her beyond measure. The Stars were teaching her how to fill the deeper Scars with golden light laced with white Stardust that would help them heal and make them bearable enough to live life as deeply.

Astrology lessons and conversations about constellations and the lore behind each were favorite topics the Stars shared with the Greyhound. The tale of the Supernova Cassiopeia intrigued the Greyhound, but the one she loved most was the tale of Pegasus.

Oh, those wings, she thought. *I wish I could fly like Pegasus, for I'd fly right up to the Stars and race around the Moon!*

That would be Magickal! The Stars twinkled their reply.

The Greyhound was enraptured by most of the stories the Stars shared, though there was one story that she did not particularly care for—the myth of Narcissus—a tale of unrequited love. That sad tale ended with the warrior loving himself more than the nymph Echo, thus causing the suffering and destruction of both. The Greyhound craved a love without a tragic ending. The Stars assured her she would find one.

When tears attacked her, she welcomed them now. She would cry, but gently, as the Willow had taught her. The Moon often reminded her to *breathe* slowly and intently when painful thoughts of the past invaded her mind or when her head hurt.

Still she battled Night Terrors. But now, she had the JeepGirl by her side, who gingerly woke her with a soothing tone saying, "BrindleMars, you are safe. Everything is okay. You were running in your dream. I love you, Girl. Go back to sleep." Cradled by that love, the two would fall fast asleep with the Mouse nestled close by, watching over them. The love, safety, and comfort the JeepGirl provided the Greyhound was a miraculous gift. The Greyhound reciprocated what she could willingly. The JeepGirl made it easier for her to cope. She understood the misunderstood. The Greyhound knew the JeepGirl was a misfit too. After the graveyard visit, the Greyhound realized how much loss the JeepGirl had suffered in her own life. Experiencing that much loss changes one. The Greyhound had changed. She hoped she would keep evolving as she learned to accept her new life. She was self-actualizing and beginning to like herself again.

The JeepGirl spoke often about maintaining inner peace. By trusting and listening intently to that inner guide and by quieting the mind, the JeepGirl said it was possible. With the Moon's and Mouse's continued guidance, the Greyhound more surely recognized and nurtured those nudges. But the JeepGirl had only filled a fraction of the Greyhound's heart with love. The greatest extension of love the Greyhound was learning to accept was the love of Self and the choice to love again was her own.

INJOY

And so it was . . . Was she dreaming? She wasn't used to being happy. This feeling had never been a constant in her life, but she knew she had found caring relationships with the Mouse and the JeepGirl, and she enjoyed her new friendships with the Yorkie and the Westie when she could.

The Greyhound loved spending evenings with the JeepGirl on the couch or when she curled up on her soft, blue blanket in her warm bed with the Mouse tucked under her chin. The warmth from the fireplace soothed her body as it healed. She settled cozily into her new life. She was home. The kind of love she felt from the JeepGirl and the Mouse was very different from the loves of the past. This kind of love was how she had imagined it could be.

The Greyhound began to feel stronger, surer of her decision to come back to the JeepGirl. She enjoyed the life they were building together. The healing practices she had learned from various encounters she experienced on her Journey had become necessary, integral parts of her life. Slowly she was healing—physically, emotionally, spiritually. Her good fortune was not taken for granted. Winter and the Bee still worried her. The days were becoming increasingly colder. She wondered if that's why the Bee had not returned, or maybe its injury had been worse than the Doe had reported. It's buzzing was still heard sometimes in the deeper recesses of her mind, but too much goodness surrounded her now to worry about it, though it did annoy and concern her.

THE KISS

And so it was . . . Just a couple of weeks before Winter arrived, on one unseasonably warm, sunny afternoon, the JeepGirl whistled for the Greyhound, who was lying on the leather couch in the living room—her new favorite place.

"BrindleMars, do you want to go for a ride in the Jeep? Let's go on another adventure. You've never been to the Beach and I want to show it to you. I have a feeling you will love the water. And guess what? There is so much room for you to run. You will be able to run fast and far, but you have to promise to turn around and come back to me," the JeepGirl explained excitedly, though the Greyhound could detect a hint of fear in her voice.

"Purr!" the Greyhound signaled a promise made. During her time on the bank of the Brook, she had reflected deeply on how fragile promises made were. The Bee's lack of follow-through on its promises emphasized how important her word was to another, and how trust was partially based on promises made and promises kept. She twirled and twirled in the middle of the living room. Her authentic Self was becoming more and more apparent as she became more comfortable with the JeepGirl. The JeepGirl giggled every time the Greyhound did zoomies. The Greyhound not only enjoyed going for rides in the Jeep and being with the JeepGirl no matter where they Journeyed, but she also never tired of the sound of her name being called.

The drive wasn't long. Once they turned onto the roadway that led directly to the shore, the Greyhound smelled a new scent—salty air. She inhaled deeply! The air had a similar effect on the JeepGirl who also drew in a deep *breath*. It was so fresh and calming. The JeepGirl parked the Jeep against the seawall, opened the hatch, and clasped the lead to the Greyhound's collar. The two walked eagerly to the sand. The Greyhound was astonished by the sight. The Beach was more Magickal than the Hill of Daisies, the stone-filled Brook, and the Meadow where she had raced the Hare, though she recognized each offered beauty in its own special way.

The dune sand felt quite different from the sand on the Track. Her paws sank into the softer sand while the JeepGirl pointed out various shells and driftwood strewn about and imbedded in it. It was obvious the JeepGirl liked what the Greyhound called WaterStones the best, because she kept picking them up and putting them in her pockets. It pleased the Greyhound that they shared an affinity for the smooth WaterStones, though the JeepGirl had that curious knack of finding the heart-shaped ones she called HeartStones.

When they reached the harder packed sand at the water's edge, the JeepGirl smiled at the Greyhound and said, "This is the Ocean. It's absolutely breathtaking, isn't it? But please don't get too close to the waves. There is a full Moon tonight, so the tide is extraordinarily rough. But when Summer comes we will go swimming. The water is too cold for that today."

Hearing what the JeepGirl said, she realized the Moon possessed and could wield much more power and influence than she had ever witnessed or imagined. The Greyhound's nose twitched as she sniffed and sniffed the salty Ocean air. The Ocean beckoned her to it. She stood clear of the waves as she became mesmerized by the ebb and flow of the tide. The JeepGirl stood still as well. It was evident the water was coming towards the Greyhound, but she was aware that it also retreated whence it came. She watched as a mighty struggle took place—the tension and relaxation of the two opposing currents converging. She observed that once the ebb and flow of the tide relaxed, the struggle ended, melding into a moment between the two waters where time seemed to stand still—there was no motion, but a stillness in motion—a moment of peaceful surrender. The Greyhound longed to be in that place.

"BrindleMars, are you ready?" asked the JeepGirl. "Remember, you promised me you would come back this time."

The JeepGirl's voice interrupted the Greyhound's contemplation of the Moon's role in the changing tide. The Greyhound looked to her left. For miles, she saw an expansive track of hard-packed sand flanked on the right by the Ocean. There was even more space here than there had been in the Circle or the Meadow. Here, she could run unencumbered without the restriction and imposition of the Fences and curves of the racing Track. She would easily be able to break out into a double suspension, full speed gallop, and she was thrilled.

The JeepGirl crouched, unleashed the Greyhound, and yelled, "Ready? Go! Go, BrindleMars! Go!"

Elated, the Greyhound bolted without hesitation, propelling herself into the air. She ran with intention and purpose and all her might, not to excel or to be perfect, but to be free in the moment and to relish in the joyful sensations enveloping her body and mind. She was enthralled by how the sand felt cool, not warm beneath her paws, how the air rushed over her as she glided through it, and how the big Birds the JeepGirl called Seagulls tried to keep up with her. She became enraptured by the serenity washing over her as she ran along the shoreline and how her mind emptied of all fear, anxieties, and pain. It was glorious to know she could easily run away and sweeter still to choose not to. This was happiness. This was living her best life. So she ran as far as compelled. With her desires fulfilled, she slowed her pace, stopped, looked at the setting Sun, contorted her position by hopping right around, and made her way back to the JeepGirl. As she neared, her gallop slowed to a trot, and with the last couple steps, she walked, winded, directly into the open arms of the JeepGirl.

"That was absolutely astonishing, BrindleMars!" said the JeepGirl, impressed by the Greyhound's grace in motion. "It's unbelievable what you just did. It's unfathomable how incredibly fast you are. It's amazing to see how all your paws are in the air at the same time when you stretch out, and then again when they contract beneath you. It's a sight to behold! I'm in awe of your ability. I'm so, so proud of you, BrindleMars!"

The JeepGirl kept stroking the Greyhound's back as the Greyhound caught her *breath*. The Greyhound even wheezed a bit, an effect of the colder air. Once the JeepGirl had given her some time to recover, she reattached the leash, and the two walked side by side across the Beach towards the dunes. Halfway there, the JeepGirl stopped, leaned over, and gently cradled the Greyhound's jaw just as she had in the Jeep the first day they met. The JeepGirl's long, dark-brown curls caressed the Greyhound's head as she lovingly and tenderly kissed the Greyhound on the bridge of her snout. Crouching in the sand, she hugged the Greyhound tightly.

The JeepGirl's voice cracked as she whispered, "I love you, BrindleMars. I love you so much."

That embrace embodied so much of what the Greyhound had searched for on her Journey and throughout her life. Her heart pounded audibly, *lub-dub, lub-dub*. Brimming with love, the Greyhound was learning that her capacity to love again was even greater than the size of her heart, which was much larger in comparison to her frame than most animals. Her jaw quivered.

The Greyhound, leaning in, requited the JeepGirl's love, "Awrrooooo!" *I love you too!*

Their embrace was significant. Upon opening her eyes, the Greyhound spied an unexpected spectacle. It was her Moon, rising in full light over the horizon. It was as if he had risen from the depths of the Ocean herself, crashing through the surface with ease and grace. The Moon's bounty of brilliant white light cascaded across the waters, like a treasure trove of dazzling diamonds dispersing their beauty far and wide along the beach. The JeepGirl tugged on the leash. It was time to go home, but the Greyhound did not budge. Turning toward the Ocean, the Jeepgirl stood by the Greyhound's side riveted. The two watched in silence as the Moon continued rising high above the Ocean. Words were difficult to come by.

"Magickal!" said the JeepGirl.

"He is," rooed the Greyhound. *You amaze me more and more every time I see you, Moon!*

As you amaze me, DearHeart, the Moon responded.

This was a day the Greyhound would not forget.

SWEET GRACE

And so it was . . . The Greyhound's heart had been broken countless times, but she was beginning to retrieve some of its pieces, one by one, as one would a delicate piece of porcelain that had tumbled off its safe place on a shelf. She learned that she did not need to retrieve all the pieces. Some were better left where they had fallen—left and forgotten, or, if not forgotten, at least her higher Self would be better served if she wrapped the pieces in Moonlight and encased them in Stardust, leaving them undisturbed. Learning to accept all the broken pieces of her Self would take time, and she knew she would never be who she had been. She would never be how others thought she should be. She would be who she was becoming. For now, she would just be.

The Greyhound felt blessed beyond words and was grateful to all who had helped her on her Magickal Journey of Self-Discovery. She knew she would never be alone again. There was the gentle nudge of the Mouse to guide her, the JeepGirl who loved her, and faithful, new friends she could trust. She practiced sustaining the peaceful stillness she had witnessed in the Ocean, and as her Magickal connection to Nature strengthened, she learned more valuable lessons about knowing *by Heart* how to live life from a place of gentleness and quiet peace. She remained in awe of her steadfast celestial guardians—the Sun who provided her with warmth and lifted her Spirit, and the Stars she wished upon and who gifted her their Stardust.

Despite all the pain, betrayal, and heartache that had plagued the Greyhound's life—all the Scars she bore inside and out, all the challenges, difficult choices, and lessons she had learned on her Journey, and those she had yet to learn—despite these and the trillions of tears shed over time, the gentle Greyhound with a heart that matched her Spirit was just beginning to accept herself, all the parts of her Self with all their imperfections. Much healing was needed, but the Greyhound *was* healing with more ease as she accepted her Scars and turned the wounds of grief into sweet grace. She began to believe she truly did deserve a healthy love—a love without conditions. And the Moon—her beloved Moon! He continued to watch over her, listen to her, guide and love her just the way she was—Scars and all.

The Greyhound, once lost, had found *the Way*.

ABOUT THE AUTHOR

—

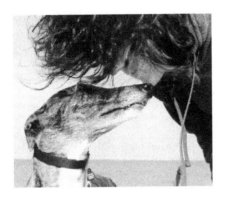

Ginamarie believes in love, magick, angels, awakenings, and serendipity. She lives in Northeastern Massachusetts along the banks of the Merrimack River with her second rescued Greyhound racer, SweetP. Serendipitously, SweetP is the niece of BrindleMars, Ginamarie's first Greyhound—the protagonist of this allegorical tale.

After graduating from Boston College, in 1988/90 with a Bachelor's degree in Arts & Sciences and Education, and a Master's degree in English, Ginamarie enjoyed a long career teaching literature, world studies, journalism, and creative writing. She attained her certification as a high school principal, and served as chair of the New England Association of Schools and Colleges (NEASC) accreditation process and the humanities department at a local high school. She is now retired.

Ginamarie's philosophy of life is drawn equally from her deep passion for singing—which led to the release of her first album, *Emerging Moon* in 2007, the confluence of Romantic authors and American Transcendentalists, her experience as a Reiki master, and the discipline and study of Martial Arts. Ginamarie ranks as a second-degree black belt in *Soo Bahk Do-Moo Duk Kwan*. These disciplines have taught her to seek solace and healing in Nature and *the Tao*.